FEARLESS, FEROCIOUS, FUBAR FICTION

Scapegoat First Published in 2018

Published by Honey Badger Press

Cover and Logo by Mike Tenebrae
http://tenebraestudios.net

Internal Design by EyeCue Productions
http://duncanpbradshaw.co.uk/eyecue-productions/

ISBN: 978-1728625355

SCAPEGOAT

March 29, 1987

For metalheads Mike Rawson, Lonnie Deveroux, and Pork Chop, an RV road trip to Wrestlemania III becomes a one-way ticket to hell. While delivering an illegal shipment of counterfeit wrestling merchandise, an ill-fated shortcut through the Kentucky backwoods leads them to a teenaged girl carved head to toe in arcane symbols. Soon our unlikely heroes are being hunted through the boonies by a cult of religious crazies who make the Westboro Baptists look like choirboys… a cult that will stop at nothing to get the girl back and complete a ritual that has held an ancient evil at bay for centuries…

Until now.

PRAISE FOR THE AUTHORS

ADAM HOWE

"Horror fans and crime fans are going to come to blows over who gets to claim Howe as one of their own but they're both going to be wrong because Howe's his own thing… One of the absolute best writers working today."

- Adam Cesare
(THE CON SEASON, TRIBESMEN)

"A fearless writer with an unfettered imagination… Lurid and elegant, trashy and witty, a literary provocateur who disturbs and entertains in equal measure."

- Scott Adlerberg
(GRAVEYARD LOVE, JACK WATERS)

"One of the funniest, sickest, most insane writers working today. The man has no filter!"

- Jeff Strand
(DEAD CLOWN BARBECUE, BLISTER)

"Adam Howe is one to watch – as in, watch your back, this guy might be dangerous."

- Eric Beetner
(RUMRUNNERS, LEADFOOT)

"Raw, punky, and genuinely surprising."

- Stephen King
(MAXIMUM OVERDRIVE)

JAMES NEWMAN

"(James Newman's work) reminds me of David Silva, but with a meaner edge."

- Thomas F. Monteleone
(NIGHT OF BROKEN SOULS; FEARFUL SYMMETRIES; SUBMERGED)

"James Newman is one of my favorite authors. His novels are always engrossing and entertaining. I can't recommend his works highly enough."

- John R. Little
(MIRANDA; THE MEMORY TREE; URSA MAJOR)

"Newman is truly a literary force to be reckoned with!"

- Ronald Kelly
(FEAR; HELL HOLLOW; UNDERTAKER'S MOON)

"James Newman is a damned fine writer. It's just that simple. He has the easygoing style of a storyteller and the sort of prose that catches your attention and keeps it. His natural sense of pace is as good as it gets."

- James A. Moore
(BLOOD RED; DEEPER; SERENITY FALLS)

"You might expect the work of a young Southern writer to show some roots, and you'll see that clearly in James Newman's writing. There's a little bit of Davis Grubb and Joe Lansdale twisting into that dark earth, and a strong straight spike of Robert McCammon digging deep. But the story tree that grows above ground belongs to a tale-spinner who can raise one mean hunk of nightmare all on his own."

- Norman Partridge
(THE MAN WITH THE BARBED WIRE FISTS; DARK HARVEST)

PRAISE FOR "SCAPEGOAT"

"A delightful backwoods detour through the three Rs of southern-fried horror: Rednecks, Revenge, and Wrestlemania! Howe and Newman pack in plenty of scares and wit, and cultists and carnage to spare, perfectly blending violence and humor in equally twisted measure. SCAPEGOAT is one of 2018's most entertaining reads, chugging along with the speed and verve of Bandit's Trans Am and fuelled by pure joy. This is one goat you'll definitely want to get!"

- Michael Patrick Hicks
(BROKEN SHELLS; MASS HYSTERIA)

"Rendered in a uniquely hip style, at a breakneck pace, SCAPEGOAT is packed with wildly imaginative events, humor both light and dark, and characters so vividly drawn they seem to materialize before your eyes. A bold romp. Refreshing and, above all, *fun.*"

- Sean Costello
(FINDERS KEEPERS; SQUALL)

"This tag-team effort between Adam Howe (whose work I know well) and James Newman (who I'm getting to know) moves so briskly through the gears of action, suspense, and horror that I felt more like I was watching a movie rather than reading a book. Indeed, Howe's M.O. of making his own highly original fiction influenced heavily by American pop culture (from AC/DC to THE GOONIES) means that SCAPEGOAT is both a much-needed breath of fresh air, and a welcome blast of nostalgia. Just beware: It's a shotgun blast."

- Joseph Hirsch
(MY TIRED SHADOW)

"SCAPEGOAT is classic, no-holds-barred Adam Howe.
Of course it begins in a motorhome headed to Wrestlemania III.
Of course it features a guy named Pork Chop with a Coors Light helmet.
Of course we end up in a chicken-fried, apocalyptic cult.
Adam Howe is his own genre. This time, he's sucked James Newman into the fold.
SCAPEGOAT is Adam Howe and James Newman's Kool-Aid and you'll want to drink it to the very last drop."

- Eryk Pruitt
(WHAT WE RECKON)

"Fully balls to the wall, mind-blowing horror… As a horror movie junkie, and someone of (ahem) a certain age, who very well remembers Wrestlemania III, this ticked all the boxes for me. Someone needs to make a movie of this - and I'll be first in line for a ticket. This is the perfect Halloween read (and Christmas, New Year, Easter, Summer solstice... any time of year, basically). If you want a truly fun and scary horror with an ending that will blow your hair back - buy it!"

- Keshini Naidoo
(HERA BOOKS)

LUST SLOTH

GREED ENVY

ADAM HOWE

SCAPEGOAT

JAMES NEWMAN

GLUTTONY

WRATH PRIDE

CONTENTS

PART ONE: HIGHWAY TO HELL - **5**

PART TWO: IF YOU WANT BLOOD (YOU'VE GOT IT) - **47**

PART THREE: EVIL WALKS – **153**

ABOUT THE AUTHORS - **187**

STORY NOTES: HERE BE SPOILERS - **188**

RECOMMENDED VIEWING - **196**

"SCAPEGOAT" PLAYLIST - **197**

ACKNOWLEDGEMENTS - **198**

For Mike & Norma

"In the traditional motion picture story, the villains are usually defeated, the ending is usually a happy one. I can make no such promise for the picture you are about to watch."

Ronald Reagan, General Electric Theater

"To all my little Hulkamaniacs: say your prayers, take your vitamins, and you will never go wrong."

Hulk Hogan

"We are here to rock you,
And to say… to hell with the devil!"

Stryper, To Hell with the Devil

The girl cowered in the mule cart. The squeaking of the wagon wheels seemed to mock her hoarse cries. The chains binding her wrists and ankles rattled and clanked as she struggled to free herself. Flies buzzed across the still-leaking symbols and words carved into her flesh. The driver of the wagon kept his eyes ever forward lest they linger on the girl's nakedness. It was vital his thoughts remained pure.

The noon sun warmed Brother Noah's face as he rode on the buckboard behind Old Moses, driving the mule through the woods with snaps of the reins.

"Please..." the girl croaked behind him. It was the first time she had spoken since they left the church. She had long since screamed her throat raw. "*Please!*"

Noah ignored her.

He began to sing:

Yes, we'll gather at the river
The beautiful, beautiful river
Gather with the saints at the river
That flows by the throne of God!

His hymn was off-key but sincere.

Dense woods choked the trail. The air smelled of pine and honeysuckle. At last they reached a clearing. Nothing living grew here. The earth had been devoid of vegetation for almost a century now. No woodland creatures scuttled in the surrounding forest; no birds sang in the trees.

In the middle of the clearing, a dozen fist-sized stones were arranged in a circle. The stones were painted chalk-white, except for seven, which were caked with sun-blackened blood. Within the ceremonial circle stood a wooden stake as tall as a grown man.

Noah reined Old Moses to a halt outside a tumbledown shack on the edge of the clearing. Climbing down from the buckboard, he stretched the stiffness from his legs.

Though he had traveled but a few miles from town, Noah had never felt so distant from his kin. A great honor had been bestowed on him, and yet the chosen one who led the 'goat into the wilderness was considered by rite to be unclean. Come the dawn, Noah would be required to wash his clothes and bathe in the creek, followed by seven days' isolation and prayer, before he was allowed to return to town and reunite with his family. Except for the blood beneath his fingernails and caked in his palms, Noah did not *feel* unclean. But as the Reverend often said, *Transference is only the first stage.* Noah's father had done the deed himself many moons ago. He told Noah he could still feel the stain all the way to the marrow of his bones. It never fully went away. Yet a few aches and pains were a small price to pay for knowing the Lord had smiled upon you.

With a rattling of chains, the girl raised herself up in the cart, peering above the slatted sides, screaming when she saw what waited to greet her.

Elsewhere within the clearing stood two wooden posts, connected by a crossbeam. Strung from the crossbeam by her ankles was a middle-aged woman. She was naked, like her daughter, and also like her daughter every hair on the woman's head and body had been shaved to the skin. She was butchered crotch to gullet like slaughterhouse cattle. What had once been inside her now lay slopped in a fly-swept pile at the base of the scaffold.

"MAMA!" the girl screamed.

Noah had never taken a life before this morning. It had not been easy. The knife had trembled in his hand as he raised the blade to the woman's throat. There he had hesitated, praying for the strength to continue. The woman wept and pleaded for her life and the life of her daughter. Noah feared he was not fit for this task. Even wished he had never been chosen. Then a beam of sunlight had winked off the blade, and God spoke to him, just as the Reverend had promised He would. The Lord had steadied Noah's hand, guiding the blade across the woman's throat, and as the arterial spray splashed his face and her screams became like the singing of angels, Noah had suddenly understood that no role was more important than his own.

He retrieved from the cart the items he would need for the coming days. *A loaf of bread, and some cheese… a water bladder… a book of matches and a dented metal canister filled with gasoline… and his Bible.* He took everything inside the shack, then returned with a bowl of water, scratching the space between the mule's crooked ears as Old Moses bent his head to drink.

Noah dragged the girl down from the cart, across the clearing to the circle of stones, and the wooden stake. He shackled her to the stake, then staggered back to catch his breath. The girl cursed and spat at him.

Clouds scudded past the sun, cloaking the clearing in shadow. The air grew cold. Noah shivered. The girl abruptly stopped screaming. She asked if he had ever been with a woman. Noah's eyes darted to her breasts. He felt himself blush. She promised to do anything he desired if he would only let her go. Noah reminded himself it was no longer the girl speaking. The Reverend had warned him that the demons would attempt to deceive him. He forced his eyes from the girl's body and said, "Get thee behind me, Satan."

Now they would wait.

There, in the Circle of Purgation, the 'goat would absorb the sins of man. Her soul would blacken, as rotting fruit. Then the ritual would end in fire.

Noah fished in his pocket for the silver timepiece the Reverend had presented to him on the day he was chosen. The ticking of the watch sounded unnaturally loud in the stillness of the clearing. He opened the watchcase. The glass face was splintered and stained with blood that Noah had been unable to remove no matter how hard he scrubbed. The cursive engraving inside the casing read:

To Eddie
My Sweet husband

The watch belonged to him now. He smiled. Hearing a droning engine noise above him, Noah glanced up and watched as a passenger plane scrolled slowly across the spring sky. The white contrail in its wake reminded him of the serpent in the Garden of Eden. *Where all this began*, he thought. His smile slowly faded. He snapped the watchcase shut and returned his mind to the task at hand. A breeze breathed through the woods, carrying with it the scent of gasoline.

He wondered what their sins would smell like, once he set them on fire.

He could hardly wait.

"Praise be to God."

PART ONE

HIGHWAY TO HELL

March 29, 1987
Morning of Wrestlemania III
Present Day

1

Mike heard the motorhome coming from four blocks away.

In case the engine wasn't loud enough – and it was loud enough to wake the neighbors, including Mrs. Peterson, and she'd died six months ago – the driver had the stereo turned up to eleven, blasting the 'burbs with heavy metal.

Power chords set off car alarms as the motorhome roared down Poinsettia Lane. Dogs barked from behind chain-link fences. A few residents, dressed in bathrobes and pajamas, peered fearfully from behind screen doors, as if the Apocalypse foretold in the Book of Revelation had come to fruition at last.

The motorhome skidded to a tire-smoking stop outside Mike's place, knocking down trashcans like a bowler scoring a strike. After some pushing and shoving and much muffled cussing, the vehicle's single side door clattered open, and a man stumbled out, wincing in the early morning sunlight. He wore a yellow muscle shirt with HULKAMANIA printed in red across the chest. The shirt did little to flatter Hulk Hogan, let alone a sack of shit like Lonnie Deveroux.

Marching onto the front lawn like a wrestler making his ring entrance, Lonnie ripped the muscle shirt from his chest in true Hulkster fashion, revealing his flabby physique in all its hairy-backed, beer-gutted, man-boobed glory.

He cupped his hands to his mouth and hollered at the house: "Mike! Mike Rawson! Yo, Mikey! Don't make me come in there and drag your sorry ass out!"

Then he spotted the lawn flamingo.

Watching from his front porch on the opposite side of the street, Mike Rawson thought: *Uh-oh.*

Lonnie hoisted the flamingo above his head, gave it a twirl, then bodyslammed the bird, shattering it to pink dust beneath his bulk as he pinned it for the count of one…two…THREE!

Mike continued watching as Lonnie staggered breathlessly to his feet and pointed to the heavens, thanking God for this hard-fought victory between man and yard ornament.

Maybe this trip isn't such a swell idea after all, Mike thought.

The warning signs had been there from the start, when Mike answered the phone in the dead of night, blearily accepting the collect call before he was fully awake and had the presence of mind to refuse.

"How's it hanging, champ?" Lonnie had slurred down the line. Shouting to be heard above the background noise. Sounded like a crowded bar. *Big surprise.*

"Lonnie?" Mike pawed sleep from his eyes, squinting at the digital display on the bedside alarm. "Do you have any idea what time it is?"

"Miller time? *Heh, heh.* One step ahead of you, good buddy."

"It's one in the morning," Mike snapped. "You just woke the baby."

"Ah, shit!" Lonnie lowered his voice to what he must have thought was a whisper but was in fact a dull roar. "Sorry, bro!"

"What's the big emergency?"

"You sitting down?"

"I'm in bed," Mike reminded him.

"What do you, me, and ringside seats for Wrestlemania III got in common?"

Turned out the answer was a broken lawn flamingo.

Mike considered ducking back inside the house now, before Lonnie spotted him. Wait for the neighbors to call the cops. The only thing stopping him was the thought of Wrestlemania III.

Mike sighed, called out: "Over here, Lonnie."

Lonnie wheeled around in surprise. He'd been eyeing a garden gnome, looked about a second away from grabbing it next. Mike suspected the gnome would have suffered simulated sodomy if he hadn't diverted Lonnie's attention.

Lonnie's face crumpled in childlike confusion when he saw Mike waving at him from the house across the street. "You move or something?"

"Nope," Mike said. "Same house we've lived in for the last five years. Though we may have to find a new place now, thanks to you."

He mentally deducted thirty bucks from his next paycheck to replace Mr. Adlerberg's flamingo. The cost of this "free" trip was already adding up.

Lonnie swaggered across the street, shirtless and sweaty.

Rachel emerged from the house behind Mike. She was cradling their bawling baby. Mike's face grew hot. She looked like she wanted to throttle the dumb bastard Lonnie for waking the kid. Lucky for him her hands were full.

Lonnie sucked in his gut and purred, "Hey, Rach." The ol' Deveroux charm working overtime. "The music didn't wake little Lonnie Junior, did it?"

The music was still blaring, of course.

Rachel said, "It was either the music, the camper, or you trashing our neighbor's yard. Take your pick."

"She's a *motorhome*, not a camper," Lonnie corrected her, with a condescending chuckle. A woman couldn't be expected to know the difference.

"And I hate to break it to you," Rachel said, "but we decided against naming our firstborn after you."

"When were you gonna tell me?" Lonnie said to Mike, in a tone that suggested his feelings had never been so viciously trampled.

"If it's any consolation," Rachel said, "it was an agonizing decision."

Lonnie missed the sarcasm. "Maybe it's for the best. These are mighty big boots to fill."

A side window on the motorhome slid open, and a fat potato head squeezed out, twisting sideways to fit through the gap. With his chubby, beer-flushed face, and a red-brown beard covering his chin and most of his neck like a thin patch of kudzu, Pork Chop resembled a debauched cherub. He wore a novelty hardhat with a can of Coors attached to each side, plastic straws dangling down from the cans to his mouth. Judging from the look on Pork Chop's face, this hat was the greatest invention since the Monster Truck.

"Hey, Mikey!"

"Hey, P.C.," Mike said, with little enthusiasm.

"See my hat?"

"I see it." How the hell could he miss it?

"Isn't it great?" Pork Chop demonstrated how the hat worked by sticking the straws in his mouth, sucking the beers dry, then belching like a thunderclap.

Mike said to Lonnie, "You didn't tell me Pork Chop was coming."

"That a problem?"

"Well, no. I just—"

"Not too good for your old pals, are you?"

"Of course not, but—"

"Then let's boogie!" Lonnie gestured to the motorhome, with more grandeur than the hunk of junk deserved. "*Monsieur* Rawson, your chariot awaits."

The '75 Vogue Villa Grande was Lonnie's pride and joy. Eggshell-white with red detail to match the rust. The vanity plate read **EZLIVIN**. A section of the RV's grille was broken on one side, giving the appearance of a snaggletoothed grin. Lonnie claimed such things gave the rustbucket "character." He'd even christened the motorhome. He called her Jezebel.

"I'd happily live in this rig," he often said.

And when his long-suffering girlfriend Wendy finally tired of his bullshit and kicked his ass to the curb, Lonnie got his wish.

Mike doubted the reality of living in the motorhome matched Lonnie's fantasy. Without Wendy, the guy had no one. He did feel sorry for his old friend. Maybe that was why he had agreed to come on this trip in the first place? Okay…the free ringside seats to Wrestlemania didn't hurt either.

Mike hugged his wife goodbye. Kissed his son's head, inhaling his powdery baby-smell. "I'll call from the arena," he promised her. "Let you know we made it safe."

Not good enough for Rachel.

"Lonnie!" she said, in the sharp tone of voice that could make Mike's balls crawl up into his abdomen.

Lonnie snapped to attention like a scolded dog.

"Have you been drinking?" she asked him.

"No, ma'am," he assured her. "Just a few beers."

"I expect you to bring my husband home in one piece."

Lonnie nodded sheepishly.

"And Lonnie." She softened her tone. "I was sorry to hear about you and Wendy."

Mike knew *that* was B.S. Rachel had often wondered aloud what was taking Wendy so long to wise up.

Lonnie puffed up his chest, flicked the tails of his mullet. "Don't be," he said. "It's *her* loss." But there was a tremor of hurt beneath the braggadocio.

Mike gave his wife a goodbye grimace as he headed for the RV.

Rachel raised her eyebrows and smirked: *Have fun!*

2

"The gang's all here!" Pork Chop cried. "The party starts NOW!"

He held out a meaty palm. Mike slapped it halfheartedly.

"Tell me I'm seeing things, P.C. You're wearing a kilt?"

"Damn straight. The ladies get one look at these legs," Pork Chop said, raking his hands through his bristles, "there won't be a dry seat in the Silverdome."

Mike shuddered. "If you say so."

"And you know I gotta show my support for my man 'Rowdy' Roddy. He's gonna destroy that fag Adrian Adonis. Just wait n' see!" Pork Chop punctuated his boast by slurping at his beer hat.

Mike glanced around the RV.

He'd been inside only once before, after Lonnie first bought it and dropped by to show it off. He didn't recall it being so...*disgusting.* Jezebel's interior reeked like a teenage boy's bedroom: Stale cigarette smoke, beer, gym socks, and jizz. It was like stepping into a time capsule from a misspent youth. Mike wondered how many brain cells had been lost in here to cheap booze and bong hits.

Lonnie's "palace on wheels" contained a cramped kitchen with a refrigerator, a gas stove, a sink, and a small dining area. The bedroom was in back, replete with double bed, which Mike thought to be wishful thinking on Lonnie's part. Tacked to the door of the bathroom cubicle (a toilet/shower combo) was a rumpled centerfold of Tawny Kitaen. Behind the driver and passenger seats was a tiger-stripe sofa with a matching blanket draped across it. Hanging from the rearview mirror was a long-expired Playboy bunny air freshener, and a rubber bat on a string, the head bitten off in emulation of Ozzy Osbourne. The gaudy wooden paneling above the stove was scorched in a hideous starburst pattern, as if Lonnie's attempt at a motorhome-cooked meal had gotten out of control.

Scuffed olive carpeting covered the floor. Except for a patch towards the rear of the rig that was roughly the size and shape of a bathmat. A sheet of blue plastic tarp covered that area. Beneath the tarp was a jagged hole where rust had eaten through to the undercarriage. Mike only knew the hole was there because the first time Lonnie gave him the "grand tour," he'd stepped on the tarp and plunged through, narrowly avoiding a broken leg and tetanus. Lonnie had laughed his ass off, claiming the hole was a doggy door. He hadn't owned a dog since he was nine.

Cardboard boxes were scattered throughout the motorhome. Mike figured they must contain Lonnie's worldly possessions. Tossed on the lawn when Wendy threw him out.

Lonnie snapped his fingers at Pork Chop. "Muscle shirt me."

Pork Chop tore the nearest box open, pulled out another HULKAMANIA shirt, and tossed it to Lonnie.

Lonnie shrugged on the shirt, eyeing Mike's duds like a sneering fashionista.

"You're not going to the rasslin' show dressed like *that*, are you, Mikey?"

Mike glanced down at his jeans and turtleneck sweater. "What's wrong with what I'm wearing?"

"What's right with it?"

Pork Chop doffed the brim of his beer hat at Lonnie's wit.

"Muscle shirt him, P.C."

"Really," Mike insisted, "I'm cool."

"Not unless they changed the definition, you're not."

"Hey! Rachel gave me this sweater."

"You look like an accountant."

"I *am* an accountant."

Lonnie threw up his hands in mock surrender. "Alright, alright. Suit yourself."

Pork Chop said, "You wanna brewski, Mike?"

Mike glanced dubiously at Pork Chop's beer hat, not sure if he was being offered one of the straws. Instead, Pork Chop fetched four beers from the icebox. One for Mike, one for Lonnie, and another two for the contraption on his head.

Mike popped his beer and took a sip. He'd quit the sauce while Rachel was pregnant. If she couldn't drink, he wouldn't either. The beer was good and cold.

Lonnie clambered behind the wheel. He took a hearty drink as if chugging beer was standard operating procedure for driving a motorhome, nestled the can in the V of his crotch, then keyed the engine. The rig rumbled to life.

"Come sit up front with the big dog," Lonnie called to Mike.

Mike glanced at the trash-strewn passenger seat. A plastic McDonald's cup lay on its side, its straw drooling something sticky across the tiger-stripe seat. "Can I get one of those muscle shirts, P.C.?"

"That's the spirit," Lonnie said.

Pork Chop tossed Mike a shirt. Mike used it to blanket the seat before sitting down. A flicker of hurt crossed Lonnie's face. Mike took a guilty swig of beer.

He glanced out his window at Rachel, who was waving the baby's tiny hand goodbye to him. But before Mike could wave back, Lonnie hit the gas and the RV roared away in a toxic fart of exhaust fumes.

3

They were on the expressway. Making good time.

Shortly after setting off, Lonnie had shoved a wrinkled roadmap in Mike's hands and informed him it was his job to get them to the Silverdome ASAFP.

"You're my co-pilot, bro." Lonnie made it sound like he was granting Mike some lifelong wish. "The Goose to my Maverick. Speaking of which…"

He winked at Pork Chop in the rearview.

The big guy was slumped on the sofa behind them.

"Say, P.C.," Lonnie said. "I feel the need…"

Together they cackled, "The need for weed!"

Pork Chop started rolling the first 'J.'

Mike continued tracing their route on the roadmap.

If all went as planned – taking into account that with Lonnie Deveroux, things rarely ever did – the drive to Pontiac, Michigan would take them no more than twelve hours, allowing for pit stops along the way. *I-40 should take us up to I-65…which will lead us into Kentucky…up through the Buckeye State…from there it's a straight shot to Michigan…*

"Something wrong with your beer?" Lonnie asked him.

Mike glanced up from the map. "Huh?"

"Your beer. Something wrong with it?"

Mike took a birdlike sip. "Just pacing myself."

"The hell for?" Lonnie slugged hard at his own beer as if he felt obliged to drink for the both of them.

Mike double-checked to make sure he had fastened his seatbelt.

"Hey," he said, "thanks for inviting me, man. I mean it. I've been going kinda stir-crazy. Haven't had a night to myself since the baby was born." Since months *before* the baby was born, now that he thought about it. Of course, Mike knew Rachel had it worse than he did. He made a mental note to return the favor and make sure she got a night to herself sometime soon.

"*De nada*, brother," Lonnie said. "It's been too long."

And it *had* been a long time. Mike wasn't proud of it. But then, five minutes back in Lonnie's company and he remembered why that was. He loved the dumb bastard and the memories they shared, but could only tolerate him in small doses these days.

"So how's daddyhood treating you?" Lonnie said with a smirk.

The answer was already written in the tired lines on Mike's face, the matching luggage under his eyes. "I'll let you know when I get a second to breathe."

"You should've taken my advice, bro."

"What's that?"

"A.P.O."

"Huh?"

"Always. Pull. Out."

Pork Chop snorted beer through his nose, half-laughing, half-choking.

"Ehhh," Mike said. "The little moments make it all worthwhile."

Lonnie looked unconvinced.

"You ever thought about it?" Mike asked him.

"What?" Lonnie sputtered. "'Bout having a rugrat?"

"Yeah. You know. Settle down, take some responsibility…" He resisted the urge to add: *Grow up.*

"Fuck that shit," said Lonnie. "I value my freedom too much."

Mike glanced around the squalid motorhome. *And give up all this.*

The pity he felt for his old pal was tempered by the question nagging at the back of his brain ever since Lonnie's late-night call: How could Lonnie Deveroux afford ringside seats to Wrestlemania? *Shit. Was he dealing weed again?*

"So," Mike said, probing for answers. "How much do I owe you for the ticket?"

"Really, Mikey? You're gonna insult me like that? Cheapen years of friendship with vulgar talk of money?"

"But…ringside seats can't be cheap."

Lonnie whistled through the gap in his front teeth. "They're not."

"You win the lottery or something?"

"Relax, Mikey. I got the tickets, okay?"

Mike mimed zipping his lips.

"Good as in my hands," Lonnie muttered.

Mike frowned. "What does *that* mean?"

"You see those boxes back there?" Lonnie said, with a jerk of his thumb. "Full of bootleg rasslin' merch. Like *this* snazzy number." He preened his HULKAMANIA muscle shirt like a Home Shopping Network model. "Bet you thought it was the real McCoy, huh? Gotta hand it to those sweatshop kids, they do great work. So anyway, this guy I know, buddy of mine, he says we deliver the merch for him to sell at the event, and those ringside seats are ours."

Mike sank down in his seat. "Jesus, Lonnie. You couldn't have told me this earlier?"

"What's the problem?"

"Leaving aside the legalities, it's a long way to drive for a promise."

"Chill, Mikey. I gotta Plan B. In the unlikely event my guy doesn't come through with the tickets, Cyndi-from-the-Bar says she'll blow Randy Savage, earn us VIP passes."

Mike wondered if the Macho Man knew about Plan B. *Ohhh, yeahhh!*

"Who's Cyndi-from-the-Bar?"

"Can I come out now?" said a voice from the back of the RV.

"Mike, meet Cyndi. From the bar."

She must have been hiding in the bathroom. And thank Christ Rachel hadn't seen her, Mike thought. His wife would have been a lot less cool about this trip had she known there were women coming. Especially a woman like Cyndi-from-the-Bar.

Shock of bottle-blonde hair held stiffly in place by enough hairspray it probably punched its own hole through the ozone layer. Fashionably-ripped fishnet tights. Butt-hugging Daisy Duke shorts held up with suspenders, and a HULKAMANIA tube-top that looked *so* much better on her than Lonnie's muscle shirt looked on him.

Mike tried valiantly to maintain eye contact as she tottered toward the cockpit. Cyndi's breasts, straining against the flimsy fabric of her tube-top, swayed with the motion of the motorhome, slapping together like a fleshy Newton's Cradle.

"Ohhhh!" she exclaimed. "He's cuuuuute!"

Her voice was a Betty Boop-on-helium squeak.

Mike flashed his wedding ring. "He's also married!"

Cyndi giggled. "You're funny."

"Why don'tcha give my boy Mikey a backrub?" Lonnie winked at Mike. "He looks a little tense."

Cyndi strutted forward.

"Not interested," Mike said. "Thanks all the same."

"What happens at Wrestlemania," Lonnie assured him, "*stays* at Wrestlemania."

"Nothing's *gonna* happen," Mike firmly replied.

Pork Chop snickered. "You turn fag on us, Mikey?"

"You found me out, P.C. The wife and kid are my cover."

Cyndi planted herself on the sofa behind the front seats and tousled Mike's hair. "You just gimme a holler you change your mind, handsome."

"I'll take a backrub," Pork Chop said, generously.

She sneered at him. "Shut up, P.C.!"

"Any more surprises you wanna tell me about?" Mike asked Lonnie.

"You gonna be like this the whole trip, Mikey?"

"Like what?"

"The word *asshole* comes to mind. You won't wear a shirt, you've hardly touched your beer, and now you turn down a backrub from a hot piece of tail like Cyndi? You're really bringing me down, man."

Was Lonnie right? Mike wondered. Was he being an asshole here? Why'd he even come on this trip if he was just gonna piss and moan?

Mike drained the rest of his beer in one long swallow, crushed the empty can in his fist, and said, "Set me up with another tall boy, P.C."

Lonnie slapped him on the back. "And a muscle shirt?"

"Just the beer is fine."

4

Four beers later, Mike quickly discovered how out of practice he was.

He'd refused the last didgeridoo-sized doobie Pork Chop rolled, at least until the second time it was passed his way. By then the motorhome was choked with sweet-smelling smoke. He figured he was getting a contact high anyway. Might as well go all in. The beer and weed went straight to his head and now his face felt tingly and warm, smeared with a sloppy smile as he melted down into the passenger seat.

Struggling to focus – *to keep his damn eyes open* – Mike marveled at how Lonnie and Pork Chop still partied like they were punk kids. They'd just never stopped, he guessed. He decided he should start pacing himself. There were still many miles ahead of them. If he didn't slow down, he'd be wasted long before they arrived at the Silverdome.

Mike glanced back at Pork Chop. The big guy looked ridiculous in his plaid kilt and novelty beer hat. P.C. was currently attempting to attach a bottle of Jack and a can of Coke to either side of the hardhat. He was already shitfaced, but if this weird science project proved successful, Mike estimated that Rip Van Pork Chop might just regain consciousness in time for *next* year's Wrestlemania.

The sound of Lonnie blatting the horn startled Mike from his reverie. With a shock of clarity he saw they were stuck in gridlock. Ahead of them, a column of black smoke billowed up from the site of an auto accident, blocking the lanes of the expressway. State troopers and EMS vehicles swarmed the scene.

"Fuck a duck," Lonnie said.

Needless to say, patience was not high among Lonnie's virtues. In fact, Mike was hard-pressed to name *one* virtue. He might have cited 'generosity with Wrestlemania tickets,' except he now knew the tickets were far from guaranteed.

Lonnie honked the horn relentlessly, to the fury of the other drivers surrounding them. They honked back, swore at him.

Mike tried to be the voice of reason: "Lonnie," he said, fanning smoke from his eyes. "You're driving a bong on wheels, carrying a load of bootleg wrestling merch. You really wanna draw so much attention?"

"Point." Lonnie laid off the horn. He glanced at his wristwatch, cursing the victims of the accident. "I didn't know any better, I'd think the cocksuckers did this on purpose! Doesn't anybody know how to drive anymore?"

"Rate we're going, we're gonna miss the undercard," Pork Chop whined.

"You think I don't know that, P.C.?"

Mike wondered how long they'd been stuck here. And more importantly…

…what the hell was Cyndi doing *sitting on his lap?*

He tried to think back, but his memory was hazy. He vaguely recalled that she had continued playing with his hair and teasing her nails down the nape of his neck until he finally consented to a backrub. *What was the harm?* That might've been the beer talking. As her fingers expertly kneaded his shoulders (*goddamn, that felt good*), she had brushed her breasts against his scalp (*goddamn, that felt even better*)…next thing he knew she was perched on his lap like a kid rattling off her Christmas list in Santa's ear.

"Cyndi," Mike said. "Would you be a doll and move back to the sofa?"

"I'm comfy right here, thank you kindly."

Mike cut a pleading glance at Lonnie: *Get her off me, would ya?*

Lonnie fired back a conspirator's wink: *What happens at Wrestlemania,* stays *at Wrestlemania.*

"Cyndi, please." Mike chuckled nervously. "My legs are going numb."

"The hell's that supposed to mean? You calling me *fat*?"

"No!" Mike stammered: "I, uh… I didn't mean… Look, I'm numb all over."

All over? Mike thought. *If only that were true.* Alcohol wasn't the only thing from which he had abstained during Rachel's pregnancy; he was hornier than a pubescent boy at the Playboy mansion, and got wood if the wind changed direction suddenly. *Please don't get hard, please don't get hard—*

"So," Cyndi said, stubbornly settled on Mike's lap, "you guys grew up together?"

"Grew up together," Lonnie said, "and we *shoulda* ruled the rock n' roll roost together. Ain't that right, Mikey?"

Here it comes, Mike thought. Lonnie's *let's-get-the-band-back-together* bit.

"One of these days, swear to God…we're gonna get the band back together."

Mike bit his tongue.

"Take a look in the glovebox, sweet thang," Lonnie told Cyndi.

She opened the glove, rooting through the clutter. "What am I looking for?"

Lonnie gestured to a cassette tape in a cracked plastic case. "Buried treasure."

Cyndi blew the dust off the case and examined the cover.

WRATHBONE was scrawled in Wite-Out across the cover image: A grainy black-and-white photo of the band loitering outside the neon-lit window of a liquor store. All glam-metal hair and try-hard macho pouts. Beneath the photo, in faded dot-matrix print, was a crooked legend:

WRATHBONE IS

Lonnie 'Love Gun' Deveroux: guitar/vox
Mike 'Roxxx Off' Rawson: bass
Pork Chop: drums

Mike snatched the tape from Cyndi's hands. "Where the hell did you find this?"

He couldn't help chuckling at his teenage self's earnest *watch out, world* expression and rooster-crest of teased hair.

"I never lost it," Lonnie said. "You think I'd just throw away an artifact of musical history?"

Rode Hard/Put Up Wet was Wrathbone's one and only demo, featuring the tracks "Well-Hung Hangover," "Just Say Yes," and "Spread 'Em Wide." The demo was never released to the public. *Probably a good thing,* Mike thought, though he hadn't heard the tape in years. Adding to the band's mystique was the fact that they'd never played a single live gig. They'd been scheduled to debut at the Battle of the Bands at the state fair. But the night before the show, Pork Chop's dad, a hard-ass Vietnam veteran, caught Pork Chop perfecting his stage makeup in the bathroom mirror. Accusing his son of being a fairy, he'd beat the shit out of him, breaking Pork Chop's wrist, before burning his drum kit out back of their doublewide, like he was back in 'Nam razing VC villes to the ground. Two weeks later, Mike left town to take a job with his uncle, and Wrathbone's legacy was over before it began. A tragic loss to hair metal.

"Whoa, Lonnie!" Cyndi swooned over his picture. "You were hot."

"The hell you mean *were*?" Lonnie double-checked his reflection in the rearview, confirming that he was as buff as he remembered.

Lonnie started telling Cyndi war stories from back in the day.

Mike felt embarrassed for them all as his old friend catalogued their punk kid escapades. It was a miracle no one had died.

"To look at him now I know it's hard to believe, but *this* guy—" Lonnie pinched Mike's cheek: "*This* guy was a motherfucking animal."

"What happened?" Cyndi asked.

"The same fate that befalls every great man," Lonnie told her. "He went and got hitched." He shook his head gravely. "Fucking tragedy."

"Hey!" Mike dragged Cyndi off his lap and teetered to his feet. "I started a family. That's hardly a tragedy!"

"You didn't have to skip town, though." Lonnie looked genuinely hurt, as if he'd been stewing on this for years. "We coulda set the West Memphis club scene on fire. Once P.C. replaced his kit and his arm healed. But *nooooo*. You decided you'd rather move to Cumdump, Tennessee and sit behind a desk all day—"

"Humboldt," Mike said.

If Lonnie heard Mike correct him, he didn't acknowledge it. Instead he glanced down at the tented crotch of Mike's jeans. "Look out! You got a concealed carry permit for that thing, Mr. Family Man?"

"Ewww!" Cyndi said.

Pork Chop pointed and laughed.

Mike felt his face burning red as he tugged his shirt down. "The fuck is the matter with you, man? I'm sorry about what happened with you and Wendy. But don't lay your shit on me." He stomped to the kitchen, fetched another beer and tried to drink himself sober, not to mention flaccid. "I knew this trip was a mistake."

"C'mon, Mikey! You know I'm just breaking your balls!"

But it was more than that. Lonnie had never forgiven him for bailing on the band. For all Lonnie's talk of fame and fortune, Mike had always known they were chasing a fool's dream with the rock n' roll stuff. Pork Chop's injury had been an easy excuse for Mike to quit, and take that job his Uncle Pat had offered him. Uncle Pat was the operations manager of a factory that manufactured golf balls in Humboldt, Tennessee. He'd told Mike that once he graduated from high school, when he was ready to 'straighten up and fly right,' there would be a job waiting for him. If Mike assumed he'd be waltzing his way to a cushy desk job in the factory accounting department, however, he was in for a surprise. While he did make a decent living as an accountant *these* days, he'd had to work like a dog to get there: Vacuuming offices, mopping floors, and cleaning toilets, while he went to night school to earn his CPA license. *We all gotta start somewhere*, Uncle Pat had told him. *Sooner or later it's time to grow up and act like a responsible adult.*

Mike wondered when that day would come for Lonnie and Pork Chop…if it ever did.

An awkward silence filled the motorhome. Lonnie took the cassette from Cyndi, slammed it in the tape deck, and cranked the volume.

A squawk of feedback… a chugging guitar riff… a heart attack blast of drums.

Wincing at the noise, Mike's first thought was that the tape must have warped with age. Then he remembered: *Nope, that's just how badly we played.* Lonnie's screeching vocal shrilled from the speakers like a metal castrato, and the rest of the group joined in an emphatic call-and-response:

Spread 'em wiiide, honey
If you got the love, then I got the money!
Spread 'em wiiide, baby
You got what I need, and I don't mean maybe!

Pork Chop started drumming an off-tempo rhythm. "Oh, hell yeah!"

"Turn that shit off," Mike said, although he couldn't help cracking a smile.

"*'Spread 'em wiiide, Mikey!'*" Lonnie sang to him.

Mike shook his head, laughed. "Asshole."

"We cool, bro?"

Mike sighed. "Yeah… we're cool."

Cyndi clamped her hands over her ears. "You guys are *so* not cool."

Mike and Lonnie laughed together.

"Alright, fuck this," Lonnie suddenly said. "Hold onto your asses, rasslin' fans!"

He wrenched the shift, throwing Jezebel into gear. Stomped the gas pedal and started bulling the rig across the congested lanes toward the exit ramp. Other drivers reacted in a fury of blaring horns and profanity.

"Lonnie!" Cyndi clutched the dash to avoid being bucked from the passenger seat. "What the hell are you doing?"

"Takin' a shortcut!"

"Don't you wanna see the wreck?" Pork Chop said.

"No time."

"But we've waited *this* long!"

"Don't worry, P.C. You'll see all the blood you want at The Fight."

Mike stifled a smirk. 'The Fight.' Like they were on their way to see Ali versus Frazier. Not a wrestling match with a pre-arranged outcome. He didn't dare say this to Lonnie, of course. Lonnie took his wrestling deadly serious. Always had. And truth be told, Mike didn't want to miss 'The Fight' either. Hogan versus The Giant promised to be a battle for the ages.

Pork Chop shoved his head out an open window and started barking at the drivers around them, "Make a hole! Make a hole!"

Gradually, Lonnie muscled the motorhome onto the exit ramp.

Before them loomed a vast sprawl of Kentucky woods.

Mike muttered something about how he'd seen enough horror movies to know nothing good ever came from a shortcut through the woods.

Lonnie laughed off his concerns. "Between being hacked to death by some kill-crazy redneck, and missing The Fight? Brother, I'll take my chances."

5

A bump in the road jolted Mike back to consciousness.

His first fuzzy thought was that Rachel had elbowed him awake, that it was his turn to check on the baby. Then his surroundings blurred into focus. He found himself sprawled on the sofa behind the front seats of Lonnie's RV. He was clutching a half-empty beer can to his chest. Must've dozed off for a second or two, the motion of the motorhome, along with the beer and weed, rocking him to sleep like a newborn in a bassinet. Faintly, on the stereo, he heard someone talking. Sounded like... *old-timey preaching?* Had Lonnie been born-again while he was napping? Mike thought it more likely he was still dreaming. He smacked his lips, swallowing back a sour taste in his mouth. He glanced at his watch and saw that nearly two hours had elapsed. It was late afternoon. *Dozed off, my ass.*

He wasn't the only one to have passed out. Pork Chop, having successfully attached the Jack and Coke to his hat, now lay poleaxed on the bed in back, snoring like someone trying to start a stubborn lawnmower. From this angle, Mike could see that Pork Chop wasn't wearing anything under his kilt. *Of course he wasn't.*

Mike heaved himself upright, blinking in confusion at the view through the windshield. Jezebel was jouncing down a washboard woodlands road, patched irregularly with blacktop and gravel and dirt. At its widest, the road was a cramped two lanes; at its narrowest, tight as a deer trail. An honor guard of looming trees lined the road. Grasping branches whipped at the windshield, snagging on the wipers and grille as the RV plowed forward.

On the radio, the preacher's thick Kentucky baritone insisted: "Brothers and sisters, so sayeth the Word: '*All things are by the law purged with blood. Without the shedding of blood there is no remission!*'"

Mike found his voice. "Where are we?"

In the passenger seat, Cyndi was scowling at the map like a cartographer studying charts from a lost world. Lonnie divided his attention between the treacherous path before them, and the jiggling contents of her tube-top.

Cyndi glared at Lonnie. "Missing Wrestlemania, is where. And would you turn that crap off? I can't hear myself think."

"The wrath of God is a-comin'," said the voice on the radio, as if in response to her insult.

"You're the one who complained about the tape," Lonnie muttered.

He switched off the radio, silencing the preacher.

They drove on. For the next few minutes, the only sound inside the Vogue was Pork Chop's heavy snoring.

"This road's gotta lead *somewhere*," Lonnie finally said. Mike suspected it wasn't the first time he had said it. As if it were a mantra that might prove true if he repeated it enough. But judging by the tremor in his voice, Lonnie was quickly losing faith.

"I'll tell you where it's leading, Lonnie," Cyndi told him, "straight to Blue Balls City!" She slapped him upside the head with the map before climbing from her seat and storming into the bathroom, slamming the cubicle door behind her.

"That girl really likes her wrestling," Mike said.

"Oh yeah, she's a regular ring rat."

Mike reclaimed the passenger seat. "Where'd you meet?"

"Cyndi-from-the-Bar?" Lonnie said, like it was a trick question. "The bar."

"And you two…you've been…?"

Lonnie cocked an eyebrow. "A gentleman never tells."

"Exactly. So spill it, sleazeball."

"Tonight was gonna be the night. I was hoping this trip would seal the deal." Lonnie glanced at his watch and then smacked the wheel in anger. "Goddamn it!"

"Relax, Lonnie. It's not the end of the world if we don't make it."

"For you, maybe."

"Huh?"

"The guy I'm delivering the merch to…"

"Your friend."

"Yeah, well. I might've exaggerated our friendship."

"What do you mean?"

"I owe the guy, Mikey. Owe the guy big. I don't deliver the merch on time…?"

Lonnie shook his head; shot Mike a somber look.

Mike exhaled through clenched teeth.

"Jesus, Lonnie. What were you thinking?"

"Beyond Wrestlemania and banging Cyndi, not much."

"Don't you ever learn?"

Lonnie's bottom lip trembled. Gone was the bravado; Lonnie had regressed to a frightened child. Tears welled in his eyes. "The hell am I gonna do, Mikey?"

Mike gave a long sigh. *Same old Lonnie. Lands himself neck-deep in shit and expects someone to throw him a lifeline. The more things change…*

He glanced at his watch. "We can still make it."

"Don't bullshit me, man."

"We can still make it!"

Buoyed by Mike's tone, Lonnie dried his eyes and nodded.

"Yeah. Right. Okay. We can still make it."

Mike fetched the roadmap.

"Now where are we? What route did you take?"

"Shit, I don't even know anymore."

Mike glanced between the map and the road. "Well, there's

gotta be a sign or some kind of landmarrr— Fuck, Lonnie, LOOK OUT!"

Something burst from the brush, darted into the road, freezing in the path of the onrushing motorhome.

Lonnie stomped the brake pedal.

The wheels locked, tires scrabbling for grip on the loose gravel, kicking up an H-bomb of dust that clouded the windshield, but not before Mike saw the thing's eyes widen, its mouth forming a shocked O, and he knew it was *human*.

Lonnie wrenched the steering wheel. The RV fishtailed. A muffled thud shuddered through the vehicle. Then the Vogue skidded to a jarring one-eighty stop that hurled Mike against the dash.

The kitchen cupboards clattered open, spewing plastic crockery out onto the floor.

Boxes overturned, upchucking a rainbow of wrestling merch.

For a moment, all Mike could hear was the blood roaring in his ears, his own Tommy gun heartbeat, and that meaty thud echoing through his mind…

Then the sound of Pork Chop snoring. He had somehow slept through it all.

Cyndi staggered from the bathroom cubicle. "What the hell, Lonnie!"

"Everyone okay?" Lonnie gasped, rubbing his whiplashed neck.

"No!" Mike and Cyndi shouted at him in unison.

Mike slumped back in his seat. He peered through the windshield. No sign of the thing (*person!*) they had hit. Only dust, swirling like mist in a bad horror movie.

"What happened?" Cyndi said.

"We hit something," Mike said.

"A deer," Lonnie said. "I think – I think it was a deer…"

Mike teetered to his feet. On unsteady legs, he kicked a path through the strewn wrestling merch to the door. "The hell it was."

"Where you going?" Lonnie called. "We don't got time for this, man. I'm telling you, it was Bambi's mother. It makes you feel any better, I'll make a donation to the ASPCA, first thing tomorrow."

Mike ignored him, shoving through the door.

"Goddamn it," Lonnie said. "Stay here, Cyndi." He went after Mike.

"Why do I gotta stay here?"

"Just make sure P.C. doesn't pull a Bon Scott in his sleep."

Lonnie found Mike standing gravely on the driver's side of the rig.

The wing mirror was shattered, hanging by a thread.

A scarlet handprint, all too human, was smeared along Jezebel's side.

"Look like a hoof print to you?" Mike said.

Lonnie bowed his head, then kicked at the gravel road in anger. "This trip has officially shit its drawers."

Mike wheeled on him. "Would you stop thinking about yourself for two seconds? This is serious, Lonnie. I think we hit somebody. Now help me look!"

They rounded the front of the RV and peered into the forest bordering the road. The woods were silent, as if even the chirring insects and scuttling critters of the forest were paying their respects for a human life cut short. It was barely four in the afternoon, yet the overhead tree canopy allowed little light, dappling the scene like a lava lamp.

Mike saw the body first, tangled in the roadside brush.

"Oh, Jesus, Lonnie… *there*!"

He was whispering. He wasn't sure why. It just felt right.

The girl was sprawled facedown in the dirt, twigs and leaves glued to her naked body. One arm was stretched above her, as though she were swimming through the undergrowth. Her head was shaved to the scalp. Hard to tell how old she was. She could have been as young as sixteen or in her early twenties.

"Fuck a duck," Lonnie wheezed.

Mike crouched beside the girl.

"Is she…?

Mike could only shake his head.

"Check her pulse."

Mike couldn't bring himself to touch her. "*You* check her pulse."

"Screw that, man. *Look* at her!"

Every inch of pale flesh – her shaved head, her shoulders and back, her buttocks, her thighs, even the soles of her feet – was carved with crude cruciform wounds.

And something else…

Mike squinted in the gloom.

Were those – *words*?

ENVY

GREED

LUST

Mike knew they would find more if they turned her onto her back.

"We didn't do that… did we, Mikey?"

"Of course not," Mike snapped at him.

"Then who did?"

A branch snapped somewhere to their left.

"That's it," Lonnie said, "I'm calling it. Back to the rig—"

A voice behind them said, "Step away from the 'goat."

6

They froze.

A shadowy figure stood opposite the road, a few feet from the RV.

Light glinted off the long metallic object in his arms.

"Do what I says," the man said. "Slow. No sudden moves."

Mike and Lonnie held their hands in the air and stepped away from the girl's body.

"Okay," Mike said. "Easy…"

"Come on over here. 'Front of your camper."

"Motorhome," Lonnie corrected the man.

"Lonnie!" Mike hissed. "Shut. The fuck. Up."

They braced themselves as the man emerged from the shadows, their guts knotted in terror as they anticipated the ghoulish features of whatever monster had butchered this poor girl…

But it wasn't a man.

It wasn't a monster.

It was only a boy.

Maybe fifteen, sixteen. Wispy hairs fuzzed his upper lip and chin in a pitiful attempt at a beard. He wore a coonskin cap replete with a striped tail, and baggy hunter's clothes several sizes too large for him. The sleeves of his flannel shirt were cuffed to the forearms. Despite his slight frame, he was country-boy strong, leveling a double-barreled Mossberg at Mike and Lonnie with barely any effort.

Lonnie gave a heavy sigh of relief, lowered his hands. "It's just a kid." He took a step toward the boy. "Careful where you're pointing that thing, son. Don't want anybody getting hhh—"

Quick as a cougar, the boy stabbed the heavy shotgun barrels into Lonnie's gut.

Lonnie woofed in pain, sinking to his knees.

The boy whipped the shotgun barrels back at Mike.

"Don't shoot!" Mike cried, hands above his head.

"Whatchoo boys doin' out here?" the kid said, in a thick backwoods drawl.

"Nuh-nothing!" Mike said. "We – we're lost!"

Still gasping for breath, on his hands and knees, Lonnie began babbling nonsensically about Wrestlemania III and the main event match between Hulk Hogan and Andre the Giant.

"Lonnie, shut up!" Mike pleaded.

"*Both* of youse shut up!" the kid said.

The boy glanced at the mutilated girl lying sprawled on the ground at the edge of the woods. "She dead?"

"I…we…don't know," Mike said.

The boy planted a boot on the girl's hip, and with a grunt, rolled her roughly onto her back.

Her front was a grotesque human doodle pad of crosses and words. **PRIDE** was carved across one of her breasts. Her nipple appeared to be dotting the '**I**.'

Mike turned his head, choking down a geyser of puke.

"Don't move," the boy warned them.

He crouched down beside the girl and pressed his fingers to her throat…

Gave a heavy sigh of relief. "Thank you, Jesus."

Back on his feet, the boy unhooked a bulky walkie-talkie from his belt. He depressed the TALK button. "Uncle Jake? Come in. I got her."

A crackle of static.

Then a man's gruff voice came over the radio: "Where are you, boy?"

"Crookback Road," the boy said. "Apiece from the old hanging tree."

"Tell me she's alive," the man said.

"She's alive," the boy said. "There's still time."

"Praise Jesus."

"There's something else. The 'goat. She ain't alone. There's two fellas here with her."

"The law?"

The boy sized Mike and Lonnie up and down.

"Naw," he said, scornfully. "They ain't nothing. They're in a camper—"

Lonnie opened his mouth to object. Mike elbowed him hard in the ribs.

"I think maybe they run her down," the boy said into the walkie-talkie.

"Well, you just hold 'em there," replied the man. "We're comin' to you."

"Yessir."

The boy hooked the walkie-talkie back to his belt.

"On your knees," he told Mike and Lonnie.

"You don't have to do this," Mike said. "We can work this out. Let's just—"

The kid ratcheted the shotgun, a bone-chilling sound in the stillness of the forest. "I said, on your knees!"

That's when Cyndi-from-the-Bar appeared behind the boy and pressed the barrel of a .38 snub to the base of his skull.

"Drop the gun, kid."

The boy turned his head slowly to see who was behind him.

While he was distracted, Mike lunged forward and snatched the Mossberg from his hands.

Lonnie staggered to his feet, and then slugged the boy square in the face with a haymaker that dropped the kid cold to the ground, his arms and legs splayed in an X shape. "Thanks for the assist," Lonnie said to Cyndi, as if he'd had everything under control, right up until the moment she'd saved their asses.

Cyndi grabbed the shotgun from Mike and checked the load with an expert's eye. She stared down at the mutilated girl, and the out-cold kid beside her.

"Not the way I expected this to go..." Mike heard her murmur to herself.

Lonnie watched as she tucked the .38 in the waistband of her Daisy Dukes. "Say, sugar. Where'd you get the pistola?"

Cyndi's face flashed with irritation, as if Lonnie's voice was a buzzing mosquito breaking her concentration. "Shut the hell up, Deveroux. Let me think."

Lonnie frowned. "Since when'd we start using last names?"

Cyndi crouched beside the unconscious kid and unhooked the walkie-talkie from his belt. She examined the device. Fiddled with the frequency dial. Punched the TALK button and said, "Mayday, mayday! Federal agent requesting emergency assistance!" She fiddled again with the frequency dial. "Does anyone copy?"

The walkie-talkie returned nothing but bursts of static.

Mike and Lonnie exchanged dumbfounded looks.

"Alright," Cyndi said, in a take-charge tone. She gestured to the mutilated girl at their feet. "You two dipshits carry her back to the camper."

"Motorhome," Lonnie said. "And, hey! Who're you calling dipshits?"

"*You*, dipshit."

Mike gawked at her. Was this the same airheaded ring rat who'd been dry-humping him just a few hours ago? Her helium-high voice had become a husky growl. She was like a different person, and a scary one at that.

"Cyndi," Lonnie said. "What the hell is going on here?"

"My name isn't Cyndi," she said. "It's Special Agent Rhonda Shaughnessy. Anti-Counterfeiting Task Force. And you two assholes are under arrest for trafficking counterfeit goods across state lines."

"The Anti-Whatting What?" Lonnie said.

Mike clenched his teeth, sighed. "The merch, dumbass."

Lonnie glanced down at his HULKAMANIA shirt. The others could almost hear the synapses firing as he pieced it all together. "But...but I'm just a mule!"

"You're a fucking jackass, is what you are," Mike said.

"Boys," Special Agent Rhonda Shaughnessy said, "once we're back in the camper you can give up your right to remain silent all you want. Right now, I suggest we shake a leg."

She peered off into the woods from which the kid had appeared.

Mike followed her gaze. An icy finger shivered down his spine.

We're coming… Uncle Jake had said over the walkie-talkie.

Whoever *they* were, Mike didn't want to meet them.

"What about the kid?" he said.

Rhonda produced a set of handcuffs from the back of her Daisy Dukes. "I'll cuff him to a tree. Once we find help, I'll send someone back for him."

Mike and Lonnie huddled over the mutilated girl.

"So, uh, you wanna take her arms or legs?" Lonnie said.

Mike didn't want to touch her at all. He tried to find a spot, *any spot*, on the girl's wrists or ankles where he could carry her without touching her wounds, but whoever had mutilated her had done a thorough job. The scabbed symbols and words covered her body like infected tattoos.

"Quit reading her," Rhonda said. "Start carrying her."

Mike's guts churned in disgust. He shut his eyes, took a deep breath. The coppery scent of blood intermingled with the pine-fresh smells of the forest. When he opened his eyes, the word **WRATH** was curved around the girl's navel like a snake coiled to strike. *The word was there before, right?* Mike wasn't sure. The girl shivered in her sleep. The scab cracked and crumbled from the wound to reveal the word in shiny red letters. Blood trickled down her alabaster flesh.

WRATH

Mike felt a flash of fury: With Lonnie for getting him in this mess, and with Cyndi, Rhonda, *whatever* the hell her name was, for making him carry—

The girl jolted awake with an ear-splitting scream.

Mike stumbled back in terror. Lonnie did the same.

Lightning-fast, the girl scrabbled across the ground towards the kid, snatched up a sharpened stick, and plunged it into his left eye. His limbs jerked like an ER patient zapped with defibrillators. His right eye opened wide, the white clouding with blood. His mouth clapped open and closed. The girl wrenched the stick in his eye. A gusher of blood erupted from the ruined socket. The boy's legs drummed the ground spastically.

Finally, he gave a gargling cry and lay still.

Heaving for breath, the girl collapsed on top of him, moaning as she sank back into unconsciousness.

"Holy…fucking…shit!" Lonnie cried.

Rhonda glanced at her handcuffs, realized they were no longer required, and slid them back into the ass pocket of her Daisy Dukes. She hitched a thumb at the RV, ordered Mike and Lonnie to carry the girl inside.

Mike gripped the girl under her arms, moaning in disgust as her wounds leaked blood through his fingers. Lonnie took her legs, turning his head and gagging as they lifted her off the dead kid. The stick waggled back and forth in his eye, like an exclamation point at the end of a violent curse.

They hefted her to the motorhome, Mike walking backwards, relying on Lonnie to steer him. Mike was reminded of the old Laurel and Hardy piano skit, with the piano replaced by a naked girl with bizarre words and symbols carved into her flesh. Rhonda followed behind them, keeping the shotgun trained on the woods.

Pork Chop welcomed them back to the Vogue with a chorus of snores.

"Where do you want her?" Lonnie asked Rhonda, panting for breath.

"Put her on the bed," Rhonda said.

"Gross!" Lonnie said. "I sleep there."

"You won't have to worry about that for the next ten-to-twenty years."

Lonnie looked like he might start crying.

"What about Pork Chop?" Mike said.

"Wake his ass up," Rhonda said.

"Good luck with that."

"Just lay her next to him. And for Christ's sake, close his legs!"

Mike fetched the largest HULKAMANIA shirt he could find from the boxes of merch and draped it over the girl. Barely covered her privates, but it would do for now. She looked tiny on the bed next to Pork Chop. Nestling in the crook of the big lug's arm like a hacked-up, blood-spattered kewpie doll. Pork Chop snuggled his arm around her, smiling contentedly.

"You got a first aid kit in this heap?" Rhonda asked Lonnie.

"Somewhere, I guess."

"Find it. Clean her wounds the best you can till we find a hospital… On second thought," Rhonda said. "Rawson, you do it. I wouldn't trust Deveroux to wipe his own ass. Deveroux, you're back in the driver's seat."

"But…where?" Lonnie said. "We still don't know where the hell we are."

"And whose fault is that? Just get this piece of shit moving!"

7

After graduating from Quantico, top of her class, Special Agent Rhonda Shaughnessy could've had her pick of plum assignments. Anti-Terrorism. Organized Crime. Behavioral Science. To the dismay of her instructors at the academy, she requested a post with the Anti-Counterfeiting Task Force. "That's where you *end* a career," they warned her, "not begin one." But her mind was set, had been long before she even joined the Bureau, ever since that fateful Halloween night. *It was all for Billy…*

The West Memphis Field Office was a single-room sweatbox above a pet-grooming parlor that resounded with constant barking and reeked of wet fur. The Resident Agent in Charge, George Hansen, was a by-the-book bureaucrat who'd had his first taste of power back in junior high, when he was appointed lunchroom monitor. He still kept the whistle from those days, displayed in a graphite case on his office wall next to a framed photo of President Reagan.

Hansen's proudest professional moment had come when, after months of painstaking surveillance, he had arrested an elderly Mexican swap meet seller hawking knock-off Cabbage Patch dolls, so shoddily manufactured they looked more like Thalidomide Tots than the must-have toy of 1984. The bust had made page four of the local newspaper. The headline read: THE CABBAGE PATCH CONNECTION. Missing the sarcasm, Hansen had framed the article and placed it on the wall next to his photo of the Gipper. When the Mexican was deported, Hansen felt satisfied he'd played his part in keeping America safe.

Now he presided over a transient staff of one. Most agents beneath him would work like hell to atone for whatever sin had cast them into this wilderness, hoping to earn eventual reassignment. But Rhonda Shaughnessy wasn't like the screw-ups the brass typically sent to Hansen for attitude adjustment.

Arriving for work one morning, Hansen was surprised to find a young woman in his office. Her makeup was part punk-princess, part streetwalker. Her gravity-defying hairdo resembled that of a bottle-blonde Bride of Frankenstein. She was scantily clad in a black vinyl micro-skirt, a snakeskin-patterned tube-top with JAKE 'THE SNAKE' ROBERTS slithering across her breasts, and killer heels.

She stood studying a collage of evidence and mugshots pinned to the corkboard. Without taking her eyes from the board, she said: "Mornin', boss."

"Agent Shaughnessy?" Hansen said in surprise. "Would you care to explain what you're doing in my office? Not to mention, why you're dressed like…"

Shaughnessy cocked an eyebrow at him. "Like?"

He cleared his throat, aware that he was blushing.

Shaughnessy directed his attention to the corkboard, and the collage of evidence. Tapped a glittery fingernail against one of the mugshots.

"Meet Lonnie Deveroux," she said.

With his greasy shoulder-length hair, reefer-reddened eyes, and delinquent sneer, Deveroux looked no different than any other wastoid the ACTF arrested regularly for hustling bootleg band T-shirts outside rock concerts.

"For the better part of two weeks," Shaughnessy said, "I've been working undercover on my own time, baiting Deveroux and his associate, one Arthur Miller – not the playwright, in case you wondered – a.k.a. 'Pork Chop,' at their sports bar hangout on Kahle Street."

She stabbed a finger at another photo. This one appeared to have been taken with a hidden camera. It captured Arthur 'Pork Chop' Miller – the poster boy for fat, drunk, and stupid – spraying beer from his nostrils as he laughed uproariously. Reacting to a pull-my-finger joke, perhaps.

"Deveroux and Miller believe I'm a ring rat," Shaughnessy went on. "That's a wrestling groupie, sir. Hence the get-up." She hooked her thumbs beneath the straps of her JAKE 'THE SNAKE' ROBERTS tube-top.

Hansen realized he was admiring the shirt's contents for longer than propriety allowed. He quickly looked away.

"Deveroux also believes I'm romantically interested in him." Shaughnessy shuddered at the notion. "He's dead wrong on both counts, especially the latter. But by exploiting this perceived mutual attraction, I've convinced him to take me with him to Michigan next weekend, where he and Miller will be delivering a shipment of counterfeit goods to Wrestlemania III at the Pontiac Silverdome."

She paused for effect, before breaking into a cat-got-cream grin.

"The dumb bastard's gonna lead me – *us* – straight to Waylon Cates."

"Let's pretend for a moment I don't know who Waylon Cates is," Hansen said.

"Only the biggest manufacturer of counterfeit goods in the Midwest, sir."

"Ah."

"They call him The Teflon Tailor. He made his bones manufacturing knock-off Halloween costumes. Maybe you remember the controversy around his Johnny Space Commander costume?" Hansen nodded, but it was clear from his expression that this was all news to him. Shaughnessy said, "Plastic fishbowl helmet, a hundred percent polyester bodysuit, Styrofoam 'oxygen tank' stitched to the back. The kids loved it. But one stray spark…?" Her voice cracked. The words died on her lips. She shook her head gravely.

Hansen grinned. "One stray spark and POOF! Johnny Space Commander was piloting the *Challenger*." He chuckled at his own wit.

"You think this is funny, sir?" Shaughnessy snapped at him. Hansen was taken aback by the anger in her voice. "The year the costumes went on sale, three children lost their lives. Another seven suffered third degree burns."

Hansen stowed the smirk and motioned for Shaughnessy to continue.

"Cates was brought to trial," she went on, "but his lawyer got him off on a technicality – hence the 'Teflon Tailor' moniker. Since then, Cates has graduated to the big leagues, manufacturing counterfeit sports merchandise through his underground sweatshop network. Shirts, caps, scarves. Those big foam hands. You name it. The NFL alone estimates Cates has cost them over ten million dollars in lost merchandising revenue."

Hansen said, "And how does your man Deveroux fit into all this?"

"Deveroux is in deep with Cates. He thinks delivering this shipment is going to dig him out of the hole. Little do they know, I'm going to bury them both."

"Exactly what are you proposing here, Agent Shaughnessy?"

"Deveroux makes the shipment. We move in and bust him. Then we put the squeeze on him till he gives up Cates. And he will, sir. Believe me. Deveroux's no stand-up guy. Just give me five minutes alone with him. Then we—"

But Hansen was already shaking his head. "No, no, no. While I appreciate the time and effort you've gone to…" He glanced once more at her undercover outfit. "You know as well as I do, the chief will never sign off on an operation like this."

"The chief doesn't have to know. Not until we bring him Cates, gift-wrapped."

"The answer is no, Agent Shaughnessy."

Shaughnessy shook her head in disbelief. "Damn it, man! What the hell are we even doing here, if it isn't taking down pukes like Waylon Cates?"

Hansen pursed his lips. "Sounds like this is personal for you?"

Shaughnessy hesitated. Thought but didn't say: *More than you could know.*

Hansen sighed. "Rest assured, I'll pass your intelligence up the chain and keep you apprised of any developments. Now if that is all, please change into more suitable attire and carry about your *assigned* duties."

But the hell with that; she'd gone it alone.

In hindsight, not the smartest move she ever made.

8

No sooner had the roar of the RV's engine faded into the distance, and silence descended once more over the forest, than four men emerged from the woods.

Breathing hard, their faces shiny with sweat, the men paused on the road less than a hundred yards from where the RV struck the girl. They wore rugged boots, dark cargo pants splotched with mud, and combat vests bulging with ammunition for their rifles and shotguns.

At the head of the pack stalked a short stocky man with buzzed hair and a pockmarked face. He wore bandoliers filled with shotgun shells and a rumpled gray T-shirt with a faded print depicting three cartoon raisins singing *I Heard It Through the Grapevine.* Though the T-shirt was a souvenir of a kind, the man had never visited California – had never left his home county, in fact – nor was he familiar with the Marvin Gaye song. A ragged circle of buckshot holes perforated the upper right corner of the T-shirt, reminding Brother Aaron of what he'd done to the shirt's original owner before he claimed it for himself.

Aaron paused in the road, clutching his shotgun tightly as he awaited further instructions from the one who led them.

An army-green four-wheeler pulled alongside him, engine puttering. Astride the all-terrain vehicle sat a rawboned man, lanky and lean with hollowed-out cheeks and a hook-like nose, his intense blue eyes cornered by crow's-feet. A blond beard covered half his face. He wore a sweat-soaked crimson headband. Scraggly graying hair fell lankly to his shoulders. Strapped to his back was a compound crossbow and a leather quiver filled with steel bolts.

Brother Jacob shut off the ATV's engine and scanned his surroundings.

Impossible. She couldn't have gotten this far. Not in her condition.

The other men stood still and silent as statues, scoping the forest for movement. The only sound was the early evening breeze whispering through the trees. Somewhere in the distance a crow croaked a doom-laden caw.

Jacob unclipped the walkie-talkie from his belt and raised it to his lips.

"Daniel? Come in. Answer me, boy. Where are you, Danny?"

Static crackled from the radio.

Jacob exhaled through clenched teeth.

"Jacob! Come look at this!" called Brother Seth. A bullish young zealot with a tuft of bone-white hair crowning his head, Seth squatted on his haunches in the road, staring gravely at a set of tracks. Jacob climbed from the ATV and joined him. Together they studied the tracks, scored in the dirt by what could only have been a heavy vehicle slamming on its brakes.

"Must be from the 'others' Danny mentioned," Seth said. "You think they took her?"

Jacob didn't answer. He turned his head to glare at a chubby man with a mop of red hair and a guilty expression. Four long, blood-crusted scratches furrowed Brother Noah's face. They started beside his left eye and zigzagged down to his chins. Unable to hold Jacob's gaze, Noah stared down at his hands, rubbing them together as if he were suddenly cold.

Jacob rose to his feet. Took in the lonely forest road and surrounding woods. *Listening.* Then he cupped his hands to his mouth and hollered at the top of his lungs: "DANNY!" His voice echoed through the foothills like unseen heathens mocking him from afar. For a moment Jacob found himself thinking of the story of Elisha from the Bible, and of the children who were devoured by bears after they dared to mock a servant of the Lord. "DANNY!"

A few feet away Aaron gave a sudden gasp. "Oh, sweet Jesus… Jacob!"

Goosebumps rippled Jacob's arms. Somehow he already knew what Aaron had found. Jacob charged forward, shoving Noah from his path, stopping in his tracks when he saw the boy sprawled beneath a towering oak tree. A stick jutted from the bloody ruins of his left eye. Jacob sank to his knees beside him.

"Oh, Daniel… what did they do to you?"

The other men shifted uneasily from foot to foot, looking off towards the horizon where the sun was now dipping behind the mountains. Noah gnawed at his dirty fingernails. Brother Seth began reaching to place a comforting hand on Jacob's shoulder. Thought better of it. Drew his hand back.

Jacob tilted his face toward the heavens, praying silently for strength. He was a hard man who rarely showed emotion even when the Holy Spirit moved him in rapturous ways, but the boy was his blood. With shaking hands, he reached for the stick in the boy's eye, took a deep breath, and then wrenched it wetly from the socket, tossing it away with a cry between grief and disgust. A thick glob of optic fluid dribbled down the boy's cheek like a ghastly teardrop. Jacob peeled off his coat, draped it over Daniel, and scooped the dead boy into his arms.

"They'll pay, Jake," vowed Seth.

Aaron grunted his agreement.

Noah said nothing.

"Whoever did this," Seth continued, "we'll drown 'em in their own blood."

Jacob only nodded. That whoever killed the boy would be dealt with accordingly was without question. There was a more pressing matter.

"First..." he said, "My brother must be told what has happened to his son."

The other men grew as pale as the corpse in Jacob's arms.

9

"We know what God demands of us, and yet we fail Him time and again."

The Reverend spoke into a vintage Cardyne radio microphone, clutching the mic's neck in a white-knuckled grip that corded the tendons in his powerful forearms. His other hand rested flat upon the cracked leather binding of his Bible. The good book's yellowed pages were dog-eared with age.

"In Corinthians, we are warned: *'neither fornicators, nor idolaters, nor adulterers, nor effeminate, nor homosexuals, nor thieves, nor the covetous, nor drunkards, nor revilers, nor swindlers, will inherit the Kingdom of God.'*"

He was a robust, broad-shouldered man; at first glance one might have assumed that Heaton Ledbetter Jr. had spent most of his life not behind a pulpit but on the football field. He was fifty-seven years old, still powerful and hale. But tonight the worry lines creasing his face made him appear a decade older. Beads of sweat glistened on his forehead. The blue veins at his temples pulsed. Perspiration darkened his black, short-sleeved clerical shirt.

He leaned into the microphone, the glow of the radio equipment bathing his face devil-red. His voice was a baritone growl, like the first rumble of thunder announcing a coming storm.

"The Lord makes no exceptions, brothers and sisters. He is not a parent who coddles His children, turning a blind eye when we stray. When we dare to live outside His grace, the punishment is severe...and His judgment is final."

The radio equipment was parked in a corner of the ascetic study. The soundboard had been obsolete for some thirty years, a jumble of wires and tubes and rusting metal knobs and whirligigs from which the paint had flaked long ago, but it served the preacher's purpose, as it had his father's before him.

There was no set schedule to the Reverend's radio sermons. Some days he preached without pause from dawn till dusk; or he might not broadcast for the better part of a week. The station had no name or payroll staff, nor did it sell advertising time. It wasn't even a station, by any official definition. There were no billboards off I-90 urging listeners to *keep that dial tuned to 1600 AM for your daily dose of Bible talk!* Though the preacher knew that folks beyond town did occasionally stumble upon his broadcasts, they were intended for his people.

And when he spoke, they listened.

Ledbetter had warned his flock that the Lord often had something to say when His faithful least expected it. There was nothing worse than being unprepared to receive His message when He was ready to give it.

So the people went about their daily lives: Teaching the younglings to read and write, feeding the chickens, milking the cows, hanging their wash, and harvesting their crops…until three high-pitched tones sounded from the speakers erected through town. The tri-toned melody alerted God's people that they should drop whatever they were doing and turn on their radios to hear His message.

No one dared ignore the summons, whether it came noon or night.

"We have fallen," the preacher said into the mic, "but we will rise again. We are in darkness, but the Lord will give us light. Have faith, brothers and sisters."

He killed the transmission with a stab of a button.

A vinyl record began spinning "I Saw The Light."

He shoved the mic aside, and raked a shaking hand through his hair.

"We are in darkness," he muttered to himself—

FOOL!

Ledbetter started at the voice – rasping and shrill, the voice of a vulture if such a creature could speak. In the decade before his death, the Reverend Ledbetter Sr. had blown out his larynx at the pulpit while delivering a blistering condemnation of the Zionists. Yet the fear his voice instilled in his son was no less potent.

Ledbetter gazed fearfully at the portrait on the wall above him.

His father had been in his grave some twenty years, yet the oil portrait was so lifelike, it appeared the old man was glaring through a window at his son. Bald on top, his pate spackled with liver spots, stringy yellow-white hair dangling down from his ears to his collar, the Reverend Ledbetter Sr. was cadaverously thin, dressed in a black suit with a string tie. The stroke he had suffered in the last year of his life had curled his lips into a perpetual sneer. But for his piercing blue eyes – eyes that both his sons had inherited – he might have been a corpse, posed like a slain villain in an Old West daguerreotype.

In the crook of his arm, clutched to his heart, was his Bible.

The same book on which his son now rested the flat of his hand.

How could you have been so CARELESS? So INCOMPETENT!

Ledbetter bowed his head in shame.

The girl could not have weighed more than a hundred pounds soaking wet! She was nothing but skin and bones, her mind addled by narcotics, and corrupted by the devil's music…and you let her get AWAY?

Ledbetter shook his head vehemently.

"No, sir. Not me—"

QUIET!

He fell silent at once, clasping his hands on the Bible before him.

Ledbetter could no longer remember when his father began speaking to him from beyond the grave. All he knew was that the old man had always been there for him. That hadn't changed since he went to live with the Lord.

On the day Heaton Jr. turned twenty-one, when most men his age would embark on a raucous night of drinking and carousing, he had firebombed an abortion clinic in East Tennessee, saving the unborn lives of so many who could not save themselves. Senior had planned the attack, but it was Junior who put it into action. It was the moment, his father told him, when he truly became a man.

On another occasion, while traveling beyond town to gather supplies, they had come across two effeminate young men whose fancy foreign sports car had broken down. Senior ordered Junior to stop the truck, but warned him not to stray too close as he carried out his necessary duty. These men and their kind were an abomination to the Lord, spreading contagion wherever they went. Junior did as he was instructed, keeping a cautious distance as Senior executed the sodomites with a double-tap shot to the chest and head. Then he hailed his brother on the walkie-talkie to dispose of the faggots, and take their car back to town, where it could be decontaminated then stripped for parts.

A few years after Senior died, Junior razed a nigger church to the ground. It was one of the rare times his father's orders gave him pause. The congregation of Grace Baptist had once visited town on their way to an outreach mission in Louisville. Ledbetter had thought they seemed like decent people, for niggers. But being shunned by his father could be worse than receiving the cold shoulder from the Lord, so he had done as he was told, and Daddy assured him that God was pleased.

Last winter the old man had spoken to him in another dream, instructing him to assemble a team of soldiers. With Jacob's help they had raided a National Guard armory and absconded with the weapons they would need to win the war of Armageddon that Daddy warned drew closer every day.

And of course, there was the ritual of the scapegoat. Daddy's voice was never more vocal than when it came time for the church to perform their sacred duty.

I trusted you to lead them, to carry on my work. So many innocent lives counting on you. And now their blood is on YOUR hands!

"Jacob will bring her back," Ledbetter insisted. "He'll find her. And when he does, we—"

Jacob? The old man cackled shrilly. *That sniveling pup? He's as worthless as you are. Both sons… wastes of seed, a disappointment to their father.*

"Don't say that. Please don't say that, Daddy. I can fix this."

There can be no Salvation without Purgation. Transference is not enough.

"Yessir."

You must finish what you started.

"I will, Daddy."

Before the wrath of God comes down upon us all.

"I swear—"

Quiet!

…Someone comes.

Ledbetter shot an uneasy glance at the door.

When he shut himself away in his study to preach on the radio or work on his sermons, his people knew his time was no less sacred than Moses's private meeting with Jehovah on Mount Sinai. No one would *dare* disturb him.

He hath made known His anger… his father said, and he was gone.

Someone knocked tentatively at the door.

"Come," Ledbetter said, hating the uncertainty in his voice.

Jacob entered, tramping mud inside.

"Heaton," his brother said. "Something terrible has happened."

"Worse than losing the 'goat? I doubt that."

Then he noted Jacob's ashen face, the tears in his eyes.

He hath made known His anger.

A chill stole through him.

"What is it, Jacob?"

10

Ledbetter clutched the lifeless body of his son and wept.

The boy had been laid in state on the communion table at the head of the church. Jacob and the other men, Brothers Aaron and Seth, now stood in silence behind their leader as he grieved.

Brother Noah huddled by himself on a church pew. The young man's chubby head was bowed. He stifled his own sobs to avoid drawing attention to himself.

Ledbetter softly stroked his son's wheat-colored hair. *Oh, Daniel... like your namesake, you walked among the lion's den, but I was not there to protect you.*

Tears spattered the boy's face, pooling in the crater of his eye socket, a crimson mirror in which the preacher could see his own features boiling with rage.

Behind them, Jacob shifted uneasily from foot to foot, cleared his throat and said, "He wanted to make you proud, Heaton. Said he was going to find the 'goat himself. Prove to you he was meant to lead us one day."

Ledbetter said nothing.

Jacob went on, "You know I loved him too, brother. Loved him like my own."

Ledbetter continued stroking Daniel's hair. The boy had never known such affection from his father while he lived. Ledbetter had feared it would make him weak. *Spare the rod and spoil the child.* Had he ever told his son he loved him? When was the last time they had talked about anything other than scripture? He forced such regrets from his mind. The Lord had commanded that he groom the boy for his legacy. It was not for Ledbetter to question why.

"I'll have Sister Sara clean him up real nice." Jacob tried to reach through his brother's grief, and spare them all his temper. "Just as soon as we find the 'goat, we'll make sure that Danny gets a decent—"

"Who allowed this to happen?" Ledbetter asked.

His eyes never left his son's face.

"My only son is dead," he said. "Someone is to blame, I want to know…"

He turned to face his men. "*Who*?"

Aaron and Seth backed up a step.

"I was in charge," Jacob said.

"Then it's you I must rebuke?"

Jacob wet his lips with a nervous flick of his tongue. Unable to hold his brother's gaze, he bowed his head…but not before his eyes darted to the lonely figure on the church pew.

"*Noah*."

The fat man exhaled sharply as the preacher said his name. He teetered to his feet, knocking a hymnal to the floor. It landed with a thump and a flutter of pages that echoed loudly in the stillness of the church.

The preacher approached, the heels of his boots deviling dust in his wake.

Noah flinched, stifling a cry as the Reverend's fingers probed the scratches on his cheek.

"She got you good," Ledbetter said.

Noah's bottom lip trembled. A single tear trickled down the unscarred side of his face. He nodded.

The Reverend placed his hands on his shoulders.

"It was the lust in your heart that got us here, Noah. She promised you something. Didn't she? Like the whore Delilah, whose seduction of Samson turned a strong man into a slave, bound in chains, his eyes gouged out."

Noah's mouth fell open. "How—?"

"Not me," Ledbetter said.

He pointed a finger heavenward; his hand was shaking.

Noah swallowed hard.

"You failed me, Noah."

Ledbetter clasped the fat man's face in his meaty hands.

"You failed Daniel. You failed your family, your friends, and your neighbors."

Brothers Aaron and Seth exchanged an anxious glance.

Tears streamed down Noah's face.

"Most importantly," Ledbetter went on, "you failed the

Lord…"

Noah gasped as the Reverend tightened his grip on his skull.

"May He forgive what I cannot," Ledbetter said.

And then he drove his thumbs deep into Noah's eyes. Noah squealed like a stuck pig as his eyeballs ruptured. Yolky-yellow fluid spattered Ledbetter's face as he drove his thumbs deeper…deeper. Blood flowed down the preacher's wrists and forearms in a twisted mockery of baptism.

Jacob let out a cry, lurched toward his brother. "Heaton, no—!"

The look in Ledbetter's eyes stopped Jacob in his tracks.

"Daniel was meant to lead us one day!" Ledbetter raged. "Who will deliver the Lord's message when I am dead and gone? That feebleminded halfwit you sired with Sister Ethel? *Hardly*. It should have been Daniel. It was his birthright!"

He returned his attention to Noah.

"And this fool has stolen that from us all!"

The preacher hooked his thumbs into claws, and with a savage wrenching motion, rent the fat man's skull with a sickening crunch of bone.

The screaming ceased at once.

Noah went limp in Ledbetter's arms.

The preacher dropped him to the floor.

Breathing hard, he wheeled toward the other men, who stood in shocked silence.

"The living embodiment of Sin will corrupt even good men. It knows its time is short. It will lie to us, cloud our minds and rob us of our reason, attempt to cripple our faith and close our hearts to the Lord. Anything to prevent us from doing His work. But we will not be discouraged…because God is with us!"

"Yes," Aaron said.

"Amen," agreed Seth.

"We are afflicted in every way, but not crushed. Perplexed, but not driven to despair. Persecuted, but not forsaken. Struck down, but not destroyed."

The preacher slashed his arms and gestured violently as he ranted.

Jacob flinched as Noah's blood flicked off his brother's fingers and spattered his cheek.

"The Rite will be completed," Ledbetter said. "God is with us!"

"God is with us!" echoed Aaron and Seth.

Ledbetter's eyes turned to Jacob. "Brother…?"

Jacob's face was deathly pale as he stared down at Noah.

The fat man's skull was like a broken coconut seeping scarlet milk across the floor.

"Should I replace you on the battlefield?" Ledbetter asked him.

Jacob took a deep breath, met his brother's eyes, and shook his head.

"I want to make this right."

Ledbetter nodded. "Go, then. Take as many soldiers as you need. Find these interlopers, whoever they are. And pray that the 'goat is with them…"

He turned his back on his men, dismissing them with a wave of his hand.

"God help us all if we fail to destroy what we've put inside her."

PART TWO

IF YOU WANT BLOOD (YOU'VE GOT IT)

11

Jezebel's shocks squealed in protest as the RV shuddered and bounced along the uneven dirt road. The Playboy bunny air freshener and headless rubber bat swung violently back and forth from the rearview mirror, as if in the throes of unnatural coitus.

"*Counterfeiting,*" Lonnie snorted, "What a crock." He glanced between the road and his passengers, tightening his grip on the steering wheel as if wishing he were wringing Rhonda's neck. "Sounds pretty bottom-of-the-barrel to me. Weren't there any openings on the Litterbug Agency or the Jaywalking Squad?"

Rhonda glared at him until he lost his nerve and looked away.

She had propped the shotgun against the bedroom wall, and now sat perched on the edge of the bed next to Mike, the unconscious girl, and the even more unconscious Pork Chop, whose snores could be heard over the engine noise.

She returned her attention to Mike and the girl. "How's she doing?"

Mike was daubing ointment on the girl's wounds, trying not to hurl.

"She's got words carved into her skin, for Christ's sake!"

"I'm no expert," Rhonda said, "but I think those are the seven deadly sins."

"So… the people who did this to her… were they some kind of cult?"

"Devil worshippers!" Lonnie called out, "I saw it on Geraldo."

"I don't know who or *what* they are," Rhonda said.

"Doesn't the FBI have some kind of special unit that deals with stuff like this?"

"Occult Crimes Division. I'm not in it."

"Right. Bootleg T-shirts, that's your thing."

Before Rhonda could retort, the girl on the bed gave a gasping cry.

Mike yelped in surprise, damn near filling his shorts.

The girl arched her back violently, shot her hand into the air and clawed her fingers as if grasping for something.

"Mama…" she croaked.

Then she gave a feeble moan, her hand dropped to her chest, and she sank back into unconsciousness. Her sudden movements had split the cruciform wound carved crookedly across her hip. Beneath the holy symbol's crossbars, pink muscle tissue glistened like an undercooked campfire frank. The wound wept fresh blood onto the bed, dyeing the navy-blue comforter deep purple.

Mike covered his mouth and retched. Rhonda took the ointment from him and continued tending to the girl's wounds. The glitter in her nail polish glistened in the overhead lights as she traced her fingertips over the symbols and words.

Many of the wounds would require stitches. The girl's tormentors had done a thorough job. She was mutilated from head to toe, literally. There was even a word carved into the dirt-caked sole of her right foot:

SLOTH

The girl whimpered in her sleep.

Rhonda's eyes welled with pity and rage. "You poor thing…"

She turned her attention to her patient's crudely-shaven scalp. As she softly fingered the ointment into the nicks and cuts stippling the girl's skull from her eyebrows to the nape of her neck, Rhonda saw that whoever shaved her had missed a quarter-sized patch of hair behind her left ear.

"She dyes her hair. Green." Rhonda spoke to herself in a solemn monotone, a detective making mental notes. "Her right ear has two piercings. Three in her left. Pale stripes around several of her fingers suggest she normally wears a number of rings. The perps removed her jewelry before they did this to her."

"You think they stole it?" Mike said.

"I don't think anything yet. I'm just making observations."

Pork Chop kept on snoring.

Rhonda said, "Could you *please* shut him up?"

"Sure," Mike said. "Can I borrow your shotgun?"

Rhonda cracked a tight smile. "How did you get yourself mixed up in this mess, Rawson?"

"Just lucky, I guess."

"You seem like a decent guy. I mean, compared to these two nutsacks."

As if in Pavlovian response to the mention of nutsacks, Pork

Chop reached a hand beneath his kilt, and began vigorously scratching himself.

"I *am* a decent guy," Mike insisted. "Married my high school sweetheart. We have a six-month-old baby." He reached for his wallet. "Wanna see pictures?"

"I'm good."

Mike looked dejected. "I swear to God, Agent Shaughnessy, I didn't know anything about Lonnie's bootlegging scheme. He invited me to Wrestlemania. I thought it'd be fun. One last hurrah with the old gang, you know? We were on the road less than five minutes before I remembered why I don't hang out with these bozos anymore. They never grew up. I did."

Mike didn't want to get his hopes up, but maybe he could convince her that he didn't deserve to go to prison with Lonnie and Pork Chop? If he felt any disloyalty to his friends, that he was throwing them under the bus to save his own ass, it was outweighed by the thought of not seeing his son again until the kid graduated high school. A choice between Lonnie and Pork Chop and his family? No choice at all. *This* wasn't what he'd signed up for.

"You lie down with dogs, you get up with fleas. Hire yourself a good lawyer and maybe you can beat this thing," Rhonda said. "Now make yourself useful: Grab me a wet washcloth from the head, then fetch the map, see if you can figure out where the hell we are."

Mike considered pleading his case further.

Instead, he sullenly did as he was told, before joining Lonnie up front.

"Sup, bro," Lonnie said, as if everything was fine and dandy and they were still on schedule for a raucous night of cheering faces, booing heels, and ogling The Macho Man's squeeze, Miss Elizabeth.

Mike unfolded the map, studied it. "What was it the kid said on the walkie-talkie? Something about a road… Crooked Road or something?"

"Crookback Road," Lonnie said.

"That's it!" Mike shook his head in amazement. "How the hell do you retain any information at all, the amount of weed you smoke?"

"It's a gift."

Mike studied the map as best he could despite the constant rocking of the RV. "We got off the interstate here…or close to it…which should put us somewhere around—" He stabbed a spot on the map with his finger. "Crookback Road!"

"Fuckin'-A," Lonnie said. "Now get us back to the main highway, Goose."

"Looks like Crookback Road is a dead end." Mike frowned at the map. "But you're gonna come to a three-way—"

Lonnie perked up. "Three-way, huh? Did I ever tell you how close I came one time? If I'm lyin', I'm dyin'. Thought I'd finally talked Wendy into—"

"Could we focus, please? When we get to the three-way, take a right on Milkweed. Milkweed eventually turns into Old Junction Nine, which should lead us back to the interstate. We've got a long way to go, though. Looks like thirty miles, at least… Jesus, Lonnie, how did you get us thirty miles out of the way?"

Lonnie shrugged. "Like I said, it's a gift."

"Good news is," Mike said, "we're gonna pass a town at some point. Place called…Little Enoch."

"Good work, Rawson," Rhonda said from the bedroom.

Lonnie cut a snide glance at Mike. "Trying to earn your Junior G-man badge?"

Mike ignored him. "When we reach Little Enoch," he said to Rhonda, "we can get help for the girl and call the police—"

"The *real* police," Lonnie said.

"Anything you say can and will be used against you, Deveroux."

Lonnie grudgingly shut his trap.

"Hey," Mike said. "Do you guys hear that?"

"Just your buddy sawing logs," Rhonda said.

Pork Chop had opened his legs again. One meaty calf slapped against Rhonda's elbow as she tended to the girl. She shoved him away with a grunt of disgust.

"Listen…" Mike said.

Rhonda cocked her head. "I don't hear any—"

Then she stopped. Stood. Squinted through the Vogue's filthy rear window.

The look of dread on her face sent a shiver down Mike's spine.

It sounded like a swarm of angry bees roused from their hive.

Growing closer… louder.

"Shit!" Mike said. "What *is* that?"

They could feel its approach now, vibrating through the RV.

Lonnie glanced in his side mirror—

And recoiled from the blinding brightness behind them.

The lights were fitted to the rusted chrome cab rack of a beat-to-hell Chevy Cheyenne. Two men stood in the flatbed, clutching the rack as the truck gained on the camper. One of the men wore a combat vest, laden with mags for the M-16 assault rifles both men carried. A pair of mud-spattered dirt bikes kept pace on either side of the truck. Two riders on each bike, the rear riders armed with Mac-10 submachine guns. The pursuers were gaining steadily on the RV.

Rhonda racked the shotgun. Held out the .38 to Mike. "Know how to use this?"

He took the gun hesitantly. "It's been a while." He neglected to mention it had also been at Space Port, the videogame arcade in the mall back home.

"Just remember," she said. "The bullets come out *this* end."

"Got it."

"Choose your shots. Make 'em count… Deveroux! Get this heap moving!"

"Ya think?"

Lonnie hit the gas. The RV rattled forward, engine whining. Black fumes farted from the exhaust like a James Bond cloaking device. The sheet of tarp tacked across the rusted-out hole in the back flapped like the wing of a frantic bat.

The truck thundered after them, dirt bikes buzzing alongside it. One of the bikes briefly took to one wheel as they gained on the Vogue. The truck driver blatted the horn. The gunmen raised their rifles and started firing.

Jezebel's rear window exploded in a storm of sparks and Plexiglas. Rubble rained over Mike and Rhonda as they ducked below the window line. Lonnie crouched low in his seat, driving blind, pedal to the metal. Bullets whipped past his head and peppered the windshield, smashing the rearview mirror from its fixture, the Playboy bunny air freshener and rubber bat tumbling to the floor.

The girl jolted awake, screaming as bullets tore through the RV.

Rhonda dragged her off the bed and wrestled her to the floor. "Stay down!"

"Is it them?" the girl cried, eyes wide as dinner plates. "Oh

God, it's *THEM!*'

Pork Chop continued sleeping undisturbed, his snoring still audible even as World War III broke out all around him.

A lull in the chaos as the gunmen paused to reload.

Rhonda fired three shots from the shattered rear window. The truck's hood cover was blasted away in an explosion of sparks. The gunmen ducked as it flipped back through the air and clattered in the road behind them.

Rhonda glanced down at Mike. "The hell are you waiting for, Rawson? Shoot back!"

Mike stopped brushing broken glass from his hair. Snaked the .38 above the window line and squeezed off a few blind shots.

Bullets punched through the Chevy's windshield and thumped into the leather seat cushion inches from the driver's head. The driver's mouth made a shocked 'O' within his bushy black beard. The truck's tires squealed as the Chevy veered violently from one side of the road to the other. But it kept coming.

The dirt bikes broke away from the truck, rocketing forward. The men in front hunched over the handlebars. The rear riders readied their weapons.

Lonnie swerved left and right, blocking the road, trying to stop the bikes from flanking Jezebel. He wrenched the steering wheel, shunting one of the bikes off the road. It slammed into a massive oak, mashing both the pilot and rear rider against the tree trunk in a bloody fusion of man and machine.

Lonnie honked the horn in triumph. "Yeah! Fuck, yeah! Did you see—?"

The second bike pulled parallel to the motorhome. Lonnie shot a glance in his side mirror and made eye contact with the rear rider. The man wore a leather flight cap and aviation goggles. He raised his Mac-10 and raked the Vogue with a burst that spewed three feet of muzzle flash.

Lonnie keened like a kicked puppy as the salvo turned Jezebel into a sieve.

Bullets tore through the boxes of wrestling merch. Shredded HULKAMANIA shirts flurried through the cabin in a yellow/red blizzard. Coors cans exploded on the kitchen counter like targets at a shooting gallery. Beer foam sprayed the walls. The Tawny Kitaen poster was peppered with holes.

Rhonda waited for the shooter's Mac-10 to empty. Once the

fusillade had abated, she shoved her shotgun through a shattered side window, fired off a blast that sheared the pilot's head from his shoulders in a Hiroshima of blood and brain matter. Piloted by a headless rider, the bike spun out of control. The man in the aviation goggles spilled from the saddle and skidded down the road, screaming as the asphalt peeled his flesh like an orange. He slid to a stop, flayed but still clinging to life…until the pickup juddered over him, smearing him along the blacktop like raspberry jelly on toast.

Rhonda tossed the empty shotgun on the bed. "I'm out!"

A desperate glance around the room—

Her eyes settled on Pork Chop.

She wrestled the bottle of Jack from Pork Chop's novelty hat.

This, of all things, almost woke him. "'S'mine."

"Rawson! Gimme one of those bandanas!"

Mike fetched a Hulkster do-rag from the mess on the floor.

He watched as Rhonda fed the bandana into the neck of the bottle and then set the end aflame with a Zippo lighter.

"Cover me!" she said, leaping up with the Molotov cocktail in her hands.

Mike muttered a curse. Broke cover. Fired his last shots at the truck.

The gunmen ducked behind the cab as the bullets whistled past them. One of the spotlights was snuffed out in a Catherine Wheel of sparks. The men took the time to snap fresh mags into their M-16s. But before they could return fire—

Rhonda hurled the Molotov cocktail like a quarterback tossing a Hail Mary.

The bottle shattered against the truck windshield and burst into flames. A wave of fire rolled over the cab, turning the two shooters into human torches. The men screamed, flailed, begged God for mercy. Even as he was roasted alive the guy with the ammo-laden vest tried desperately to remove it. But not soon enough. The mags detonated in the fiery heat, spraying bullets that tore both men into flame-cooked chunks of meat, sizzling on the griddle-hot flatbed. Shrapnel ripped through the cab and turned the truck driver into a human pincushion. He slumped lifelessly over the steering wheel.

The burning truck rolled to a lazy stop in the middle of the road.

Jezebel tootled triumphantly away.

12

"That was fuckin' rad, man!" Lonnie cried. "Like something from a Schwarzenegger movie! *'I'll be back.'* Not this time, pal! You guys see me steer that sucker into a tree? Fuckin' BOOM!" He glanced at Rhonda. "You're welcome for that, by the way."

"There may be others," Rhonda reminded him.

The gloating expression vanished from Lonnie's face. He shifted up a gear and floored it.

The motorhome surged forward…but then shuddered violently. The engine sputtered and coughed. Black smoke spewed from the exhaust. Steam billowed from under the hood. The Vogue went into convulsions, losing speed fast, like a sci-fi movie spaceship snared in an enemy tractor beam.

"No, baby, no!" Lonnie cried. "Don't do this to me! Not now!"

Ceding defeat, Lonnie eased the rig to a jerking standstill, gunning the engine for fear it would conk out completely and leave them stranded in plain sight.

Without considering the pros and cons, Lonnie shifted into reverse, and backed the rig into the roadside brush.

"What are you doing?" Rhonda cried.

Jezebel reverse-plowed through thick vegetation that crunched back into place behind them, concealing the vehicle from the road.

"Saving our asses again," Lonnie said to Rhonda.

Suddenly the ground fell away beneath them.

The RV lurched sickeningly.

Started tobogganing downhill.

"Oh, shit! Oh, shit!" Lonnie cried, desperately stomping the brakes.

The RV slid some more, then shuddered to a tentative stop on the slope.

Lonnie collapsed over the steering wheel with a heavy sigh.

"Now what, genius?" Rhonda said.

Panting for breath, Lonnie said, "Now…I fix the engine…if I can."

Pork Chop awoke with a heavy snort. "We there already?" He lifted the brim of his novelty hat, yet to realize the bottle of Jack was gone. His bleary eyes took in his shot-to-shit surroundings.

"Whoa, mama… what happened to Jezebel?"

He saw the girl huddled in the corner. Her HULKAMANIA shirt, hanging off her skinny frame like a nighty, was Dalmatian-dotted with blood where her wounds had soaked through the fabric. "Whoa, mama," Pork Chop said again.

"Bro," he whispered to Mike. "What'd I miss?"

Mike gave a bark of unhinged laughter. "Nothin' much, P.C."

13

Lonnie sat perched on a cooler between the two front seats, inspecting the Vogue's exposed engine, located at the front of the rig between the front seats.

"Can you fix it, Deveroux?" Rhonda asked him.

Lonnie pushed aside a hose, straining for a closer look.

"I don't know," he said. "I think maybe a bullet went through the engine block."

They spoke in hushed tones, fearful that another gang of lunatics with guns might blitz the RV at any moment.

Mike said, "C'mon, man. Back in the day you could fix anything."

Like the first car Mike ever owned, a '69 Cutlass.

The day Mike and Lonnie met, the piece of shit had crapped out again, choking the high school parking lot in an environmental disaster of thick black smoke. Lonnie had appeared through the noxious cloud like a denim-clad demon summoned by the heavy metal blasting from Mike's stereo.

Lonnie Deveroux was a recent transfer to West Memphis High. Mike had seen him around school, but never had cause to talk him till now.

"Heard your tunes, dude," Lonnie said. "Had to come n' see who was jamming Angus and the boys. The Deece are my favorite band." He pointed out one of many band logo patches sewn onto his denim jacket.

"Mine too," Mike said.

They shook hands, Mike anointing Lonnie's palm in engine grease. Lonnie didn't seem to care, just wiped the grease on his jeans.

He nodded at the Cutlass. "Sweet ride, man."

"When she's running."

"I'm pretty good with cars. I could take a look," he said, "if you'll give me a ride to rehearsal?"

Mike had nothing to lose, except his job slinging pizzas if he was late for work again. He stepped aside to let Lonnie work.

"Rehearsal?" he asked, watching as his new friend tinkered under the hood.

"I'm in a band," Lonnie said, without looking up from his work. "You play bass, right?"

"A little, I guess." Mike frowned. "How'd you know that?"

"My drummer told me," Lonnie said. "Art Miller. You know him?"

"Pork Chop Miller?"

Everyone in school knew Pork Chop Miller; the poor bastard was West Memphis High's whipping boy.

"That's the guy. He can't keep time for shit but he bangs the skins louder than Bonham. Looks like he's having a seizure. It's funny as hell— Hey! You should jam with us sometime. Just so happens we're looking for someone to hold down the low end."

Against his better judgment, Mike had agreed, and before the year was out, he and Lonnie and Pork Chop were inseparable.

Mike shook his head wistfully as the memories came back to him.

He glanced at Rhonda, saw her swipe sweat from her forehead, her hands shaking with adrenaline. For the first time, he thought she looked truly worried...which scared the hell out of him.

While Lonnie worked on the engine, Pork Chop wandered outside to take a leak; the bathroom door had been blown off its hinges, and P.C. was surprisingly bashful for a guy wearing a kilt sans underwear. The tension inside the RV was broken by the sound of Pork Chop pissing. Heavily. And apparently endlessly.

Then a tiny voice said, "Th-thank you..."

Everyone turned to stare at the girl.

"For not letting them get me," she said.

Rhonda sat with her. "What's your name, hon?"

"Rebecca. My... my friends call me Becca."

"Becca. I'm Special Agent Rhonda Shaughnessy. FBI."

Lonnie gave a mocking snort.

"You're FBI?" the girl said, a glimmer of hope in her eyes.

"That's right. This is Mike... Lonnie... and that's Pork Chop outside."

The girl frowned. "Pork Chop?"

"Don't ask," Rhonda said, rolling her eyes.

That actually earned a smile from the teen, though she winced as if the smile had caused her great pain. She wrapped her arms around herself and shivered. Wearing only the HULKAMANIA shirt, she was probably freezing.

"You need pants," Rhonda said. "Deveroux, you got a clean pair somewhere?" She thought but didn't say: *Something she can throw on without needing penicillin shots for the next six months?*

"Check the closet."

Rhonda scrounged around, found some sweatpants that didn't smell too wretched, and gave them to the girl. "Here, honey. Put these on."

Mike watched the girl take the sweatpants with a silent nod of thanks. They were easily three sizes too large for her. WEST MEMPHIS MUSKRATS read the logo along one leg. Their old high school football team.

Outside, Pork Chop shook off his main vein and started loudly belching his ABC's. His alphabetic burps echoed through the forest like the mating call of some brain-damaged bird.

He made it to 'M' before Rhonda lost her cool. "You wanna tell your friend to keep it down out there?" she spat at Lonnie. "I know he slept through the whole thing but someone just tried to kill us. We're supposed to be *hiding*."

Lonnie shouted out his window: "Hey! Keep it down out there, dumbass!"

He winked at Rhonda, even as his "dumbass" echoed over the woods.

Rhonda gave a withering headshake.

"Lonnie?" Pork Chop called from outside. "You think we'll still make it to the 'Dome in time for Piper's Pit?"

"Doubtful, big guy." Lonnie sounded as upset about it as Pork Chop looked.

Pouting, Pork Chop picked up a stick and started swishing it around like a lightsaber.

Rhonda returned her attention to the girl. "Becca, how old are you?"

"Six...sixteen."

"I need you to tell me what's going on. Can you do that? Who were those men? What did they want?"

"Me," Becca said. "They… they wanted me."

"Are they some kind of cult?"

"Devil worshippers," Lonnie said, "am I right?"

"No," Becca said. "Nothing like that. They don't worship the *devil.*"

Rhonda said, "Help me understand what's going on, Becca. Tell me what you know about those men. If I'm going to get us out of this, you need to tell me everything."

The girl's eyes welled with tears as she struggled to process everything that had happened to her. She stared down at her bloodstained hands.

"It all started with Pastor Joe," she said. "I wish…wish I could say he deserved what happened to him. It would've been easier if he were some kind of pervert trying to get in my pants, instead of getting me right with God. But I know he meant well. Mama did too. We didn't always get along…but I loved my mother…and I never…oh, G-God…I never wanted anything to happen to her!"

She started sobbing uncontrollably.

After a few seconds, she took a deep breath and managed to compose herself.

"Mama took me to see Pastor Joe two weeks ago. I wish I hadn't been so…so mean to them. But how could I know what was coming? Mama used to drag me to church with her every Sunday. When I got older I guess she got tired of fighting about it all the time. I only went with her to see Pastor Joe because it was her birthday and I wanted to do something nice for her. I knew it would make Mama—"

14

"—so happy, Rebecca, that you came to see me!"

Pastor Joe beamed at Becca from behind his desk. He was an insufferably cheery fellow with a push-broom mustache, wire-frame eyeglasses, and a gaudy maroon sweater (over shirt and tie) that looked like he'd raided Bill Cosby's wardrobe. "I remember when you were just *yea high.* Rosy cheeks, head full of golden curls. Cutest kid in church."

Becca pushed a spiky strand of hair from her eyes. Gone were the golden curls the preacher once adored. These days she dyed her hair a different color every week, depending on her mood. Today it was Dark Blue A41. Drove Mama crazy. They'd fought about it that morning, in fact. Not about the dye job itself. Her mother knew she'd have more chance of changing the weather by shaking her fist at the sky. Mama got pissed because Becca always left dribbles and splashes of dye all over the bathroom sink. Last night, by the time she was finished, the bathroom had looked like someone butchered a Smurf.

"Remember when she used to sing for us in the church choir?" Pastor Joe asked her mother. "Those hymns were never quite as sweet once Rebecca stopped coming to practice." He gave a burlesque sigh of regret.

"She did have the voice of an angel, didn't she?" Mama said. She was sitting right next to Becca, but the distance between mother and daughter might as well have spanned a thousand feet. "If only she still used it to praise the Lord."

"You can stop talking about me like I'm not in the room," Becca said.

Pastor Joe leaned forward, resting his elbows on the desk. "Rebecca, I invited you here because I'd like you to consider something. Consider it with an open mind, if you will."

He opened a drawer, pulled out a green sheet of paper, and slid it across the desk. The slogan at the top read:

JOIN US…
AND FIND WHAT YOU'VE BEEN MISSING!

In the middle of the page was a crude illustration depicting two stick figures on either side of a large wooden cross. The cross had giant cartoon eyes, a bucktoothed grin, and gloved hands sticking out of it. The stick figures walked arm-in-arm with the cross. Best friends till the end.

Becca snickered. "You gotta be kidding. Is this for real?"

At the bottom of the flyer big bold letters advertised something called:

T.T.I.F.U.C.

"Tittyfuck, huh?" Becca said. "Gotta admit, I'm intrigued."

"Rebecca Ann Fennimore!" Mama gasped.

"I beg your pardon?" stammered Pastor Joe.

"T-T-I-F-U-C." Becca's black-painted fingernails (oh, how Mama loved *them!*) tapped out each letter on the flyer. "Mom already told me what this was about. But dude...someone should've taken the time to think through that acronym."

Pastor Joe's face went pale. He snatched the flyer back. "It stands for 'Troubled Teens Interventional Faith and Unity Camp,'" he said, sounding flustered.

Mama's face was redder than the pastor's Cosby sweater. She clutched one hand to her chest as if fearing her heart might explode. "Rebecca, you apologize to Pastor Joe right this second!"

"I'm just messing with you guys," Becca said. "Sometimes it's fun to see you look so shocked, Mom. If it gets you off my back, then fine, I'll go to T.T.I.F.U.C. Camp." She made the acronym sound filthy. "I'll hate every second of it, but I'll go. Whatever." She thought, but did not say: *Maybe I'll meet a cute guy at this thing, hook up with some other bored misfit.*

Tears welled in Mama's eyes. She pulled Becca into an awkward embrace.

"Oh, honey! You won't regret this. Just wait and see."

*

The next week, driving through the wilds of Kentucky on her way to Tittyfuck Camp, Becca was in a wretched mood, dreading whatever was in store for her.

No weed or rock music, that was for sure, but what other tight-ass rules and regulations would this place impose upon her for the next ten days? Her mood only darkened as she listened to the conversation between Pastor Joe and her mother from the back of the preacher's station wagon. Becca had been dozing on and off since they hit the road. Apparently they thought she was still asleep.

"It really is a wonderful place," Pastor Joe was saying. "I think it's just what she needs."

"I didn't realize it was so far from home," Mama said.

"A three-hour drive is nothing. As long as there are youngsters who need my help to lead them to the Lord, I would gladly travel twice that distance."

"You said you were friends with the owner in college?"

"Seminary school. He inherited the property from his father in the late 70s. He originally intended to build a church on the property but that never panned out. He opened the camp in '83. I'm proud to say I'm the one who gave him the idea."

"The name, though. Four years running and your friend never noticed?"

"An unfortunate oversight," Pastor Joe agreed.

"I pray this works, Joseph. It's my last resort. Her behavior has only gotten worse since her father left. Every other word out of her mouth is eff this, eff that. She comes home smelling like beer and the marijuana. I lie awake at night and I ask myself: What's next? A child out of wedlock? Some unsightly tattoo etched into her skin?"

"Have faith, dear. The sheep that stray from His flock will always find their way home. Sometimes they just need a little nudge in the right direction."

The sound of lips touching in a chaste kiss.

Becca opened her eyes. She watched the woods go whipping by outside her open window. A strand of her hair – Apple Green #1446 – rode the updraft.

"Well, hello, sleepyhead," said Pastor Joe from the driver's seat.

Mama quickly snatched her hand off his thigh.

Gimme a break. As if Becca hadn't known for months that they were boning. Truth be told, she was cool with it. Pastor Joe was the world's biggest dork and his breath always smelled like onions, but he was basically a good guy, and Mama was lonely. If they made each other happy, it was no skin off Becca's tits. *Just keep it down when you're bumping uglies, would ya? The walls in our trailer are thinner than you think...* She shuddered at the thought. *Ewww.*

Mama, searching for something to do with her hands, turned on the radio.

A deep country baritone crackled from the stereo speakers:

"*—the Lord will come in fire, and His chariots like the whirlwind, to render His anger with fury, and His rebuke with flames, and He will execute Judgment by His sword on all flesh, and those slain by the Lord will be many—*"

Pastor Joe frowned. "Mmm. Heard this fella the last time I came up this way. He's a little whack-a-doodle for my tastes. Talk of blood atonement, sin-eating rituals..." He shook his head sadly. "Turn the page, pal. We're no longer living under Old Testament law." He turned off the radio before glancing in the rearview to give Becca his best *Christ-is-cool* grin.

She grimaced back at him.

That's when the station wagon's right rear tire blew out.

Minutes later, Pastor Joe was rummaging in the back of the Oldsmobile for the tools he needed to fix the flat. His cheerful mood had not abated. Mama plucked a compact mirror from her pocketbook, started fussing with her hairdo while mumbling how she couldn't believe their luck. Becca wandered on the opposite side of the road, craving a cigarette while she fantasized about hitching a ride to somewhere far from here in an RV full of buff metal hunks.

"That ol' Devil is nothing if not predictable," Pastor Joe said, panting as he hauled out the spare. "Remember the Turn Away From Rock rally a few years back? Satan placed obstacles in our path every step of the way. He lost that battle though. And I'm confident he'll lose this one too."

Held the summer before Becca's sophomore year, the Turn Away From Rock rally was a weeklong youth revival, a series of sermons warning of the dangers of secular music. Pastor Joe's presentation included a slideshow that enlightened parents to the diabolical sabotage at work: Judas Priest cavorting onstage like leather-clad sadomasochists, replete with whips and chains… Ozzy Osbourne biting the heads off bats… Mötley Crüe tossing fistfuls of cocaine around like crossdressing freaks engaged in an infernal snowball fight… The preacher had played clips from rock songs over the church P.A. system. His congregation was shocked to discover that the degenerates who created this racket were placing hidden messages of drugs, deviant sexuality and devil-worship into the recordings. The process was called backward masking and it attacked the listener's brain by invading the subconscious. Led Zeppelin sang odes to Satan under the guise of building stairways to Heaven. Queen urged children to smoke marijuana – as if the singer's blatant homosexuality was not enough to damn them already. Countless others encouraged impressionable young fans to wallow in sin. If parents didn't act quickly it was only a matter of time before the homecoming queen swapped her textbooks for the Satanic Bible…A's and B's became STDs…and the band captain wrapped his lips around the business end of a shotgun, or worse yet, another boy's penis, instead of his beloved trombone.

Pastor Joe had planned to conclude the revival with a mass record burning where parents and teens would join together to rebuke rock n' roll. Local youth were invited to dedicate their lives to Christ while purging themselves of the mind-poisoning filth via the Flames of Forgiveness. Alas, Pastor Joe's church sat next door to a car dealership. When the car dealer caught wind of the record burning he argued that the smoke and ash would damage his inventory. Local politicians intervened, and ruled that the record burning would indeed affect not only the vehicles on the adjacent property but also the environment. Much to Pastor Joe's chagrin his main event was cancelled. He didn't blame the car dealer, or the politicians who made the decision. Joe knew it was that old rascal Lucifer pulling the strings. Throwing a monkey wrench into God's good work, it's what the Devil did best. But when all was said and done, the controversy had been great free publicity for Turn Away From Rock. Who needed a heavy metal bonfire when the number of souls saved from eternal torment in the Lake of Fire reached triple digits in just a matter of days?

It made Pastor Joe smile every time he thought about it. He was smiling even now as he lifted the tire iron and a small hydraulic jack from the trunk. He whistled an upbeat gospel hymn as he rounded the car…

Then he froze, frowning at the flat.

"Is something wrong, Joseph?" Mama called from the car.

"I, uh… darnedest thing," he muttered, crouching to examine the flat.

Sticking from the tire was a…

What is *that?*

No sooner had he identified the shiny silver object as a crossbow bolt—

Than a second arrow slammed into his upper thigh. The arrowhead punched through the back of his leg, pinning him fast to the side of the car. Blood gushed from the wound, spattering his Hush Puppies.

Joe barely had time to register the pain, much less scream, before the men came charging from the woods on all sides of them.

15

A scream echoed over the forest.

"What's that?" Becca gasped.

No one made a sound. Lonnie stopped tinkering with the

engine and strained to listen.

Mike said: "Sounds like…"

"A train," Rhonda finished for him.

The whistle wailed once more.

"Maybe we can ride the rails outta here?" Rhonda said.

Mike didn't wait to be told. He quickly searched the cabin for the map. Found it crumpled between the passenger seat and a bullet-riddled duffel bag crammed with kiddy-size Champion wrestling belts. There was a crosshatched line on the map, indicating railroad tracks running parallel to Crookback Road before they curved north toward Louisville.

"How close?" Rhonda asked him.

"Three miles… maybe four."

"With those crazies out there!" Lonnie said. "Screw that, man."

"He's right," Mike said to Rhonda. "We're out of bullets."

"We could improvise some weapons." No sooner had Rhonda said the words than she glanced outside and saw Pork Chop slashing his stick at a crow in the lightning-blackened branches of a birch tree. The bird squawked at him. Pork Chop staggered back in fright, snagging his kilt on a thorn and nearly tripping. Rhonda sighed; the idea of fighting their way out of here was folly, especially with the likes of Pork Chop in tow, not to mention a grievously wounded girl.

The train whistled again, sounding more distant now. It seemed to Mike like their only tie to the ordinary after all the crazy shit they had been through…

And away it went.

"Let's get our heads back in the game," Rhonda said.

Mike nodded grimly.

"Deveroux, fix that engine."

"Oh yeah, sure, piece of cake."

Rhonda rejoined Becca at the back of the Vogue. She wished she could comfort the girl. Put an arm around her shoulder or even just hold her hand. But it was hard to see anywhere that wasn't scarred with Sin. She'd only end up hurting her more than she already was.

"Tell us what happened next," she said, softly.

The girl swallowed hard.

"Pastor Joe got hit with the arrow," she said, in a hoarse monotone. "Then the men came rushing from the woods. They dragged Mama from the car…broke the window…dragged her out by the hair. She yelled at me to run, but before I could, someone hit me with something…back of the head… knocked me out. Next thing I know I'm waking up inside—"

16

—a church.

A small-town country church.

Not unlike dozens of other hick houses of worship Becca's mother had dragged her to through the years: A barn-sized rural gothic with high cathedral ceilings and polished hardwood flooring. Votive candles lined the walls between stained-glass windows. Not the usual benevolent Bible scenes – Joseph with his coat of many colors, Moses and the burning bush, David defeating Goliath with a rock flung from his slingshot – instead they depicted nightmarish creatures laying waste to humanity. Cities crumbled beneath the beasts. Flames consumed civilization in their wake.

Twelve long wooden pews filled the hall, six on either side of the aisle that stretched from the double-door entrance to the pulpit.

The congregation sat elbow-to-elbow among the pews. Perhaps fifty or sixty people in all. Men, women, and children wearing their go-to-meeting best.

They sang from hymnals, a song Becca remembered from church as a kid, one she'd always found creepy despite its uplifting message:

Would you be whiter, much whiter than snow?
There's power in the blood, power in the blood!
Sin stains are lost in its life-giving flow!
There's wonderful power in the blood!

Becca stood before the congregation at the head of the church.

Stood? No… it felt almost as if she were floating. She felt strangely weightless.

Where am I? This can't be Tittyfuck Camp.

She tried to raise a hand to her face and brush away the dried tears crusting her eyes—

But something *clanked* on her forearm.

She blinked dumbly at the strange jewelry she wore…

Steel shackles bound her wrists, and her ankles.

The bracelets were connected to chains, looped over the rafters and bolted to an eyelet in the floor.

Suspended like a marionette, with her arms outstretched and her weight pressing down on the balls of her feet, Becca stood on display for all the congregation to see. She was naked. And shaved completely hairless from head to toe.

With a flash of panic, she pulled desperately at the chains, which jangled like mocking laughter at her pitiful attempts to free herself. The steel shackles bit sharply into her wrists and ankles. She cried out in pain, but something was wedged in her mouth, muffling the sound. She assumed it was a gag – then realized it was her bone-dry tongue, cemented to the roof of her mouth. Exhausted, her struggles gradually ceased, until she could only dangle from the chains, sobbing as her shoulders took her weight.

The congregation continued to sing.

In a corner of the room, an old woman – so old she might have been a passenger on the *Mayflower* – sat hunched over a small organ, working its keys with arthritically clawed fingers, pumping the foot pedals like she was driving the instrument. Her skull was visible through her white, cobweb-thin hair. The old crone grinned at Becca, saliva glistening on her horsey yellow dentures as she nodded in encouragement, apparently expecting the shackled girl to join the congregation in song.

In front of the organist stood a little girl. Maybe five or six years old. Her long blond hair was in pigtails. She wore a peach-colored dress and knee-high socks, her black buckle-shoes polished to a shine. She sang another verse, her angelic voice delighting the congregation, who now joined her for the chorus:

There is power…power…wonder-working power in the blood of the Lamb!
There is power…power…wonder-working power in the precious blood of the Lamb!

When the song was finished, the little girl curtsied, the gesture as practiced as her singing. Then she took a seat next to a beaming young couple at the back of the hall. Becca read the mother's lips: *Mommy's so proud of you…*

She thought of her own mother.

"Where's my Mama?" Becca sobbed. "Won't someone speak to me? *Please!*"

But no one answered her cries.

She sensed a looming presence behind her then.

With a start, she turned her head, as much as her bonds would allow—

And cried out in horror at the bloody, pain-wracked face gaping back at her.

The giant crucifix hung from the ceiling by three chains, two attached to its crossbeam, with a third shorter chain at its top. The dying Christ nailed to the holy symbol was startlingly realistic. Painstakingly carved from a single piece of wood, the sculptor had captured His likeness to the finest detail. Beads of sweat stippled the Savior's naked torso. Drops of dark brown blood oozed from beneath His crown of thorns, trickling down His furrowed forehead. His eyes peered upward, silently imploring His father to forgive those who had done this to Him. His lips were slightly parted, as if He were about to whisper a secret of salvation in Becca's ear…or perhaps a promise that her predicament would only get worse from here.

"He will deliver us!"

Becca startled at the booming voice.

The preacher emerged from a darkened doorway behind the pulpit.

The congregation rose with a heavy stamp of feet, like soldiers standing to attention.

"He will deliver us!" they echoed.

He was perhaps the biggest man Becca had ever seen. Yet it wasn't so much the man's height, or his bulk – and he was built like a football linebacker – than the powerful aura that radiated from him like heat from a bonfire, which made him seem so much larger than life. This man was Paul Bunyan wearing a preacher's collar. Pastor Joe on his best day in church had never possessed such force of personality. His black hair was streaked with silver at the temples, and brushed back from his forehead in a rockabilly pompadour. Thick muttonchop sideburns framed his face, reminding Becca of her mother's favorite musician, Elvis (though Mama called his on-stage gyrating "distasteful," she had once admitted to her daughter that Elvis was the prettiest man she had ever seen, and she had wept for days after the King was found dead on his porcelain throne). The preacher wore a short-sleeved black clerical shirt and a white collar above dark brown slacks. His eyes were electric – bug-zapper-blue – but the leathery bags beneath them suggested his dedication to the Lord had denied him sleep for many days.

The preacher took his place at the pulpit.

He gazed down over the faces of his flock. One by one, as his eyes fell upon them, they looked away, as if he had seen into their very souls, and the darkness that dwelt there. Husbands grasped their wives' hands for comfort. Women's cheeks reddened. Children buried their faces in their mothers' skirts.

"Be seated," the preacher told them.

They obeyed.

No one made a sound. Not a cough, or a rustle of clothing. Even the children fell silent; not a single toddler squirmed in her seat or tugged at his mother's skirt, pleading to use the bathroom or asking when service would be over.

"Brothers and sisters… once again it falls to us, the few, to make recompense for the wickedness of the many." The preacher raised his Bible above his head and shook it emphatically. "So He hath commanded, so it shall be done!"

"So He hath commanded, so it shall be done!" echoed the congregation.

"The first goat has been slaughtered," the preached said. "The offering has been made—"

Becca's mind raced.

First goat?

Slaughtered?

"What are you saying? Where's my mother? Where's Pastor Joe? What did you—?"

The preacher glanced at a young man sitting ramrod-straight at the front of the flock. More boy than man, dressed in a pressed shirt and slacks, his wheat-blond hair neatly combed, his resemblance to the preacher was unmistakable. At the glance from his father the boy rose from his pew. Approaching Becca without a word, the boy whipped the back of his hand across her face, grimacing as he performed this unpleasant but necessary duty. The blow rattled Becca's brain. Her cheek blazed. Rubbing his knuckles, the boy nodded to his father before returning to his seat. The preacher beamed with pride.

"The first goat has been slaughtered," he said once more. "The offering has been made… now the second goat shall be brought forth for expiation."

The preacher peered down from the pulpit, his blowtorch-blue eyes boring into Becca, and she understood at once why his people could not hold his gaze.

Hot urine squirted out of her.

The preacher smiled, his teeth white as the pearly gates.

Becca had never seen such love as in his eyes.

"A great honor has been bestowed on you, my child. The Lord has delivered you to us to absolve His people of their sins. Accept this gift, and thank Him for deeming you worthy."

He turned back to his people.

"Brothers and sisters, are you ready to do your duty?"

The congregation cried out as one: *YES!*

"Then come! Bring forth your sins. Cast them unto this vessel so that we *all* may enter the Kingdom of Heaven. It is time…for the Rite of Transference."

The congregation began to file from either side of the pews, marching to the front of the church with a mix of purpose and somber reverence for the ritual at hand. They came for Becca, carrying knives. Men, women, children…the preacher's son, the ancient organist, the little blond songstress and her parents…each of them wielded a shiny silver blade. Candlelight shimmered off honed steel. Some smiled as they approached; tears of joy glistened on the faces of others. They gathered around Becca in a sea of bodies.

And one by one they began to—

17

"—cut me…" Becca said. "Put these words on me…"

She spoke in a numb monotone, her eyes gazing off into nothingness as she relived her ordeal. "I don't remember much of it… I passed out after the second or third one."

Mike shot a horrified glance at Rhonda.

The color had drained from the Fed's face.

"When I came to," the girl went on, "I was on a wagon…a mule wagon…like something from the olden days. A fat man was driving us through the woods. I keep drifting in and out, but I remember we rode for what seemed like forever…till we got to where he was taking me."

The girl shuddered. "He called the place…the Circle of Purgation. He was going to burn me there. It was some kind of ritual." Becca shook her scarred and shaven head, struggling to comprehend everything that had happened to her. "I don't know how I got away. I remember the fat man kept staring at my boobs. I think… I think maybe I pretended to like him."

Becca's cheeks flushed with shame.

"And somehow…somehow I got away…got away and never looked back. I just ran…ran and ran until I heard an engine…and you guys came along and you—"

BAM! Lonnie slammed down the engine cover between the front seats.

Everyone jumped.

"Sorry," he muttered.

The girl fell silent.

No one spoke for some time.

Then Lonnie said, "That's gotta be the craziest fucking thing I ever heard."

"It's true!" Becca cried. "All of it!" She thrust her arm toward him, the word GLUTTONY sliced into her forearm from wrist to elbow. "You think I did this to myself? I didn't do this to my fucking self!"

"Guys," Rhonda said, "we have to keep our voices down."

Pork Chop had by now returned from outside. He was slumped on the tiger-stripe sofa, still clutching the stick he'd found, sliding it down inside his sock to scratch at an itchy spot on his ankle. Mike heard him mutter, "Worst road trip *ever*," and wondered how much the big guy even understood of what was going on here. Was it even worth trying to explain?

Rhonda took the girl's trembling hands in her own and gently squeezed them.

"Becca," she said. "I think you're braver than you could possibly know. And I promise you…I'll do everything I can to make sure these bastards pay for what they did to you and your mother…just as soon as we get out of here." She glanced at Lonnie. "Deveroux?"

Lonnie climbed back in the driver's seat. "Here goes nothing. This doesn't work, I'm outta ideas." He took a deep breath before keying the ignition, pumping the gas pedal with his foot. "Come on, baby! Please!"

Something rumbled under the floorboards. The RV began to shudder and quake. The engine whinnied and whined, coughed and sputtered…then died.

"Fuck!" Lonnie slammed his fist against the steering wheel. "Anyone else wants to give it a shot, be my guest—"

"What's that?" Mike suddenly said, straining to listen.

"Mikey hear another choo-choo?" Lonnie said. His voice was distorted as he mashed his face against the steering wheel in defeat. "Nobody gives a shit."

"Quiet!" Rhonda snapped. "Someone's coming!"

She rushed to the front of the Vogue and peered through the windshield.

"Who is it?" Becca cried. "Is it them?"

"Becca," Rhonda said, "you need to keep your voice down—"

"Oh, God! It's them, isn't it? They're here!" The girl teetered to her feet and stumbled across the cabin, falling to her hands and knees with a thud. "I wasn't supposed to get away!" she sobbed, dripping tears and snot. "They're gonna finish what they started! They're gonna buh-buh-burn me!"

"Becca, please—"

"There can be no Salvation without Purgation! That's what the preacher said!"

"Make yourselves useful," Rhonda barked at Lonnie and Pork Chop. "If someone doesn't shut her up right now *we are dead*."

Becca slapped at the men as they approached her. "Don't touch me! *Don't touch me!*"

Mike joined Rhonda at the front of the RV. They peered out the windshield. Watching in silence. Hardly daring to breathe as three men moved along the road above them. Two men astride a dirt bike. A third straddling an ATV four-wheeler. Strapped to the latter's back was a crossbow.

The men continued slowly along the road. The slightest glance to the right, a glint of light off Jezebel's body, and the hunters would surely see them.

18

The four-wheeler skidded to a stop beside the smoking wreck of the Chevy Cheyenne. Jacob raised his hand from the throttle, shielding his face from the heat of the flames. The dirt bike pulled alongside him. Brother Aaron muttered a sibilant prayer as he climbed from the back. Brother Seth let the bike fall into the weeds on the side of the road.

Hunched inside the truck, still clutching the melted steering wheel, the blackened skeleton of Brother Luke grinned through the flames like the devil's own chauffeur. (Jacob could only guess it was Brother Luke; it was hard to tell for sure.) Further down the road, scattered along the tree line like garbage strewn about by a passing litterbug, mangled chunks of man and motorcycle were all that remained of the other four soldiers. The air was choked with burnt rubber, scorched earth, and gunsmoke, and the intermingled scents of blood and grill-cindered meat.

Aaron stumbled to the side of the road, sank to his knees, and brought up the lunch that Sister Sara had prepared for him earlier that day. Jacob shot him a withering look. Aaron wiped the bile from his mouth with the back of his hand and grimaced apologetically.

Jacob returned his attention to his fallen brethren. Good men, fine soldiers and righteous Christians all. How many was that now? Seven dead. Good Lord in Heaven. Not forgetting Daniel, of course. And Brother Noah. How could he possibly forget Noah? His brother's temper was fierce, even more wrathful than their father's had been; some of the stories Jacob had heard from the elder churchgoers could turn a man's hair white as snow. Yet the sight of Heaton gouging his thumbs into Noah's eyes…Noah's shrill, hog-like screams…the splintering of bone as Heaton wrenched his skull asunder; Jacob knew the memories would never leave him.

The walkie-talkie trembled in his hand as he raised it to his mouth.

"Heaton? Come in."

The Reverend's voice crackled over the radio. "Tell me you found them."

"Something went wrong," Jacob said. "Whoever we're dealing with here…they must be professionals. They took out seven men, an entire squad of soldiers!"

A long pause.

"Then you don't have the 'goat?"

"I need more men," Jacob said. "More time."

"Men I can give you; time is running short. Must I remind you what happens if the ritual is not completed? God is good. But He is also vengeful. He is to be feared…as am I, brother. Find the 'goat. And do not fail me again, Jacob."

The radio went silent.

Jacob glanced at Aaron and Seth.

"How long we got before it's too late?" Aaron asked him.

Jacob shook his head. "You think I got all the answers?"

"You're his brother. What'd he tell you?"

"He didn't tell me nothin'. Just that we gotta find her. This ain't never happened before. It had, we wouldn't be standin' here."

Jacob turned his eyes toward the black clouds gathering in the darkening sky.

In the distance, thunder growled like the hunger pangs of some ravenous beast.

"Let's move out," he said, "and keep looking. This won't get any easier once that storm hits."

19

"They're gone," Rhonda said. Mike exhaled loudly in relief. Hadn't even realized he'd been holding his breath. Turning back to the others, they found Pork Chop on his butt in the middle of the galley. The girl lay limp in his lap. Her head was gripped between his meaty forearms. Her eyes were closed; her tongue lolled from between parted lips. Easing Becca to the floor, P.C. stroked the side of her bristly head like a doting daddy nursing his sick child. He looked up at Rhonda and Mike and grinned.

"Sleeper hold," he said. "Always wanted to try that."

"I said shut her up," Rhonda said, "not choke her out!"

"She ain't screaming no more, is she?" Lonnie said in P.C.'s defense.

Rhonda and Mike huddled over Becca and checked to make sure she was still breathing.

"I swear to God," Rhonda said, "I've never met a bigger bunch of idiots in my life!"

Mike opened his mouth to object.

"And yes, that includes you, Rawson, for being friends with these clowns."

"They're coming…" Becca moaned in her sleep.

Rhonda softly stroked the girl's cheek.

"No, hon. The bad men have gone. We're safe."

"For now," Mike muttered, and Rhonda shot him a hard look.

Becca smacked her cracked lips together. "Not them," she rasped. "Something worse…"

Mike glanced nervously at Rhonda. "What's she saying?"

"She's delirious. After everything she's been through, I'd be worried if she wasn't." Rhonda brushed broken glass from the bed, smoothed the sheets, and fluffed a pillow. "Put her back on the bed. We'll let her rest awhile."

The bottom of Becca's HULKAMANIA shirt had ridden up when Pork Chop executed his sleeper hold, exposing her scarred belly. Mike shuddered in disgust upon seeing her wounds again. He reached to pull down her shirt—

Something moved inside of her.

"Holy fuck!" Mike lurched back in horror, thudding against the kitchen counter. Empty beer cans clattered to the floor.

Rhonda wheeled around, fearing the crazies had found them. "What is it?"

Lonnie snatched P.C.'s stick, gripped it like a club. "Are they back?"

The color had drained from Mike's face. He pointed a shaking hand at the girl's belly. "It… she… it looked like her…"

The words died on his lips.

"Like what?" Rhonda said.

"*Her belly moved.*"

Mike remembered Rachel's third trimester. How the baby would make its presence known as they cuddled in front of the TV, its tiny hand bulging against the drum-tight skin of her swollen belly. He had joked about how the kid was high-fiving his pop from the womb after their beloved Lakers hit a buzzer beater in the final game of the playoffs. Rachel just rolled her eyes like she always did when Mike made some lame joke, which were the only kind he knew.

What Mike had seen was like that. Except… the girl *couldn't* be pregnant. No way. She was junkie-thin, couldn't weigh more than a hundred pounds soaking wet. And that was *before* whatever blood loss she'd suffered when those psychos carved her up. Anything that might have lived inside her, there was *no way* it could have survived after everything she'd endured. A girl twice her size would have miscarried long before Lonnie hit her with his motorhome.

And yet... *her belly had moved.* There was something *inside* the girl. What Mike didn't dare tell Rhonda, for fear she would think he'd lost his fucking mind – and maybe he had – was *exactly* what he had seen. Something inhuman...a claw...pressing up against the inside of the girl's stomach.

Which was crazy!

Mike took a deep breath, reminding himself that as scared-sober as he might feel right now, just a few short hours ago he'd been blitzed. Hadn't tied one on so tightly in years, and now it was obviously cutting off the blood to his brain. The girl's insane story had only tangled the knot even tighter. That explained it. *Had to.*

Rhonda sighed. "Don't go losing your shit on me, Rawson."

Mike nodded shakily.

"I need at least one borderline intelligent person to help get us out of this mess," she said.

Lonnie must have mistaken the borderline intelligent person for himself. "And just how do you suggest we do that?" he asked her.

Rhonda hesitated, before unhooking the walkie-talkie from her Daisy Dukes and raising it to her lips. "Mayday, mayday. Federal agent requesting emergency assistance—"

Lonnie laughed. "Oh, man. That's it? *That's* your plan? *Fuck a duck.* We might as well just click our heels and say 'There's no place like home.'"

"Don't you have any backup?" Mike asked her. "A partner or something?"

"This wasn't an official investigation," she admitted.

"*No one* knows where you are?"

"Rawson," Rhonda said, "not even *we* know where the hell we are."

Mike sank down on the tiger-print sofa. "Then we're really on our own here."

Just them, a cult of kill-crazy Jesus freaks...and whatever was inside the girl.

Outside, it began to rain.

20

Brother Jeremiah hit his windshield wipers as he swung a hard left onto a gravel road cutting through black trees. He was ready to be done with this business. Surely his talents could be better served elsewhere? Yet once again it was left to him to take out the trash. It was hard not to feel unappreciated, even if the Reverend did assure him that the Lord would reward him one day for his selfless dedication and willingness to "get his hands dirty for the greater good."

Still, it rankled. "Man of the law oughta be with Jacob and his crew," he grumbled. He often talked to himself while alone in the patrol car. The habit was so deeply ingrained that he was no longer aware he was even doing it. "Should be in charge of the whole ball of wax, you ask me." He sucked his teeth, sighed. Gripped the steering wheel tighter as he gassed the engine and roared down the tree-shrouded trail.

Brother Jeremiah was a flabby man in his early fifties, mostly bald but for an island of thinning brown hair above a deeply-lined forehead. He drove a black-and-white 1967 Dodge Polara that had seen better days. The engine made a maddening ticking sound any time the speed dropped below twenty; anything above fifty and the whole vehicle began rocking n' rolling like a tumble dryer on wheels. But the car was his, unlike any other in town, and he cherished it. When Jeremiah patrolled the roads outside Little Enoch, he could picture himself driving one of the fancy new Mustang SSPs driven by his big-city brothers in blue.

Like his ride, his uniform wasn't perfect – always smelled of sweat, always looked like he'd slept in it, and every year it fit a little tighter in the gut. The gold star pinned to his left breast, however, was shined to perfection. The name engraved upon the star was M. CORDELL but shortly after it came into Jeremiah's possession he had covered the name with a strip of electrical tape and carefully printed his own in its place. The tape remained there to this day, like the patch of brown crabgrass that now covered the missing M. CORDELL's shallow grave somewhere off I-80.

Rain plinked on the roof and hood of the patrol car as Jeremiah drove on. The wipers *swish-kathump-swish-kathumped* back and forth. He hunched forward in his seat, scowling at the stormy sky. A little less than twenty-four hours ago he'd been clearing a fallen power line out by Osborne's All-You-Need, when the 'goat arrived with her party. He wished he'd been there to help wrangle her. Least someone could have done was hail him on the radio. Not that he'd complain to the Reverend about being left out. No one dared question the Reverend's decisions. To do so would have been to doubt the Almighty Himself. "We all have our responsibilities," was another thing the preacher often said. "Duties handed down to us from on high." And like it or not, this was Jeremiah's.

He heard a *thump* behind him, as something shifted in the Polara's trunk.

The *other* preacher. The one who'd been traveling with the 'goat and her mother. The one Reverend Ledbetter had called the "false prophet."

Every time the patrol car hit a bump, Jeremiah heard the body rolling around back there, almost as if the dead man was wide awake and thumping on the underside of the trunk lid, pleading for someone to let him out.

Jeremiah shuddered at the thought.

The false prophet – the 'goat had called him "Pastor Joe" – had met a gruesome end. Crying out for mercy, begging for the congregation to spare the green-haired girl and her mother, to take *his* life instead. The Reverend had thrown back his head and laughed when he said that, as if the phony holy man had told the funniest joke he'd ever heard. Then he'd taken a blade from his pocket, and sliced the man's tongue down the middle, the two sections thrashing and spraying blood as they darted back inside the charlatan's mouth.

"Now thy tongue is forked," the Reverend had told him, "like that old serpent who first tempted Eve."

Ledbetter had ushered the congregation outside, to a spot behind the church. A hole had been dug a few feet from a large pile of rocks. He'd instructed his deacons to bury the false prophet up to his chest, binding him tight in the earth. The men had obeyed without speaking. The only sounds were the grunts of their labor and the false prophet's pained whimpers. When they were finished, the Reverend had addressed the congregation: "Let he who is without sin cast the first stone."

The first to step forward was the Bartlett boy, five-year-old Solomon. The Bartletts lived next door to Jeremiah, and were his oldest friends. He supposed this made Solomon his godson, though the two families had never used that word, as godparents were a Catholic construct and thus of the Devil's design. In any event, Jeremiah loved the kid like he was his own. He wasn't the only adult in the crowd who beamed with pride as the boy stepped forward and flung a rock at the false prophet's forehead. It had done no real damage, merely caused the man to gasp and grit his teeth, as if he'd been stung by a honeybee.

Then the Reverend announced, "And now the rest of us shall take our turn, for the ritual draws near, and thus our sins will soon stain the soul of another."

The adults lined up then, rocks in hand.

Ten minutes later, the false prophet's face was a mangled mess of blood and tattered skin. Stark white bone shone through multiple cracks in his forehead. Teeth lay scattered around him like pebbles among the larger rocks that had ended his life. One of his eyes oozed like a slug from the socket, slid down his cheek, and slopped to the ground in a puddle of bluish-gray slime. Then the man's broken body slumped forward, crumpling like a water-starved sunflower.

It had been left to Jeremiah to dispose of the body.

Same as it ever was, he thought, as he reached his destination.

His patrol car skidded to a stop on the edge of the property. He knew his task would be easier if he backed up closer to the place, but the last time he was here he'd gotten stuck in the mud, and he didn't plan on letting that happen again. He killed the engine and climbed from the car. Grimaced as he gazed out over the hog farm. The rain was picking up, but even the clean, earthy smell of an afternoon storm did nothing to cover the stench from the pigpen. A dank and primal stench – dirt and filth, vegetables gone to rot – it always turned Jeremiah's guts, no matter how many times he came here. As he clamped his uniform hat to his head, he realized his hands were shaking.

Ever since he was a tyke, the Brunswick family hog farm had given him the creeps. He knew it was silly – especially now that he was a hardened officer of the law – but he couldn't help it. The ravenous sounds the swine made as they rooted around in their own waste…rubbing against one another like lust-drunk sinners in some hellish orgy…their bloated bodies driven by gluttonous hunger…there was something about them that always made him break out in a cold sweat.

The stories Cousin Eli told him when they were kids hadn't helped. They'd lived not far from the Brunswick property and the older boy had enjoyed nothing more than scaring ten-year-old Jerry with spooky stories about the place. Eli would tell him that "at least a dozen men, women, and children" had lost their lives to the Brunswicks's pigs. He warned young Jerry never to stray too close to the pens, because the beasts were ready and waiting for some tasty morsel to fall in, where – like bloated, four-legged piranha – they would devour the sorry soul faster than you could say "Jesus once cast a bunch of demons into a herd of swine, and they've been waiting all this time for revenge."

It was only years later, when Jeremiah was appointed Little Enoch's one and only officer of the law, that he learned Eli had been right. Brunswick's pigs *did* have a taste for human flesh. The speed at which they could strip a man to his skeleton had been an exaggeration, but there was a good reason Jeremiah was tasked once a year with lugging cargo out here to feed to the hogs.

The farm sat on an acre of scrubland, all rusted barbed wire and ramshackle wooden fencing. The pigpen itself was little more than a quagmire of thick black mud, and a long metal feeding trough. To the left of the pen was a small lean-to shack with a battered tin roof. Farther back, on a slight rise, squatted Malachi Brunswick's clapboard home, barely twice the size of the lean-to. White with gray trim. Smoke snaked from the chimney into the roiling gray sky.

Jeremiah heard the beasts snorting excitedly as he approached. They always knew when it was feeding time, Brunswick once told him. "They're smarter than most folks think, maybe even smarter than most folks!" Jeremiah wondered if they were smart enough to recognize the sound of his patrol car, the ticking under the hood as it eased to a stop at the edge of the Brunswick property. Or were the fevered grunts that greeted his approach no more than an overactive imagination forged by childhood tall tales?

Jeremiah shook his head, gave a nervous chuckle, before calling out, "Mac! You around? Malachi! I got something special for your girls!" For reasons known only to him, Brunswick always referred to the creatures as his "girls," and Jeremiah had picked up the habit.

The hog farmer emerged from the lean-to, hiking suspenders over his broad shoulders, and clawing the seat of his coveralls from the crack of his ass. He squinted through the sheeting rain and raised a meaty mitt in greeting. He was a husky man with a ruddy rectangular head, like a house brick gouged with crude facial features. He wore a weathered baseball cap with the words GO WITH GOD embroidered over the bill.

"Jerry," he said. "Good to see you. You're gonna make my girls real happy."

Moving quickly for a man of his size, Brunswick joined Jeremiah at the back of the patrol car. Jeremiah opened the trunk. The one called Pastor Joe gazed up at the men with his one lifeless eye. Brunswick sneered at the dead man. "Burn in hell, false prophet." He punctuated his curse by spitting a wad of brown tobacco-juice that splashed the ground and the toe of Jeremiah's boots. Jeremiah stifled a sigh but didn't complain.

"You get his arms, I'll get his legs?" he suggested to Brunswick.

"Works for me."

They lifted the dead man out of the trunk, and began carrying him toward the pigpen.

"A real fine mess young Noah's got us into," Brunswick said, barely breaking a sweat as they carried the corpse, while Jeremiah wheezed like an old codger with emphysema. "Anyone coulda known that boy wasn't fit for the job."

"It ain't up to us who gets chose, Mac. The Reverend says—"

"The Lord decides," Brunswick finished for him, nodding. "I just wish He'd picked someone with half a brain, is all." He cast an anxious eye at the stormy sky. "This ain't good, Jerry. I ain't never seen it like this."

Jeremiah aimed for a reassuring smile. "We'll get the 'goat back, Mac."

Brunswick perked an eyebrow. "*We?*"

Jeremiah felt his cheeks burn. "Jacob's out there lookin'. Don't you worry none."

They reached the pigpen.

One…two…three!

They heaved the dead man over the fence and into the enclosure.

Four of the fattest hogs waddled forward, snorting with porcine gratitude. They descended upon the dead man as if they had not eaten for weeks. One bit at his lower lip, tearing it away from his face along with most of his cheek.

"Eat well, ladies," Brunswick said with a smile, leaning against the fence to watch his girls feast, like a spectator at a sporting event.

But Jeremiah had seen enough. "I oughta head back."

"You don't wanna stay for supper?"

Jeremiah gave a nauseated glance into the pigpen. "I'm gonna get. This town ain't gonna police itself."

Brunswick gave a loud "Haw!" of laughter. Then he realized Jeremiah hadn't been joking, wiped the smile from his face, and cleared his throat awkwardly.

Jeremiah trudged slump-shouldered back to the car. *No respect.* The sheriff's star on his chest might as well have been a toy, for all the authority it lent him in the eyes of others. He was reminded of a picture show he saw one time while on church business in Bowling Green. The movie was about a dedicated peace officer, and his determined efforts to apprehend a Trans Am-driving moonshiner called the Bandit. *What we got here is a complete lack of respect for the law*, the officer said at one time. Jeremiah could sympathize. Boy, could he ever…

Thunder rumbled overhead as he slammed the car door closed. He was about to key the engine, when static squawked from the dash radio, and a woman's voice said: "Mayday, mayday! Federal agent requesting urgent assistance!"

Jeremiah hesitated. He knew what he *should* have done, which was to report to Jacob at once. But maybe this was his chance to finally prove his worth to the Reverend? Maybe this was the Lord sending him a sign?

Brother Jeremiah cleared his throat, and reached for the radio with hands that were no longer shaking.

21

"Mayday, mayday!" Rhonda said into the walkie-talkie for what was surely the hundredth time. Static crackled back at her. She fiddled with the frequency dial and tried another channel. "Federal agent requesting emergency assistance!"

Lonnie said, "Give it up, Shaughnessy." He was slumped in defeat in the driver's seat. He popped the top off a lukewarm can of Coors and sprayed beer foam everywhere. "No one's gonna save us. We're screwed. And not in a good way."

Rhonda hated to admit it, but maybe Deveroux was right. Resisting the urge to smash the walkie-talkie in frustration – perhaps over Lonnie's head – she lowered it to her lap and clenched her teeth, took a deep breath and composed herself.

"Rawson," she said.

Mike stood at the foot of the bed, staring down at the girl, struggling to cling to a rational explanation for what he had seen move inside her.

"Rawson!"

Mike startled to attention.

"What's with you, man?" she said.

Mike just shook his head.

"Time to start thinking about finding those railroad tracks," Rhonda said. "It's probably too much to hope another train will come along. But maybe we can follow the tracks to something like civilization. Where's the map?"

Before Mike could find it—

The walkie-talkie crackled to life: "This is Sheriff Goosen of the Carmel County Sheriff's Department. This frequency is restricted to law enforcement personnel only. Please identify yourself."

The voice was so cornpone, it was easy to picture Foghorn Leghorn, the good-ole-boy rooster from the Looney Tunes cartoons, on the other end of the radio.

Rhonda nearly dropped the walkie-talkie in surprise. She glanced at Mike to make sure she wasn't imagining things, that he'd heard the voice too. "Special Agent Rhonda Shaughnessy," she said into the radio. "I'm a federal agent."

Mike and Lonnie crowded around Rhonda and the radio.

"F.B.I.?" Foghorn said. He pronounced it with a drawl, *Eff-a-Bee-Eye*.

"Anti-Counterfeiting Task Force."

A long pause.

Then the lawman said, "If this is some kind of joke…?"

Lonnie snickered. Rhonda glared at him.

"Just listen. Please. I have an injured girl in my party. She's been attacked."

"Attacked by who?" Foghorn said.

"It's a long story. I don't have time to explain. But the people who did it, they carved her up like a Thanksgiving bird – and they want her back."

"The girl's alive, you say?"

"For now. She'll need a doctor."

"And a shit-ton of therapy," Lonnie said.

"Who's that?" asked the lawman.

"No one," Rhonda said, shooing Lonnie away.

"How many in your party, ma'am?"

"Three civilians, plus the girl."

"And what is your location?"

"I don't know exactly. We exited I-65 about twenty miles south of Munfordville and got lost."

"That's easy done. It's a dang maze out there."

"No kidding."

Mike thrust the map in Rhonda's face, indicating the nearest town.

She said, "We think we might be close to a town called… Little Enoch?"

"Lil' Enoch, sure. I'm maybe twenty minutes from there."

Mike mouthed to Rhonda: "Crookback Road."

Rhonda said into the radio, "Does 'Crookback Road' mean anything to you?"

"Sure does," Foghorn said. "That where you is?"

"We were. Now I'm not so sure. But I'd say we're close."

"Alright. You folks sit tight, I'm on my way."

"Just Deputy Dawg?" Lonnie muttered. "I feel safer already."

The lawman must have heard Lonnie. He sounded offended as he said, "We're just small town law, son. But I'll call it in, don't you worry, just as soon as I get your location to give to the emergency services. Meantime, you folks armed?"

Rhonda glanced at the stick Pork Chop was clutching.

"Negative."

"That's too bad. Then just keep your heads down till I get there. I can only guesstimate 'bout where you are, so you're gonna have to flag me down when you see me."

"Watch your six," Rhonda told him. "I don't know how many more of those crazy sonsofbitches are still out there."

"Roger that, ma'am."

Rhonda gave a heavy sigh of relief as she lowered the radio.

Mike realized for the first time how scared she was; she'd just been holding it together better than the rest of them.

Rhonda saw Mike staring and forced a strained smile. "Looks

like our luck's finally starting to turn, Rawson."

He wished he could believe her.

22

Help arrived twenty minutes later. It felt like twenty years.

Rain drummed the roof of the RV like impatient fingers on a desktop.

Lonnie sat up front, keeping watch…for the fuzz or the psychos, whoever came for them first. It was hard to tell how much Pork Chop understood what was going on, but even P.C. seemed unusually subdued. He sat slumped on the tiger-print sofa, quietly wringing his stick.

Rhonda sat on the edge of the bed next to the sleeping girl.

"How's she doing?" Mike asked, nervously eyeing Becca's belly.

Rhonda handed him the washcloth, which was now stiff with dried blood. "Clean this and wet it again. She's burning up."

Mike nodded, stole another glance at the girl's belly before shuffling away.

"Hang in there, Becca," Rhonda whispered. "*Please…*"

She had rehearsed in her mind what she would say to the cop when he finally arrived. It would be a good dry run for when she reported this clusterfuck to Hansen and her superiors. Going off grid like this, she'd be lucky to keep her job when all was said and done. They could hardly punish her with demotion to some lonely outpost, though; outposts didn't come much lonelier than the West Memphis Field Office. It had been her choice to sign up with the section of the Bureau devoted to fighting T-shirt bootleggers, but she couldn't imagine what they would stick her with if they wanted to teach her a lesson. She remembered Lonnie's dig about the Jaywalking Squad and the Litterbug Agency and figured he might not be too far off once her bosses got through with her.

The thought struck her as funny. She let out a tired chuckle. It felt good to release the tension, despite the fact that she was laughing at the probable crash-and-burn of her own career. She shrugged, without realizing she was doing it. At least if she got that far, it would mean that she had made it out of this mess alive.

Mike glanced at her. Offered her a sympathetic look. But he quickly looked away when their eyes met, as if he had witnessed something he wasn't supposed to see.

"Hey!" Lonnie said. "Someone's coming!"

Rhonda collected herself, scrambled to the front of the RV.

Mike joined her. "Is it them? Are they back?"

Rhonda squinted through the gloom. "I can't tell."

At the top of the hill, headlights ghosted across the forest.

A distant crunch of tires, on gravel and broken asphalt…

Then the vehicle rumbled into view.

Mike let out his breath. "Thank Christ."

"Never thought I'd be so happy to see a cop," Lonnie said.

The weather-beaten cop car could have driven straight from the set of *The Dukes of Hazzard.* CARMEL COUNTY SHERIFF'S DEPARTMENT was printed in faded paint on the dented door. The gumball light appeared to be fastened to the roof with duct tape, cocked at a rakish angle like a red bowler hat.

"Who is this guy," Lonnie said, frowning. "Rosco Coltrane?"

"What do you want?" Rhonda said. "He's small town law." She raised the walkie-talkie, said into it, "I see you!"

The cop car shuddered to a stop.

Foghorn's voice crackled over the radio, "Where are you, ma'am?"

"Coming to you," she said.

"The injured party," asked the lawman. "Is she okay?"

"I think she'll make it, yeah. Everyone's okay. And ready to get the hell out of here."

"Roger that," Foghorn said. "Ready when you are, ma'am."

Moving fast, Rhonda ransacked Lonnie's closet, salvaging a pair of scuffed engineer boots with rusted buckles. She elbowed Pork Chop along the sofa and sat down, ignoring his eyes on her legs as she pulled on the boots. They were several sizes too large, and heavy enough the Mafia could've used them to drown stoolies in rivers. But they'd do in a pinch.

She checked out the windows on both sides of the RV, scoping the forest for movement. No sign of those crazy fucks. But even with the lawman waiting on the road above them, she didn't like the idea of venturing outside with just her tits in her hand. She snatched Pork Chop's stick.

"Hey!" the big guy cried. "That's mine!"

She ignored his protests. "Rawson, you're in charge of watching the girl while I'm gone. Make sure Miller doesn't choke-slam her and I think she'll be okay for now."

Pork Chop gave an offended snort. "Like I'd even do that."

23

The Vogue's bullet-riddled door was jammed in the frame. Rhonda put her shoulder to it, the broken glass in the porthole window crumbling away as she forced it open. She stepped outside into needling rain. Something moved to her left, and she wheeled around, hefting P.C.'s stick like a club…sighing with relief when she saw it was only the passenger-side mirror dangling by a thread.

The earth was slick beneath her boots. The hillside angled sharply down, a pitch-black gullet descending to the guts of the forest. The camper clung to the slope like a barnacle to a ship hull. All four tires were bogged deep in mud. Even if Lonnie *had* managed to get the engine started, they wouldn't have gone anywhere; they were literally stuck here. Thank God the cavalry had arrived…

Using Pork Chop's stick as a climbing pole, Rhonda began scaling the slope. She moved between trees, propping herself against them and checking her footing before continuing her slow ascent. Rain hissed through the trees. More than once she slipped, sank to one knee, the mud squelching obscenely beneath her.

She was panting for breath as she crested the hill, clawing through a tangle of brush to emerge onto the road. The cop car idled forty or fifty yards ahead of her. She raised a hand to shield her eyes from the glare of its headlights.

Even with one headlamp missing (*that's a little strange,* the thought flashed through Rhonda's mind), it was hard for her to discern the lawman's features beneath the rain streaming down the patrol car's windshield and the wipers swishing back and forth. From where she stood, he appeared to be a heavyset man. He tapped a two-finger salute off the wide brim of his uniform hat.

She took a deep breath and started forward. Lightning flashed. Something glinted on the lawman's chest. His badge? A tiepin? No… Something else. Hanging from a chain around his bullish neck. She stopped in her tracks.

A cross.

Something Becca said earlier echoed through her mind: *They don't worship the devil...*

"Shit—"

The lawman shifted the car into gear and hit the gas. The vehicle surged forward, the grill looming toward her like a ravenous mouth. Before she could leap from its path, the lawman threw his door open, the window glass fracturing as the frame slammed into Rhonda and hurled her to the ground like a ragdoll. She skidded through a puddle with a spray of muddy water. He hit the brakes and the car slewed to a stop. Rhonda hacked for breath, facedown in the mud, the left side of her body ablaze where the car door had struck her.

The lawman climbed from the car. He hitched up his belt in a practiced sawing motion. With a passing scowl at his splintered window, as if estimating the cost of the damages, he stalked down the road toward Rhonda, one hand resting on the butt of his holstered sidearm.

"Alright," he drawled, "now where's the 'goat?"

He planted his boot on Rhonda's hip and rolled her onto her back—

And she used the momentum to swing P.C.'s stick, connecting with the cop's knee. His kneecap shattered like glass. He hit the ground screaming. She slithered away through the mud. Still howling with pain, the lawman snatched his sidearm and fired wildly at the fleeing Fed. Bullets ripped past Rhonda's head as she stumbled to her feet and bolted into the roadside brush, branches lashing her face and tearing at her clothes before whipping back into place behind her.

The lawman let out a curse as she vanished into the woods. He lowered the smoking revolver and bent to clutch his throbbing knee. The car was just a few yards away but with a busted leg it might as well have been the distance to the moon. Thankfully the Fed had abandoned the stick she'd used to hobble him. Using the stick as a crutch, Jeremiah eased himself to his feet, favoring his good leg and choking down the pain as he crabbed to the car.

He snatched his radio. "Jake. It's Jerry. I got 'em. They're on Dogwood."

24

Rhonda scrambled back down the slope to the RV.

It wasn't supposed to go down like this. By now she should have been sweating Deveroux under an interrogator's lamp in a room with no windows. Scaring him into giving up the goods on Waylon Cates. Building an airtight case. Charges that would finally stick to the Teflon Tailor. If everything had gone as planned, this time tomorrow she would have been shopping for a snazzy new pantsuit to wear when she testified for the prosecution. She'd lost count of the amount of times she'd imagined herself sitting front and center in court, staring Cates cold in the eye as the judge threw the book at the bastard. Maybe then, with the sonofabitch behind bars where he belonged, the nightmares would finally stop.

Nightmares of Halloween night, ten years ago…

Mom had made her take Billy trick-or-treating. While all of Rhonda's friends were planning to party like it was 1999 at the old water tower on the edge of town, *she* was stuck babysitting her kid brother. The little dork was wearing a cheap knock-off costume from his favorite Saturday morning cartoon, *Johnny Space Commander*. He looked ridiculous in the fishbowl helmet, the white bodysuit with phony NASA insignia, and the Styrofoam 'oxygen tank' strapped to his back. Rhonda could have *died* with embarrassment.

Scuffing her Converse down the leaf-strewn sidewalk, Rhonda skulked behind Billy as he raced from house to house, his trick-or-treating bag growing fatter as the night bored on. She checked her watch, counting the seconds till she could bring Billy home without Mom bitching at her. Maple Street swarmed with costumed kids. Rhonda glared daggers at every four-foot Frankenstein's Monster and toddler princess and pint-size Darth Vader. She even pointed out to Billy one or two other Johnny Space Commanders wearing *genuine* costumes. She knew she was being a bitch, but what else were big sisters for?

And just when she thought her night couldn't get any worse—

A cherry-red Camaro screeched to a stop beside her. "Cat Scratch Fever" blasted from the stereo. The driver climbed coolly from behind the wheel. Todd Matthews. The reason Rhonda had wanted to go to the party tonight in the first place. He was dolled up like Dracula. Black cape, white pancake makeup, fake blood dripping from the corners of his mouth. He spat plastic fangs into his palm and gave Rhonda his best panty-soaker grin. It didn't matter to Rhonda that beneath the vampire-paint, he had a rash of zits on his forehead like a fleshy game of Connect Four. He was still *fine* with a capital F. Todd Matthews could suck her neck *anytime*.

"Hey, Rhonda."

"Hey, Todd."

Awkward silence.

Rhonda's little brother glanced back and forth between them like a midget spectator at a tennis match. *Bigger kids were so weird.*

"You going to the kegger later?" Todd asked her.

"I have to babysit," she said, like it was a death sentence.

Todd glanced down at Billy. "Bummer."

"I'm not a baby!" Billy protested. "I'm Johnny Space Commander, savior of the galaxy!" He zapped Todd with his ray gun. "*Pew, pew, pew!*"

Todd halfheartedly mimed being shot. "You got me."

Rhonda cringed. "Go get some candy," she snapped at her brother.

"You coming?"

"I'll be right here."

"But Mom said—"

"Just *go*, dork! I don't wanna be out here all night!"

He zapped her with his ray gun (*pew-pew-pew!*) and then scuttled away to the next house on their route. The jiggling of his Styrofoam backpack was affecting his balance, and Rhonda couldn't help snickering when he tripped over his feet and almost ate a faceful of sidewalk.

Todd waited till the kid was out of earshot. "Sucks you're stuck with the brat. But, hey… if you can't go to the party, then maybe the party can come to you?"

He pinched a joint from behind his ear. Lit it. Took a dramatic toke, then offered it to Rhonda. The rolling paper was slightly sticky from the hair gel he had used to slick back his Dracula 'do. Rhonda glanced over her shoulder and made sure Billy wasn't spying. She knew the little booger would rat her out to Mom in a heartbeat. She took a deeper hit than she'd intended, trying to give Todd the impression she was a seasoned pro at this…and started coughing violently and spluttering smoke in his face.

Todd just laughed approvingly. "So, I was thinking," he said, when her coughing fit subsided. "Like, maybe if you're not doing anything next weekend, we could—?"

The sound of small feet slapping excitedly up the sidewalk.

"Rhonda, look! Look, Rhonda! I got your favorite! Charleston Chews, the strawberry kind!"

She felt a pang of remorse for being so mean to her little brother. He'd remembered the sticks of chocolate-coated nougat were her favorite candy in the world, especially the strawberry-flavored ones, which were nearly impossible to find. Billy *never* shared his candy. This simple gesture spoke volumes about how much it to meant to him that his big sis had taken him trick-or-treating.

Feeling like the world's biggest asshole, Rhonda wheeled around, whipping her hands behind her back and dropping the joint before Billy could see it—

And her life was changed forever.

The burning coal hit the ground, exploding into embers that swirled through the air like fireflies. A single spark struck the thigh of Billy's spacesuit…

PWOOF! It was as if the costume had been lacquered in gasoline from collar to cuff. The boy became a human fireball, the Styrofoam backpack blazing like a barbecue briquette, the plastic helmet melting on his face. Todd stripped off his Dracula cape, started beating at the inferno, which only fanned the flames. Billy screamed and flailed as the helmet melted on his face like a molten plastic caul. A homeowner charged across his lawn with a garden hose and doused the fire, but by then it was too late. When the smoke cleared, Billy lay curled in agony on the sidewalk next to his spilled bag of Halloween candy. Most of the sugary treats had turned to sticky puddles in the heat. Only Rhonda's Charleston Chews, scattered next to Todd's Camaro, lay untouched by the tragedy.

Had Billy died there and then, it would have been a mercy.

But next came the long months at the ICU: Mom praying outside the oxygen tent erected around Billy's hospital bed… Dad clutching his hipflask tighter than Mom clutched her rosary beads, already disappearing into the bottle that would corrode his liver and kill him within five years… and Billy, *poor Billy*, a grotesque phantom behind the opaque walls of the oxygen tent, swathed from head to toe in surgical gauze that would yellow with the pus oozing from his blistered body. The bandages required changing twice a day, a process that made the seven-year old scream in agony. His head was completely covered in bandages, except for one bloodshot eye that glared out at Rhonda like something from an Edgar Allan Poe story. At last, mercifully, he took his final breath. After the closed casket funeral, where Billy was burned for a second time in the crematorium, Mom and Dad demanded once more that she tell them what happened. But Rhonda could never bring herself to tell them the truth. All she could think about was Todd's joint, still smoldering on the ground, which she had kicked into an open sewer grate, disposing of the evidence even as her brother burned.

What happened, Rhonda? Tell us what happened!

What happened?

What—

25

"—happened?" Mike said, as she staggered inside the RV. "Where's the cop? Are we getting out of here?"

She slammed the door and collapsed against it, barely able to stand, heaving for breath. She was soaked to the bone. Rainwater flooded from her hair, down her face. She snorted some, started choking. Mike might have slapped her on the back, cleared her airway, if he hadn't thought she'd add 'striking a federal agent' to the list of charges against him.

"I fucked up," she said at last.

Mike shot a nervous glance at Lonnie and Pork Chop.

"The cop… he's one of them."

"And you led him right to us?" Lonnie booted a box of wrestling merch across the motorhome. "That's just great! Who the fuck are these fucking fuckers?"

Pork Chop broached a delicate subject: "Uh…Cyndi?"

"If you ask me about that stick," she said, "I swear to Christ…"

"Never mind," he muttered.

Something caught Rhonda's eye at the rear of the cabin—

An oxygen tent encased an ICU hospital bed. Her brother lay there like a nightmarish mummy. Billy glared at her hatefully through the slit in the pus-yellowed bandages that turbaned his head. Slowly…he raised one skinny arm and pointed at her…as a dark, bottomless 'O' opened up in the gauze covering his mouth, and an ear-splitting shriek filled her skull.

Rhonda stumbled, grabbing the edge of the kitchen counter to stay on her feet. She shut her eyes, choked down a scream. Mike clutched her arm to keep her from falling. The men glanced back at the bed. Becca was still sleeping off Pork Chop's chokehold. Lonnie looked at Mike, twirled a finger by his temple and rolled his eyes in the universal mime for *this bitch is loco.*

"What is it?" Mike asked her. "What's wrong?" *Had she seen the girl's belly move,* he thought. *Had she seen the clawed hand too?* It would have been a relief to know he wasn't the only one losing his mind here.

Rhonda slowly opened her eyes. Now she saw only the girl on the bed. She shuddered with relief. Nodded at Mike – *I'm okay* – and he relaxed his grip on her arm.

"Are you hurt?" he asked her.

Rhonda glanced down at herself. The rain had rendered her tube-top transparent. Her arms and legs were scratched where she'd clawed through the brush – a pale imitation of Becca's wounds – and the limbs on her left side were already started to bruise where the cop had struck her with the car door.

"I…I don't think so," she said, teeth chattering as her adrenaline buzz faded.

"Just cold by the looks of it," Lonnie smiled, ogling her rock-hard nipples.

"Damn it, Lonnie!" Mike snapped at him. "Make yourself useful and find her something dry to wear!"

Lonnie fetched a rumpled *A-Team* T-shirt from the closet.

Rhonda threw it on.

"So what's the plan?" Lonnie asked her.

Rhonda shook her head numbly. "I…I need a minute to think."

They heard the sound of engines approaching.

"I don't think we've got one," Mike said.

26

Jeremiah perched inside the open door of the Polara, splinting his busted leg with the stick the Fed had left behind, and cinching it in place with his belt. Hearing engines approach, he eased himself to his feet, gutting down a yelp of pain. Jacob skidded the ATV to a stop. Behind him, a half-dozen armed men poured from the back of a stake truck. Jacob marched towards the cop; despite Jeremiah's uniform, it was clear who had authority here. Lightning flashed above them.

"Where are they?" Jacob shouted above the rumble of thunder.

Jeremiah pointed sheepishly into the woods where the Fed had escaped.

"Damn it, Jerry. Why didn't you call me the second you found 'em?"

"I called as soon as I could," the lawman insisted.

Jacob glanced scornfully at his wounded leg. "Figured you'd play hero, is what you did."

Found out, Jeremiah hung his head in shame.

"Heaton's gonna be mighty displeased," Jacob said.

The color bled from Jeremiah's face. "Heaton don't gotta know about this, does he, Jake?"

For several seconds, Jacob allowed the threat to hang above Jeremiah's head like a guillotine blade. "Just pray your pride hasn't damned us all."

Jacob peered down the embankment then, shielding his eyes from the stinging rain. The RV clung precariously to a hillside that was quickly turning into a mudslide in the rain. He cupped his hands around his mouth. "Hello, the camper!"

Silence at first. No sound below except for the rain hissing through the trees.

Then a man's voice shouted back, "It's a motorhome, motherfucker!"

Muffled arguing below.

Now a woman's voice: "You assholes are in a world of trouble! I'm a federal agent!"

Jacob perked an eyebrow at Jeremiah, who wrinkled his nose and shook his head.

"The Anti-Counterfeiting Task Force, wasn't it?" Jeremiah called down the embankment. (Jacob frowned: *The what-now?*) "Yeah, we're mighty impressed!"

"You will be!" the woman shot back. "I've called for reinforcements. Any minute now this forest is gonna be crawling with G-men. The best you fucksticks can hope for is spending the rest of your sorry-ass lives in prison. Now make it easy on yourself and lay down your weapons!"

"She's bluffing," Jeremiah said.

A thin-lipped smile teased through Jacob's beard. "Girl's got sand, don't she?"

"Ask me, she needs her mouth washed out with soap."

"Listen here, missy!" Jacob called out. "You folks have stumbled onto something here that's got nothing to do with you, something you can't begin to understand. All we want is the girl. She's not who you think she is. Turn her over right now and the rest of you are free to go. You got my word on it."

Even as the lie left his lips, Jacob nodded to the men prepping their weapons outside the stake truck. Jeremiah, too, reloaded his sidearm, before reaching inside the cop car to fetch a pump shotgun.

Jacob glanced dubiously at his wounded leg. "Sure you're up to this, Jerry?"

Jeremiah racked the shotgun defiantly. "I owe this harlot."

Jacob nodded. "Go on, then. I'll keep 'em busy."

Jeremiah and the other men began making their way into the woods.

27

"Well," Lonnie said, "I say we vote on it."

"Vote on what?" Rhonda said.

"The hell you think? Giving 'em the girl. All in favor say *fuckin'-A*."

Pork Chop raised his hand without hesitation. "Fuckin'-A!"

Rhonda couldn't believe what she was hearing. "Look what they did to her!"

"This has nothing to do with us. P.C., Mikey, tell me I'm wrong?"

"Rawson, please don't tell me you agree with these assholes?"

Mike said softly, "I got a wife and kid to think about."

"Damn right you do," Lonnie said, perhaps the first time he'd shown any real interest in Mike's family.

Rhonda said, "Do you honestly believe they're just gonna let us leave here?"

Mike didn't want to abandon the girl any more than she did. But doing 'the right thing' took on a whole new meaning when it was a matter of life and death. In a hypothetical situation, everyone was the bravest, most virtuous S.O.B. who ever lived; thrown back into the jungle, the old lizard brain took over and it all boiled down to self-preservation at whatever cost.

Rhonda and Lonnie crowded Mike, talking over one another as they each pleaded their case: Give up the girl, get home safely, and eventually learn to live with their decision…or flee with her and allow her to slow them down while psychotic hillbillies pursued them through the woods. Even Pork Chop got in on the act, although he didn't seem to know what the options were, and just pleaded with Mike: "We gotta stick with Lonnie, man!" Mike backed away with his palms held out. Their words merged with the pounding rain on the RV's roof, creating an incomprehensible, static-like buzz in his head. As the trio bullied him to the back of the motorhome, Mike could think of little else than what the man had said…

She's not who you think she is.

What did that *mean*?

Mike shuddered, remembering whatever it was he had seen move inside Becca's belly.

Lonnie said, "Think of your kid—"

Rhonda said, "You'll never forgive yourself—"

Pork Chop said, "When has Lonnie ever let us down—"

"Would you just give me a minute?" Mike pleaded. "I can hardly hear myself th—"

And suddenly Mike was gone.

One second he was fending off Lonnie and Rhonda…the next he had disappeared.

Lonnie and Rhonda exchanged a baffled glance. Pork Chop chuckled dumbly.

Something wheezed below them.

Glancing down, they saw Mike splayed on his back in the mud beneath Jezebel, where he had plunged through the rusted hole in the floor. Lonnie's so-called 'doggy door.'

Rhonda crouched above the hole.

"Rawson," she grinned, "you are a genius!"

Mike could only reach a trembling pain-wracked claw toward her and wheeze like Dom DeLuise being slowly asphyxiated.

"How's it look down there?" she said.

Mike was in so much pain he hadn't thought to admire the view. "Cold and wet."

"Can we get downhill, you think?"

"I don't know. Maybe. I guess."

Rhonda looked at Lonnie. "Here's our chance, Deveroux. What do you say? Even *you're* not dumb enough to believe they're letting us walk out of here."

Lonnie hesitated. He knew she was right...but it chafed his nuts to admit it.

"Hey," Pork Chop said, gazing idly out the window. "There's a buncha guys outside." He glanced at Rhonda. "Maybe it's those reinforcements you called?"

Rhonda gave a withering headshake. "I was bluffing."

"Oh," Pork Chop said. "Remind me never to play poker with you."

Rhonda scrambled to a shattered side window and peered outside. Slinking through the dark, stalking between the trees toward the RV, she saw...

"One. Two. Three. I count four. Armed. Shotguns and assault rifles."

"I got another two this side," Lonnie whispered from the opposite window.

"And that's just the ones we can see," she said. "Don't be stupid, Deveroux. I know that's hard for you. But come on, use your head, man."

Lonnie gave a heavy sigh. "Fuck it. Grab the girl and get moving."

His unexpected chivalry raised Rhonda's suspicions. "What about you?"

"I'll be right behind you," he said. "As soon as I leave these bastards something to remember me by."

Rhonda shook her head. *Whatever.* There was no reasoning with stupid.

She moved quickly to the bed, staring down at the unconscious girl.

"Miller," she snapped at Pork Chop. The big guy seemed surprised, as if it had been many years since anyone called him by his name. "Give me a hand with her."

Pork Chop hooked his arms under Becca's shoulders. Rhonda took her legs. Together they lifted the girl gently off the bed, and carried her to the hole in the floor. They lowered Becca down through the hole, careful not to scrape her wounds against its circumference.

She murmured in her sleep, but otherwise didn't fight them.

"Got her," Mike said, laying the girl on the ground beside him.

Rhonda passed the first aid kit down to Mike, then perched herself on the edge of the hole. Before lowering herself down, she glanced back at Lonnie. *What the hell was he doing?* He moved with purpose, gathering the boxes of wrestling merch into one large pile at the front of the motorhome. Little late to start getting house-proud, Rhonda thought. "Deveroux!"

He upended another bullet-riddled box of muscle shirts onto the mountain of merch he was building. "Right behind you."

Rhonda lowered herself down through the hole, squelching in the mud on her back next to Mike and Becca.

"You made the right choice, Rawson."

Mike didn't remember making *any* choice. He'd just fallen through a hole in the floor. If anyone deserved credit, it was gravity.

A massive shadow loomed over them. They glanced up and saw Pork Chop preparing to lower himself down through the hole. The big guy's kilt fanned out around his meaty thighs and bristly legs, presenting Mike and Rhonda with a commode's-eye view of cock and balls and bunghole.

Mike retched. "Damn it, P.C.! Would it have killed you to wear boxers?"

"Little help here, Mikey?"

"I'll leave you to it," Rhonda said, dragging the girl through the mud toward the backend of the RV, where the ground sloped down and away.

"Yeah, right," Mike grumbled. "Thanks for nothing..."

Inside the cabin, Lonnie had finished building his pile of wrestling merch. He stepped back to admire it for a second, before hustling to the kitchen stove and turning all the gas dials to HIGH. He did the same on the oven control, opening the oven door to allow the gas to escape. The unlit hobs hissed like a feast of snakes. The air soon shimmered with fumes.

Hurrying back to the pile of wrestling merch, Lonnie fished his lighter from his pocket. It was one of those novelty things in the shape of a bikini-clad babe. The babe's titties flashed with red LED lights as he sparked the lighter and set fire to two giant foam hands on top of the pile...the fuse for his makeshift time-bomb.

The speed with which the merch caught fire took Lonnie by

surprise. He staggered back, raising a hand to shield his face from the heat of the flames.

He glanced around his beloved motorhome, wishing there was more time to savor the moment, knowing this was the last time he'd ever see Jezebel.

Lotta mammaries in this ol' rig. I'm sure gonna miss you, girl…

A crack of thunder ripped the world in two outside. Lonnie felt the vibrations shudder through the motorhome from end to end. He imagined the rumbling of the storm was not unlike the sound of ninety thousand wrestling fans stomping their feet on the floor of the Silverdome right this second.

The flames grew higher. Higher…

Time to go.

Lonnie moved toward the doggy door—

And stopped in his tracks.

Pork Chop was buried waist-deep in the floor.

He grinned up at Lonnie. "I'm kinda stuck."

"When you say 'kinda'…?"

"I'm stuck."

"Mikey!" Lonnie shouted through the floor. "We gotta move, man!"

"I'm working on it!"

Lonnie cut an anxious glance between the burning merch and the gas-hissing oven. "Work faster, dude!"

Mike gripped Pork Chop's legs in a tight embrace, struggling desperately to yank him down through the hole. Pork Chop's kilt draped over his head like a cloak. Mike gave a cry of disgust as Pork Chop's junk slapped down upon his head.

Lonnie said, "What're you homos doing down there?"

"Just say the word and we can switch places!" Mike shouted.

Lonnie swiped the sweat from his face as the fire leapt from the burning merch to the sofa. The flames lapped at the ceiling and left black streaks there like demonic claw marks. "Ah, Jesus! You gotta hurry, Mikey!"

Pork Chop screeched in pain as Mike tugged on his legs and Lonnie attempted to cram the flabby folds of his gut down the hole from above. Its jagged edges scraped the skin from his belly. "I'm not gonna fit," P.C. cried. "Just leave me!"

"You die, I die!"

"Don't be a hero, man!"

"No, you dumb shit, you're blocking my way out!"

Pork Chop gasped as something cold and wet slapped against his legs. He feared he'd been disemboweled on the twisted metal; that it was his own guts he felt slopping down his legs. "Mikey? Mikey, what is that?"

"Mud," Mike said, slapping another fistful onto Pork Chop's ample hips.

Pork Chop giggled girlishly. "Kinda tickles!"

Choking down his disgust, Mike continued slathering Pork Chop with mud.

When that was done, he shouted up at Lonnie five words he never thought would come from his own mouth…but tonight was just full of surprises: "He's all greased to go!"

"Here goes nothing!" Lonnie said.

Lonnie took a running start and kicked P.C. in the gut, his foot sinking ankle-deep in doughy flab. Pork Chop gave a pained woof and plunged down through the hole, landing splat on his back in the mud next to Mike. Before he could catch his breath, gravity shot him down the slope like a cannonball. *"Shiiiiiiiiit!"*

Lonnie scrambled down through the hole. Noxious black smoke poured out after him. "Close call," he wheezed as he joined Mike beneath the RV.

"Jesus, Lonnie. What the hell did you do?"

"Seemed like a good idea at the time."

Mike shook his head. "You're incredible."

"That's what your mom sss—"

"Just move, asshole!"

They slithered through the mud to the rear of the motorhome. There the ground angled sharply down, like a gut-check Wet N' Wild ride. Confirming that the coast was clear, as much as they could in the dark and pouring rain, they exchanged a steely nod before breaking cover and sliding down the slope to the bottom of the embankment—

Where a heavyset man wearing a tan county sheriff's uniform waited for them. He was favoring one leg; the other was splinted with a stick, strapped with a belt.

His pump shotgun was pointed their way.

Rhonda lay crouched at the cop's feet, her arms wrapped protectively around the unconscious girl, her eyes betraying what she knew was a futile gesture. Pork Chop was sprawled a few feet away. One side of his face was smeared with mud. He was staring jealously at the stick the cop had used to splint his leg.

"Glad you could join us," Jeremiah said to Mike and Lonnie.

28

On the hillside above, the soldiers converged on the motorhome.

Through the vehicle's shattered windows and the bullet holes riddling its battered body, Brother Seth saw flames inside, flickering like lantern light. With a frantic hand signal, Seth ordered the charge. The men kicked down the door and swarmed inside, recoiling from the intensity of the blaze.

Then they smelled the gas. Looked to Seth for guidance.

Seth's shoulders slumped. He lowered his rifle with a sigh of resignation.

Even the most pious man will resort to profanity to mark his final words:

"Well, *shit*—"

The motorhome exploded into hellfire.

*

On the road above, Jacob reeled back from the force of the blast, shielding his eyes as a great mushrooming fireball billowed up above the forest canopy.

Something whistled down from the heavens, plummeting toward him at great speed. Jacob dodged from its path. The license plate *thunked* into the earth where he'd been standing. It quivered there, hissing at him in the rain, the smoldering metal scorched and red-hot in one corner. Jacob's lips curled into a sneer as he read the words embossed upon it:

EZLIVIN

"Godless heathens."

*

The shock of the blast tore through the woods, uprooting

undergrowth and stripping leaves from trees, startling sleeping birds from their roosts.

Jeremiah grunted as the blast knocked him back, throwing off his aim. Before he had time to regain his senses, Pork Chop exploded to his feet like a linebacker from the scrimmage, slamming him against a tree. Jeremiah's eyes went wide. He gave a gasping cry. Blood sprayed from his mouth, spattering Pork Chop's face. P.C. glanced down and saw the broken tree branch spearing Jeremiah's belly. He staggered back in horror at what he had done. Jeremiah clutched at the jagged wooden spike jutting from his abdomen. He struggled uselessly to free himself. At last he ceased struggling – resigned to his fate or exhausted, maybe both – and simply dangled there like a coat on a rack.

Mike and Lonnie climbed to their feet.

Lonnie slapped P.C. on the back. "Nice work, dude. I was just about to make my move."

P.C. had tears in his eyes. "I never meant to *hurt* him."

"You did good, Miller," Rhonda told him.

"What about me?" Lonnie said, jerking his head toward the flaming wreck that was Jezebel. When Rhonda refused to compliment him, he said, "Well, sorry your evidence got blown sky-high." He gave her a shit-eating grin.

Jeremiah's dimming eyes moved slowly from Pork Chop…to Mike and Lonnie…until at last they came to rest on Rhonda, and the unconscious girl in her arms. "Fools…" he croaked, hacking up blood. "You…got no idea…what you're dealing with…"

Rhonda propped the girl against a moss-cushioned tree stump before climbing to her feet. She fetched the lawman's shotgun from the ground, racked a round in the chamber, and approached him.

"How do we get out of here?" she said.

He bared his bloodstained teeth in what might have been a smile. "*Behold! The Lord cometh out of His place…to punish mankind for his iniquity… The earth shall disclose her blood…and shall no more cover her slain.*"

"Is that from *Master of Puppets*?" Lonnie said.

Jeremiah coughed up something long and wet and red and stringy. His face a mask of pain, he gnashed his teeth and groaned, fighting to keep his head from sinking to his chest. "The girl…must…die—" And then he demonstrated how dying was done by slumping lifelessly from the tree branch.

"Jesus," Mike breathed.

Rhonda said, "Let's move, people. Before they have time to regroup."

She took the sidearm from the dead cop's holster and held it out to Mike.

Blood drizzled off the butt.

Mike's stomach flipped a cartwheel. "I… I don't want it."

Lonnie stepped forward eagerly. "Shit, I'll take it."

"The hell you will," Rhonda said. "Two words: Friendly fire."

She stuffed the revolver in the waistband of her Daisy Dukes. Then she salvaged all the ammo she could find on the lawman's utility belt, shoving bullets in her pockets like a shoplifter who's just realized the guy behind the counter has stepped out for a smoke.

"Miller," she said, "you're carrying the girl."

"Why me?" Pork Chop whined.

"Call it your penance for choking her out."

Bitching under his breath, Pork Chop hauled the girl onto his shoulder in a fireman's carry.

They started walking.

29

Jacob gazed in horror at the carnage strewn across the hillside. His friends and neighbors, men with whom he had worshipped since they were old enough to voice their love for the Lord…their bodies were now reduced to charred and smoking meat, food for scavengers and decay.

The stench of burning rubber and roasting human flesh cloyed the air. Seth sat slumped against a smoldering tire, the tuft of blond hair atop his skull burning like a candlewick, wisps of smoke rising up from his body. Brother Seth had spent his free time painting harrowing scenes of the Apocalypse, gifting his art to friends and family on anniversaries and birthdays; but even Seth's most vivid depiction of the End of Days paled in comparison to this hell-on-earth… Aaron and his wife had been blessed with triplets less than a month ago; now the young father's lifeless body hung from the highest branches of a maple tree like a trapped kite… Micah could take apart and piece together any mechanical contraption put in front of him, but the pieces of him now scattered all over the hill, not even Micah could possibly reassemble… Brother Jordan's angelic singing voice had belied the man's three-hundred-pound frame; now his decapitated head gawked at Jacob, fused to a slab of blackened metal that was once the motorhome's hood, like a nightmare ornament, and his mouth was open wide in a silent scream as if he sang a song only the dead could hear.

Jacob could barely recognize the cindered remains of the other men.

He raised his eyes to the heavens.

"So much killin', Lord. Where does it end?"

Lightning lashed the night sky. Jacob started at the boom of thunder, as if rebuked by the Lord. He took a deep breath, reminding himself that his brothers were casualties in a war that surpassed all human understanding. There was so much more at stake than the life of any one soldier. Not that he felt their loss any less. But there would be time to mourn them later. *God willing, there will be time…*

Jacob steeled himself for what he knew he must do next. A lump formed in his throat, big as one of the apples that grew in Sister Sara's orchard on the edge of town. It took three tries for him to swallow it down.

With trembling hands, he unhooked the walkie-talkie from his belt.

"Heaton," he said, "we got a problem."

30

Ledbetter sat alone on the floor of the church, his back resting against the communion table on which lay the shrouded body of his son. He held a framed photograph. It showed Melissa, pregnant with Daniel, her hands clasped over her pregnant belly, standing outside the church on a bright summer's day. The slight downward tilt of her head and her self-conscious smile reminded Ledbetter of how much she had loathed having her picture taken. He'd never understood it. She was the most beautiful creature he had ever laid eyes on.

In the photo Melissa wore a light green dress that fell properly past her knees. Her long golden hair cascaded to her waist. Ledbetter had never met a woman with hair as long Melissa's, and when she passed before her time, in tribute the Reverend had decreed that no female church member should grow her hair longer than shoulder length.

As Ledbetter stared at the photo, he remembered Melissa singing in the choir as a child, the way the sun shone down on her through the windows, on her and her alone, making her long golden hair shimmer and glow. Even then he had vowed to make her his bride. He had of course conducted himself accordingly. Courting the girl with long walks and prayer sessions, waiting patiently until her first flow, when she became woman, before taking her to the marriage bed.

In his weaker moments, Ledbetter sometimes wondered if the Lord had taken Melissa before her time because He coveted her for Himself; or had He punished the preacher for daring to share his soul with another after promising it to God?

He had never asked permission to take a wife. Perhaps that was why they had struggled so hard to produce a child; why, when at long last Melissa fell pregnant, there were complications. The doctor had warned them the child could be stillborn. And on the day his wife went into labor Heaton was given a choice. The doctor was a good man, with a strong basso timbre that never failed to boom "AMEN!" during sermons, but he could barely find his voice as he gave Ledbetter the terrible news. *I can only save one of them. Mother or child. I'm so sorry, Reverend. You must make a decision.*

Ledbetter did not hesitate. Someone had to lead his people after he was gone. He had held Melissa's hand to the very end, when she took her last breath, and Daniel his first.

Now mother and child were reunited in the Promised Land.

His deepest fear was that he might never join them there; not unless the 'goat was recaptured, and the ritual completed.

As if to confirm his fears, the walkie-talkie on the floor beside him gave a sudden belch of static.

"Heaton?" Jacob's voice crackled over the radio.

Ledbetter depressed the TALK button. "Speak."

"It's bad. The outsiders set some kinda trap. I—" He gave a choked sob. "I'm the only one who made it."

"And the 'goat?"

"She got away with the outsiders."

Ledbetter exhaled through clenched teeth. "I trusted you, Jacob."

"And you were right to. I just need more—"

"Time? *'Watch therefore, for you know neither the time nor the hour.'* There is no more time!"

"I can still fix this, brother."

"God help you if you don't," the preacher said. "God help all of us."

"I'll regroup with more men and keep look—"

Ledbetter switched off the radio.

He heaved himself to his knees. Turning towards the figure of the crucified Christ, he clasped his hands, closed his eyes, and said, "All my life You've been there for me. In moments of fear and doubt You were there. I need You now more than ever. Please, Lord. Guide me. Tell me what to do."

He remained there on his knees until his muscles throbbed and his bones ached. He remembered the times his father had forced him to kneel in prayer as a child, usually bare-kneed on grains of rice, punishing him for some transgression.

"Do not forsake me, Lord. Not now. With so much at stake..."

Still the Lord would not answer.

Unspooling his belt from the loops of his pants, he wrapped the buckle around his fist, and began thrashing the leather strap against his back. "*Speak* to me! *Speak! Speak! Speak!*" The belt was a furious blur as it bit into his back, ripping his shirt to ribbons and scoring his flesh, flinging blood across the room. A fine red mist spackled Daniel's funeral shroud. Soon the flesh of Ledbetter's back hung in raw tatters, as new wounds opened alongside old scars.

With every strike he wailed like a man possessed, yet he wept not from the pain, but with the knowledge that he was alone. His movements slowed as fatigue overwhelmed him. Sweat dripped from his face, pitter-pattering the puddles of blood that had pooled on the floor. Lightning flashed, the stained-glass windows turning neon in the stuttering light, seeming to animate the abominations that surrounded him.

The belt slid weakly from his hands.

He cast his eyes heavenwards.

"Where are You?"

*

Ledbetter hastened to his study.

The open wounds in his back blazed with pain, leaking blood with every move he made, yet the preacher was calm, his hands were steady. He ignored his father's glare as he swung aside the portrait on its single rusty hinge. Secreted behind the painting was a small metal safe, built into the wall. Decades had passed since he last touched its dial, but the preacher knew by heart the combination that would open it: 04 – 05 – 99. To most, the numbers would mean nothing. But to father and son, they meant everything. April 5th, 1899. The month, day and year that Little Enoch became an official township.

The safe was empty save for a small stack of papers – some dog-eared legal documents and a handful of savings bonds that had been accruing interest through the years. But it was the item on top of the papers that had his full attention.

An old reel-to-reel tape, on its round metal spool.

Delicately – as if he were handling a volatile incendiary device, which, in a manner of speaking, he was – Ledbetter removed the tape from the safe, shut and locked the door, and then replaced his father's portrait in front of it. He moved to his desk, and began threading the tape ribbon through an old Revere recorder, stored among the jumble of radio equipment.

His father's portrait glared down as he worked, the old man supervising his son from beyond the grave.

Before the day is done, Daddy said, *God's people shall hear His message.*

Not looking up from his work, Ledbetter said, "I'm praying it doesn't come to that, Daddy. Jacob will find the girl. And when he does, we—"

If the Lord commands it, you will not hesitate!

Ledbetter flinched at his tone as if struck by a blow.

'In their hearts humans plan their course, but the Lord establishes their steps.'

"Yes, sir."

'For as by one man's disobedience many were made sinners, so by the obedience of one shall many be made righteous.'

"I'll do what I must."

He finished loading the tape, and shifted the recorder close to the radio microphone. Then he stood gazing down at the machine, as if admiring some holy relic, remembering the day his father had recorded the message on the tape.

The old man had been not long for the grave. The last stroke he'd suffered had all but broken him, leaving him confined to a wheelchair and requiring air from a tank just to breathe and praise the Lord. The left side of his face looked like it was melting; his hand was a misshapen claw. The church physician had informed him – warily, fearing the messenger would be shot for delivering bad news – that nothing more could be done. He would soon be traveling on the Road to Glory. The old man had taken the news stoically. He had retired to his study, demanding that he not be disturbed. But after several days, and having seen neither hide nor hair of his father, curiosity had gotten the better of Heaton Jr.

Approaching the closed door to the study, he could hear his father's voice echoing from within, screeching and shrill, like carrion crows warring over a carcass. Unable to summon the nerve to knock, Heaton had knelt before the door and put his eye to the keyhole. The old man sat hunched in his wheelchair. The tape recorder whirred on the desk before him. His yellow-white hair stood in wild tufts from his head, his skull so emaciated that his eyes bulged from the sockets like bloodshot eggs. Spittle sprayed from his lips as he raged into the microphone, pausing only to suck air from his oxygen mask. Occasionally he would angle his ear toward the heavens, with his eyes squeezed shut, straining to hear a voice only he could hear, as if he were merely a conduit for someone else speaking through him.

He had looked, Heaton thought, like a madman. And for the first time in his life he had doubted his father, and the church, and their duty to God. It was only a fleeting thought, and one for which he would punish himself most severely in time to come.

As if sensing the Doubting Thomas spying through the keyhole, the old man's one good eye had snapped open, and he stared directly at his son. The old man may have had one foot in the grave, but his eyes had lost none of their intensity. Heaton Jr. was by this time almost thirty years old, and had already inherited his father's mantle as leader of the church. Still, he shrank under the old man's gaze, reverting to a frightened child as he was summoned inside.

God's people may one day need to hear this, he had said, gesturing to the tape recorder with the misshapen claw that was his left hand. *My final sermon.*

Heaton had promised his father he would not let him down…

Now he stared at the tape recorder.

He did not wish to press PLAY.

Yet he feared he would soon have no choice.

31

"Guys," Pork Chop whined. "Can someone else take this chick for a while? She's heavy as hell."

"We've been walking less than fifteen minutes," Mike said.

"But she's really heavy! I don't know how much longer I can do this!"

Rhonda snapped, "Quit being such a pussy, Miller. She probably weighs less than your head."

That made Mike and Lonnie laugh.

"He does have a giant noggin," Lonnie said.

P.C. muttered something about infant encephalitis.

"I can't believe we're laughing," Mike said.

"Yeah, well, I don't laugh about this I might go fuckin' crazy."

Rhonda led the way through the woods, Mike and Lonnie behind her. Pork Chop lagged a little ways back, lugging the unconscious girl on his shoulder.

Mike unfurled the map, struggling to read it in the dim light.

"Which way to the railroad tracks?" Rhonda asked him.

"North, I think?"

"Great. So, who brought their compass?"

"Shit," Mike said, resisting the urge to tear the map to shreds.

"Wait," Lonnie said. "I remember something from Boy Scouts..."

"Reading *Guns & Ammo* doesn't make you a Boy Scout, Lonnie."

"Dude, I'm serious. I helped out my nephew's troop one time when they went on a camping trip."

"It's true," Pork Chop said, wheezing for breath as he struggled to keep up. "I went with him. It was fun. Funner than this, that's for sure."

"Jesus," Rhonda said. "Those poor kids."

Lonnie let that slide. "I remember the Scoutmaster teaching the kids something about the North Star. It's near Polaris, I think, next to the Little Dipper's handle. If we can find the North Star, and follow that, we'll know we're headed north."

"There's just one problem, Deveroux. You see any stars in the sky? 'Cause all I see is a bunch of storm clouds. And would you even know the Little Dipper if you saw it? Something tells me you wouldn't know the difference between the moon and your ass."

They walked on.

The only sounds were their footsteps scuffling along the forest floor, Pork Chop's obscene-phone-caller-breathing, and the distant rumbling of thunder.

Then a man's deep voice crackled over the walkie-talkie hanging from Rhonda's belt loops: "*Vengeance is mine…and retribution… In due time, their foot will slip… The day of calamity is near… And the impending doom that is hastening upon them.*"

The group froze.

Rhonda raised the walkie-talkie hesitantly to her lips, "Who is this?"

"Who I am is unimportant," the voice said. "What is important is that you surrender the 'goat while there's still time. You don't know what she is."

"Not the first time I've heard that tonight," Rhonda said, regaining her composure. "Care to tell me what this is about? Maybe if I knew exactly what she is – apart from a goat, whatever the hell *that* means – we could reach some kind of agreement."

The man sighed sorrowfully through the speaker.

"I implore you," he said. "Surrender the 'goat…or know suffering the likes of which you never imagined."

"Let's talk consequences, shall we?" Rhonda said. "Your people – I'm guessing I'm talking to the man in charge – your people attempted to murder a federal agent. That's not even counting what you did to this poor girl and her mother. You're in a world of trouble, mister. Now I suggest you cut your losses and work with me here."

"Enough fucking around." Lonnie snatched the walkie-talkie from Rhonda's hands. "Listen up, shithead!" Spittle sprayed from his lips as he shouted into the radio. "We already sent a bunch of you bible-thumpin' sons of whores to hell and we're good and goddamn ready to go again! You don't got the faintest idea who you're dealin' with here, pal: We're motherfuckin' Wrathbone! Born to chase tail and raise hell! And if you don't clear a path and let us leave here, I swear we'll—"

Rhonda clawed the walkie-talkie from Lonnie's hand. "Idiot!"

Lonnie snatched it back. They played tug-of-war with the radio for a few seconds, until Rhonda jabbed him in the gut with the butt of her shotgun, and Lonnie woofed and gave it up.

Rhonda thumbed the TALK button. "Are you still there?"

A long silence.

The walkie-talkie hissed with dead air.

Mike glared at Lonnie. "Nice going, asshole."

The man spoke one last time, his voice eerily calm: "Before this night is through, boy, I shall have that blasphemous tongue plucked from your mouth."

32

All Arthur 'Pork Chop' Miller ever wanted was to see Wrestlemania III.

Pork Chop loved wrestling almost as much as beer and titties. The only thing he could think of that might beat seeing Wrestlemania live was sucking on a titty filled with beer instead of milk. He would've given his left nut for ringside seats. And thanks to good ol' Lonnie, the tickets hadn't cost a dime, much less one of his balls.

He'd been so pumped to see in person not only 'Rowdy' Roddy Piper (his fave!), but also the Macho Man, George 'The Animal' Steele, 'Hacksaw' Jim Duggan, and the Junkyard Dog. There were even rumors that Alice Cooper was gonna be in attendance, hanging out with Jake 'The Snake' Roberts. It didn't get any cooler! Pork Chop couldn't remember the last time he'd been so excited…

He should've known it was never gonna happen. Oh, for ninety thousand other lucky fuckers, the party was still on. The main event was probably getting started right now – P.C.'s money was on Andre the Giant pulverizing The Hulkster – while he and his friends wandered through the woods in the middle of nowhere. Same old story for Arthur 'Pork Chop' Miller. Ever since he was a kid he always got a raw deal. If happiness was a drum solo, someone stole his sticks long ago.

"This is a hot load of bullshit…" Pork Chop grumbled, shifting the girl's deadweight on his shoulder. "What'd I ever do to deserve this?"

The others paid him no attention, if they heard him at all.

Mike, Lonnie, and Cyndi – Pork Chop still didn't understand

why the others were calling her Rhonda – were thirty feet ahead of him now, and the distance was growing with every step. It was almost as if they'd forgotten he was part of the group, or they were trying to ditch him. "Guys? Guys, wait up! This chick's a lot heavier than she looks!"

He was reminded of his days banging skins for the band. Couldn't remember a time when he wasn't left behind to haul his own gear. Always treated like a second-class citizen, the butt of every joke. (*How do you tell if the stage is level?* The drummer's drooling from both sides of his mouth… *What's the funniest thing a drummer ever said?* Hey dudes, let's try one of *my* songs!) It wasn't fair. He did a good job of hiding it, but Pork Chop was a sensitive guy. That shit hurt. And he'd never had a choice but to bend over and take it.

He wondered how the others would react if he just put the girl down and refused to carry her any farther. Let someone else lug her heavy ass. "Betcha they wouldn't like *that* shit," he said to himself. "Maybe *then* they'd start appreciating the old Chopster." P.C. groaned, staggered beneath her weight. "Damn, girl. Whatchoo been eatin'?"

It didn't make sense how she could weigh so much. Pork Chop's cousin Buzzy made his living on the carny circuit guessing people's age and weight, and while P.C. had never mastered the skill himself, it didn't take a brainiac like Buzzy to estimate this skin-and-bones girl at barely one hundred pounds. But after carrying her for a few miles, Pork Chop was convinced she would have tipped the scales at twice that number. A real porker this one, despite her skeletal frame. "Yep," P.C. decided. "Two hundred pounds, at least."

Impossible as it seemed, the proof lay slung across his shoulders, forcing him to walk with a lopsided gait like Igor in a Frankenstein movie. "Guys! Please! I'm really struggling here!" *Nada.* Like he didn't even exist.

The girl was still unconscious on his shoulder. If not for her ragged breathing on the back of his neck, Pork Chop might have thought she'd succumbed to her injuries and that for the last half-mile he'd been unwittingly carrying a corpse.

Weird thing was, though…she never seemed to stop *moving.*

It was like he was lugging a sack full of rats; the way her muscles quivered and twitched and her flesh writhed and squirmed. Something pulsed beneath her skin – her heartbeat, P.C. guessed –

undulating like topsoil rippling with worms.

And the smell…

Kee-rist! The *smell* of her—

He fanned the air as it hit him again. His guts roiled. Bile rose in his throat. He choked it down with a hoarse "gahhh!" Years had passed since the last time P.C. tossed his cookies. His ability to drink any man under the table without hurling was a thing of legend on the bar scene back home. But he feared that record was about to end, thanks to the stench seeping from Becca's pores.

It was the stink of something dead. Reminded him of the roadkill littering the highway near the trailer park where he'd been raised. That road had claimed the lives of countless critters: Dogs and cats, possum and raccoons. Usually the animal carcasses would have lain there for days before Pork Chop and the other trailer park kids discovered them and whiled away the hours poking at their guts with a stick. The smell choking the air as they'd desecrated and dissected those sun-baked bodies was foul yet strangely sweet.

That's what the girl smelled like.

At times Pork Chop was forced to hold his breath while he walked, but the stench still burned his nostrils, and oozed down his throat like ghastly slime.

"Miller!" Cyndi called from somewhere in the darkness ahead of him. "You wanna put some fire in your ass?"

"I'm…coming!" he called back, panting for breath.

He shifted the girl once more on his shoulders, shuddering in disgust as her wounds brushed against his skin. Felt less like the nubile flesh of a teenage girl than a piece of soggy sandpaper scraping across his neck.

He could barely see the others through the darkness anymore, couldn't tell Lonnie and Mike's silhouettes apart, Cyndi identifiable only by her luscious hooters and long hair. Panicking at the thought of being abandoned, P.C. began hiking faster.

As he clawed through the overhanging foliage, trudging through the rain-slick undergrowth and mud, he remembered a song his Pop used to love. "Run Through the Jungle" by Creedence Clearwater Revival. It came out around the time Stan Miller was shipped off to 'Nam for his first tour. An appreciation for good music and championship wrestling were about the only things P.C. and his dad ever had in common.

Most fathers would bond with their sons over a football, or a V-8 engine; Pop liked to ramble drunkenly for hours about all the things he had done in the war.

Pop's favorite story – P.C. knew it by heart, though he wished he didn't – was the one where his platoon stormed a V.C. village. After a brutal firefight in which they lost several men before emerging victorious, they were itching for payback.

She couldn't have been older than thirteen, fourteen. Who could tell with a gook? Even Cousin Buzzy would have struggled to guess her age right.

The whole squad took a turn. And when the last man was spent, and the girl little more than a bloody bag of bones, PFC Miller cut her throat with his cane knife, painting the walls of the hootch with an arterial spray.

"Best night of my life," Stan Miller would say to cap his charming anecdote.

And P.C. could see it in his eyes…Pop meant every word.

Pork Chop pushed the memories away and continued walking.

The chirring of crickets greeted P.C. as he staggered from the woods into a clearing. A steep rise loomed before him. Far ahead of him, three vaguely humanoid shapes – little more than splotches of darkness moving slowly in the darkness – slogged up the weed-choked slope.

Pork Chop sucked a deep breath and started up the rise, weeds raking against his bare legs and reaching beneath his kilt to fondle him like slender fingers.

"Guys! Wait up! *Please!* I can't—"

He slipped on something slick, nearly turning his ankle. Catching himself before he fell, he saw that he had stepped in the bloated belly of a raccoon carcass. The animal had been dead for some time. Half its head was rotted, leaving the critter with a toothy sneer. Stark white ribs poked through what was left of its fur, snagging Pork Chop's ankle in an organic trap. Maggots churned around his shin like a thick white broth brought to boil. "Gross!" He snatched his foot from the critter's innards. A loop of grey intestine stuck to his sneaker like an untied shoelace. He kicked it away with a cry of disgust. And when he looked up again—

The world as he knew it was gone.

The sky was the color of a vicious raw wound. Crimson clouds roiled above him like a tempest-tossed sea of blood. Instead of a grassy hill, Pork Chop climbed a mountain of rotting corpses. It stretched as far as he could see, an Everest of death and decay that topped the scarlet sky. The lifeless eyes of legion dead glared up at Pork Chop as if blaming him for their fate. Monstrous carrion birds circled above the deathscape, swooping down to pick at the endless feast, shreds of meat dangling from ebony beaks.

Something bellowed in the distance. Something huge. The thunderous roar dislodged dozens of corpses from the pile and sent them tumbling down the mountainside into black nothingness.

Pork Chop pissed himself at the sound, an involuntary reaction of which he was unaware until he felt the warm stream soaking through his socks.

Glancing down, he saw that he no longer stood inside the festering guts of a dead raccoon, but the corpse of a fat man with matted hair the color of old pennies. With a sickened squeal, he tore his foot from the man's belly. Soupy black viscera slopped from his sneakers. Pork Chop ran. Tears blurred his vision as he fought to find purchase on the mountain of corpses. Bodies flopped and flailed as he scrabbled across them, their death-stiffened arms groping and clawing at him, eager to drag him down among them. Bloated bellies burst beneath him, spilling maggots like piñata prizes, belching fetid gas.

He tripped on something – some*one* – and fell to his knees, his left arm sinking elbow-deep into the liquefied flesh of a corpse that could have been male or female, P.C. couldn't tell. He struggled to stand, almost made it, then slipped and went down again, face-first, his lips mashing against the muddy mug of a grinning skeleton attached to nothing more than a gnarled spinal cord. He lurched to his feet, spitting putrescence from his mouth.

"Oh, God!" Pork Chop sobbed. "What is this? What's happening? Someone help me…please…SOMEONE HELP ME!"

The girl was no longer on his shoulder.

Had he dropped her? Fuck! He must have dropped her. He looked back in the direction he had come, his sanity stretching like a rubber band as he searched the rotting sea for a pale hairless figure carved head to toe in scars. He half-expected to glimpse the girl's hand sinking down into the quicksand of bodies.

A girlish giggle behind him.

He wheeled around.

Was she *laughing*? What in the literal hell was she *laughing* at?

"Where are you, girl?"

He scrambled blindly up the mountain of death, scrabbling for purchase on the helter-skelter bodies, faces sliding from skulls like rubbery masks as he touched them, glazed gray eyeballs bursting like berries beneath his fingers.

By now he barely registered his disgust, benumbed to the horror.

Until, among the multitudes, he started seeing familiar faces…

Here was his MeeMaw. The mean old bitty became his legal guardian after Pop got drunker than usual one night and ate the Colt .45 he brought home from the 'Nam. When Pork Chop was a child, she'd often threatened to pinch his pee-pee shut with a clothespin if he didn't quit wetting the bed. There was little left of her than a pile of crumbling bones, but Pork Chop knew it was his MeeMaw because of the tattered WORLD'S BEST GRANDMA nightgown clinging to her skeleton. As he stumbled over her body, his kilt rode up, and for a second he was sure he would feel a desiccated claw reach up and grab his junk, MeeMaw making good on her threat from beyond the grave…

There was Danny Kilmer, the retarded kid who lived in the trailer park next door to Pork Chop when he was nine, the one who eagerly traded comics with P.C. despite always getting the worst end of the deal. While the other kids were scavenging the highway for roadkill, Danny used to like to watch the big rigs thunder past. He'd pump his arm and make honking noises and sometimes the truckers would respond with a blast of the air horn. Danny loved that sound, and it was probably the last thing he heard before one eighteen-wheeler hit him and left him smeared on the blacktop, just another piece of roadkill. Pork Chop could still see the tire marks on the dead boy's crumpled face as Danny lumbered through the sea of corpses toward him, dripping maggots in his wake…

There was his late Uncle Marcus, the man who had shown Pork Chop his first picture of a vagina in a well-thumbed copy of *Hustler* magazine. Pork Chop remembered being grossed-out more than anything. The thick bush the centerfold sported looked just like Uncle Marcus's beard. Decomposition had turned Uncle Marcus's face blacker than the cancer that took his life. His eye sockets were empty black pits that matched the ragged open cavity between his legs, where the carrion birds had devoured the softest parts of him…

"Please," Pork Chop sobbed. "No more!"

But there *was* more; he tripped and fell and came face-to-rotting-face with the only person whose death he had ever celebrated.

There wasn't much left of Pop. But Pork Chop recognized his father instantly. The dogtags Stan Miller had worn since his soldiering days dangled from around his skinny neck, though they were now too rusted to read. His oil-stained work shirt, with his name embroidered over the left breast pocket, had melted into his rotten flesh and become a part of him. Cobwebs of snow-white hair clung to his skull, which wore a crown of shattered bone where the suicide-bullet had exited the top of his head. Unlike his older brother, Stan Miller had always kept his face clean-shaven, but now he wore a full-beard of furry green moss.

Pop spoke without moving his lips. Yet inside Pork Chop's head the thick Tennessean drawl was as loud and mean as it had ever been in life.

There's bad things comin', boy. Bad things like you ain't ever seen. And you brung it on yourself. When you took that gal from those meant to have her. You n' them worthless fuckin' friends of yours. You deserve everything you're gonna get—

Then his jaw levered open, and he laughed, and an enormous copper-colored centipede skittered from his mouth like a grotesque tongue.

Pork Chop screamed.

32

"Dude! Over here!"

Pork Chop started at the voice, his daddy's mocking laughter still echoing through his mind. He clutched at his chest, gasping for air as he took in his surroundings. He was back on the grassy hill, struggling to keep up with his friends. What the hell just happened? Did Lonnie spike his beer with Yellow Sunshine (again)? The girl still lay across his shoulders, unconscious. She made a noise in her sleep that sounded for a second like malicious laughter. Pork Chop flinched as if someone had stuck a wet finger in his ear.

The ground sloped down before him. Through the gloom he

could see the silhouetted shapes of the others, huddled together beneath a bridge at the bottom of the hill. They sat on a cluster of boulders. A gently flowing stream trickled nearby. P.C. felt the sudden urge to pee.

"There's something…seriously wrong…with this bitch," he gasped for breath as he joined his companions beneath the bridge.

Rhonda cleared some space on the ground for the girl. She fished inside the first aid kit for whatever dressings they had left for her wounds. "Set her down here," she said. "Let me take a look at—"

Pork Chop dumped the girl at her feet.

"Easy!"

"I'm telling you…" Pork Chop pointed a trembling hand at the girl. "She ain't right."

Rhonda saw the fear shining in the big guy's eyes. *Dumb bastard probably doesn't even know what's happening here. Might even be in shock.* She softened her expression. "You're really sucking wind, Miller. Rest up for a few while we figure out where we are."

Pork Chop nodded gratefully.

Lonnie clapped him on the shoulder and he gave a little squeal of terror.

"Took you long enough," Lonnie said. "Stop to rub one out along the way?"

For once, P.C. didn't laugh at his friend's crude humor. There wasn't anything the least bit funny about this trip anymore.

Lonnie winced in disgust at the hand he'd used to slap P.C. His palm was slick with blood. "Gross."

Pork Chop made a retching sound and shouldered past Lonnie, scuttling to the stream to wash the girl's blood off his chest and shoulders.

*

Mike glanced up from the map and considered the bridge above them.

"We found the railroad tracks, at least. That's something…right?"

No one else shared his optimism.

"Take a look?" Lonnie said, reaching for the map.

Mike handed it over, waited. Lonnie gave it back after a minute or so, offering nothing new.

With a sigh, Mike slid from the butt-numbing boulder to the muddy ground. He fished in his pockets, found his wallet, and pinched a photo from inside the clear plastic sleeve. In the photo, he and Rachel stood atop a sandy dune in Myrtle Beach, South Carolina. They'd spent a week there the previous summer. Rachel wore tortoiseshell sunglasses and a blue one-piece bathing suit. Mike wore shorts and a Hawaiian shirt that would've put Magnum, P.I. to shame. Embracing Rachel from behind, his arms couldn't quite reach all the way around her pregnant belly. The wind was tossing her reddish-brown hair over her shoulder and into Mike's face, blinding and choking him. The boardwalk photographer had offered to take another picture for half-price – a real prince, this guy – but Rachel said this one was a keeper. Mike could still hear her laughter when she saw the photo, Mike all squinty-eyed and upchucking hair.

He brushed away a tear. *Why did I ever agree to come on this trip?*

He wondered what Rachel was doing now. Probably stealing an hour or two of much-needed rest before the baby woke up hungry. Or perhaps she lay awake in their queen-size, worrying why her husband hadn't called from the Silverdome as he'd promised. He imagined her gnawing her nails, wishing for a cigarette – two habits she had kicked shortly after they were married – fretting about this adventure he had embarked on with friends she had never trusted.

"You really lucked out, dude."

Mike glanced up at Lonnie. "Huh?"

"Rachel. She's the best."

"Oh. Right. Yeah."

"Can I see?" Lonnie held out his hand for the photo. His forearm was crosshatched with vicious scratches and welts, courtesy of the briars and branches that had slashed at them as they trekked through the forest.

Mike handed him the photo, reluctant to give up his totem. For the first time he noticed that his own arms sported similar injuries. He'd feel those in the morning… assuming he lived to see morning. He glanced at Becca's wounds and felt like the world's biggest asshole for thinking his own scrapes and bruises were anything to whine about.

Lonnie looked at the photo long and hard.

"What a great life you've got, Mikey. Don't you ever take for granted what the good Lord has given you here."

The only time Mike had ever heard Lonnie Deveroux refer to a higher power was back when they used to rock n' roll all night and party every day and Lonnie ended up praying to the porcelain throne, swearing he'd never drink again if only the Man Upstairs would make the sickness go away. But Mike supposed a situation like the one they were in could make a believer out of even the most godless heathen. What was that old saying about atheists in foxholes?

He reached to take the photo back.

Long seconds passed before Lonnie gave it up.

"Rachel's the best, man," he said again. "I mean, I know she hates my guts—"

"She doesn't hate your guts."

"You don't have to lie to me."

"Fine. She hates your guts."

Both men chuckled softly.

"She called me, you know," Lonnie said.

"What?"

"Last week. She called me."

Mike frowned. He scooted around and put some space between them so he could face Lonnie. He fully expected this to be another inappropriate joke at his expense, one with a vile punchline that suggested his old friend and his better half were boning behind his back. But now wasn't the time. Mike was in no mood.

"What the hell are you talking about, Lonnie?"

"She called me and asked me to get you out of the house, let off some steam."

Mike sat back, stunned.

"Wait. What? This was *Rachel's* idea?"

"Well," Lonnie said, "I don't think *this* was exactly what she had in mind."

Crazy as it sounded, Mike knew Lonnie wasn't lying. That explained why he'd found his address book on Rachel's nightstand, instead of in the drawer where he kept it. She must've been looking for Lonnie's number to arrange this trip. Despite everything that had happened, it made him love her all the more.

Lonnie gazed at the bridge above their heads. Slats of moonlight peeked through the beams of the railroad tracks. "Remember when we used to park in that vacant lot off Sycamore and walk the tracks? This reminds me of that."

"Minus the girl with the seven deadly sins carved into her?" Mike said. "And the lunatics trying to kill us?"

"I remember the first night Rachel came with us," Lonnie went on. "I was with some slut, don't even remember her name. But you two, somehow I knew even then that you and Rachel were gonna be together forever."

The first few months after they graduated high school, they had often walked the railroad tracks outside their hometown after dark. For Mike it was a period of existential disorientation during which he tried to figure out what to do with his life. There was something strangely exhilarating about exploring abandoned property. Lonnie tagged along out of boredom, and the opportunity to vandalize shit. Pork Chop called it 'gay.' There was no logic to that statement, since Mike and Lonnie would often bring their girlfriends, incurable romantics and big spenders that they were. P.C. was just jealous because, since the opposite sex rarely gave him the time of day, they never invited him along on these excursions. They'd build a fire beneath a bridge just like this one, drink beer, smoke weed, and a do a little heavy petting if their dates allowed it.

Those were some of the best times Mike remembered from his youth, especially when he and Rachel started going steady and he discovered she enjoyed these late-night walks as much as he did. She was a girl who appreciated the simple things in life: The night breeze teasing its fingers through her hair…the smell of pine trees and honeysuckle…the distant sound of traffic on the interstate, as if the rest of civilization existed on another planet entirely.

After one such night, Lonnie bragged to Mike that his date had allowed him to finger her – he'd held up two fingers as if they were gilded – and later gave him a handjob before he took her home. When he asked if Mike had at least gotten to second base with Rachel, he'd scoffed at the answer. *A kiss? That's all? Blue balls are a bitch, bro. Sucks to be you!*

But Mike never regretted anything. Then or now. Because the blue balls had been worth it, in the long run. A small price to pay for finding his soulmate.

"Don't take this the wrong way," Lonnie said to Mike now. "But sometimes I look at what you and Rachel have and I get so jealous I can hardly see straight. She's perfect, Mikey. What I wouldn't give to have a broad like that waiting for me at home. I thought me and Wendy mighta had something special. We were together four years, on and off. That's a record for me, ya know. But guys like me…we always manage to fuck it up. Maybe it was for the best. A few months before she split, me and Wendy had a little scare. She was late. We thought she was pregnant. Turned out she wasn't. You woulda thought she'd won the damn lottery or something. She told me she was scared to have a kid with me, in case it turned out like its daddy. Like *she* was so damn perfect. But deep down I knew she was right. The world's better off without a little Lonnie Junior on the rampage. There's no way that kid would turn out to be anything other than a piece of crap like his old man."

"Don't be so hard on yourself, Lonnie. I'm sure you'll make a good father some day." Actually, Mike wasn't sure about that at all. "Kids don't come with an instruction manual. We do the best we can and usually things turn out fine."

"If you're *Mike Rawson* they turn out fine."

Mike was surprised to hear the bitterness in his friend's voice.

"Nobody from the Deveroux clan ever amounts to shit."

"Look," Mike said. "Maybe things didn't pan out the way you wanted with Wendy. But there's always a bright side." Lonnie looked at him, all ears. "What happened to the guy who was bragging just this morning about how he finally got the freedom he always wanted? The dude who told me, 'always pull out.' Back in the day, I lost count of the times you said, 'All I want in a woman is a good rack and low self-esteem.' Some guys would kill for what you have, Lonnie. Spreading your wild oats. Raisin' hell and chasin' tail… remember?"

Mike boxed him on the shoulder.

Lonnie forced a smile, but his eyes were anything but gleeful. "Maybe I was full of shit, Mikey. Ever thought about that? Freedom ain't all it's cut out to be. It means being alone. I never wanted to be alone. I'd rather have someone to come home to, someone who looks at me the way Rachel looks at you. Last time I got anything close to that, it cost me a hundred bucks and she was gone in the morning. Only thing I had to remember her by was a rash on my dong."

Mike made a face like he'd bitten into a piece of rotten fruit; he thought he heard Rhonda mutter "Ewww" in the background.

Lonnie gave a sigh like a slashed tire. "All I'm saying is, treasure what you got. 'Cause one day? *Poof!* Just like that, it can all disappear. And brother…you got a whole lot more to lose than I ever did."

Before Mike could find any words of comfort—

Lonnie's lips pulled back from his teeth, lending him the appearance of a ravenous predator about to pounce on some smaller prey. Something in his eyes made Mike uneasy; they seemed to burn with an insatiable hunger. He wasn't looking Mike's way. He was staring at Becca, at a wound on the girl's left leg. The word carved down her shin seemed to glow in the gloom, as if embers burned beneath her flesh:

ENVY

Still staring at the girl, Lonnie said to Mike in a guttural voice, "When you quit the band and moved away…was it because you thought you were too good for us?"

"What?" Mike tried to laugh off the accusation, but his laughter sounded hollow, even a little guilty. "Where's *this* coming from, man?"

But before Lonnie could answer, they heard the train approaching.

33

Rhonda leapt up, knocking over the first aid kit, spilling Band-Aids across the ground, a roll of gauze unfurling like a long white tongue.

"It's a train!" she cried. "There's a train coming!"

Mike rose, staggered, his legs prickling with pins and needles. He stomped his feet, trying to coax life into them. "You think we could flag it down?"

"We're sure as hell gonna try," Rhonda said, quickly checking the loads in the shotgun and the revolver.

"One way or the other," Lonnie said, "I'm hitching a ride on that sucker."

"Miller," Rhonda said. "Bring the girl."

Pork Chop shook his head in childlike defiance. "I don't wanna."

"Bring the fucking girl!"

P.C. did as he was told, grumbling and grunting with effort as he hefted Becca back onto his shoulders, his knees stiffening beneath her (*impossible*) weight.

Rhonda led the group from under the bridge, splashing through the stream into the overgrown field on the other side. From there she hoped they might flag down the train or attempt to jump aboard.

They scrabbled uphill, hollering for help, the roaring train engine muffling their cries. The ground quaked beneath them as the train approached. The bright light on its nose speared the night. Its whistle banshee-wailed over the forest.

"Hey!" everyone screamed. "Stop! Help us! HEY!"

The train thundered past, a clanking steel centipede of flatbed trailers, double-door boxcars, and open wagons loaded with coal.

"They're not stopping!" Mike cried.

"We can still jump aboard!" Lonnie shouted, pulling ahead of him.

"Guys!" Pork Chop gasped. "Please wait up!"

Rhonda fired a shot from the revolver into the air.

"Try the shotgun!" Mike called to her. "They can't hear—"

Then his foot sank ankle-deep in the earth, and down he went. He ate a faceful of dirt, tasting blood as his teeth snapped shut on the tip of his tongue. Foggily aware of P.C. lumbering past him, Mike cried out for help, but his cries were swallowed by the noise of the train and Rhonda firing another shot in the air.

He rolled onto his back, clutching his ankle and hissing in pain. Must've stepped in a gopher hole. No way could he jump a train now. His ankle had already swollen to the size of a grapefruit, and even through his socks it felt warm, like something ripe and fit to burst. Mike braced himself, tried to stand, fell back on his butt. Salty tears burned his eyes as he cried out for help. But the others were too far ahead to hear him. He couldn't even see them in the darkness anymore. The train clattered on, wheels sparking on the tracks. The ground thrummed beneath him. *Did they make it onboard? Did they leave me?*

A pair of hands grabbed him, fingers digging into his armpits.

Mike cried out in surprise, glanced behind him.

"Used to be I was the one who was too fucked up to stand," Lonnie said.

Mike choked down a sob of relief. "I thought you'd bugged out on me, man."

"Never." Lonnie gave a shit-eating grin. "The hell kinda friend you think I—?"

Something whisked through the air above their heads.

The arrow *shunked* into the dirt behind them.

Lonnie dropped Mike to the dirt. Mike landed on his ankle and screamed in pain.

"Oh, shit! They found us!" Lonnie cried.

Whiiiiisk!

Another arrow ripped past Lonnie's head, lifting his hair off his shoulders.

"They're here!"

Four figures stalked from the woods. The bearded man at the head of the pack was loading another steel arrow into his crossbow.

Mike clawed at Lonnie's legs. "Get me up! Get me outta here!"

But Lonnie was already backing away. "They'll kill us both…"

"Lonnie…?"

"I'm sorry…"

"Lonnie!"

Lonnie turned and ran.

Mike tore up a fistful of dirt and flung it at his fleeing back. "Lonnie, you piece of shit! Get back here! *Lonnie!*"

But Lonnie was gone.

34

Mike crabbed across the ground away from his pursuers, dragging his wounded leg behind him like a tail. The relentless crunch of their boots through the overgrowth grew louder as they gained on him. He glanced back. They were almost upon him. He cried out in terror and scrabbled faster on his hands and knees, ignoring the agony in his ankle as he scraped it across the ground.

One of the men – blond, bearded, armed with a crossbow – brought his boot down hard on Mike's ankle, pinning it to the ground and grinding the bone beneath his heel as if he were crushing a cockroach.

Mike screamed, a salt-and-pepper blizzard clouding his vision.

The man with the crossbow kicked him onto his back. Shoved the weapon in his face. The razor-tipped arrow hovered inches before Mike's bulging eyes.

"Don't you move," Crossbow growled at him.

Mike showed the man his palms, his hands shaking wildly.

"I…p-please…don't—"

A kick in the gut stole the breath from his lungs.

All four men crowded around Mike, looming over him with glaring eyes.

Crossbow unhooked a bulky walkie-talkie from his belt.

"Heaton," Crossbow said into the walkie-talkie. "We got one of 'em."

Static hissed from the radio.

Then a familiar voice crackled through the speaker: "The 'goat?"

"Negative. One of the outsiders. Maybe the fella who killed Daniel."

Mike cried out, "What? No! It wasn't me—"

Crossbow slammed the butt of his weapon into Mike's face, bursting his nose.

The last thing Mike heard before he lost consciousness was the man on the radio saying: "Bring him to the church."

35

Rhonda watched helplessly as the train disappeared into the darkness.

Pork Chop stood gasping for breath on the tracks behind her. The girl was slung across his shoulders like a grisly human stole, her wounds dripping down his front and back.

Footsteps behind them…

Rhonda wheeled around, shotgun raised.

"Don't shoot!" Lonnie cried. "It's me!"

She lowered the gun with a hiss of breath. "Damn it, Deveroux! That's a fine way to get your head blown off."

"They're back! They're here!"

She looked past him. "Where's Rawson?"

"He…" Lonnie swallowed hard. "He's gone. Mikey's gone."

"What do you mean he's gone?"

Lonnie's bottom lip trembled. "Gone…"

"Mikey's *dead*?" Pork Chop said, in a tiny voice.

"There was nothin' I could do," Lonnie said, tears in his eyes. "I did everything I could." He glared at Rhonda accusingly. "Maybe if you'd given me that gun I coulda done something to stop it. It wasn't my fault."

Rhonda hefted the shotgun, stepping past Lonnie in the direction he had come from, as if she was tired of running and ready to meet their pursuers head-on.

Lonnie grabbed her arm. "Are you nuts? There's too many of them! We gotta get outta here!"

Pork Chop said, "But Mikey—"

Lonnie wheeled on his friend. "He's dead, P.C.! Mikey's dead! And I'm sorry as hell about it. But there's no sense in us dying too."

Rhonda took a second to think about it. "Alright," she decided. "Everybody back to the woods. We're in plain sight here. We'll hug the tracks as best we can and keep following the railroad. These tracks gotta lead us somewhere."

They returned to the woods and kept moving. The thickness of the forest made traveling in a straight line impossible, as they were forced to circumvent deadfalls of branches and logs, and impenetrable tangles of vines and thorny briars. It was almost as if Mother Nature herself conspired with the men who hunted them. Before long they had lost sight of the railroad completely.

Rhonda led the way, the shotgun cradled in her arms.

Pork Chop continued to whine about the weight of the girl on his shoulders and at least once every two or three minutes he begged one of the others to take a turn carrying her.

Like a mantra, Lonnie kept muttering: "Nothing I could do… *nothing…*"

Rhonda suddenly stopped, held up one hand like a soldier on point.

"Everybody shut up," she said, tilting her head to listen.

Something crunched through the undergrowth, hurtling through the midnight woods towards them. The men cowered behind Rhonda. She raised the shotgun and sighted down the barrel, finger teasing the trigger…

The mule burst from the brush, its eyes bugging wide with panic, its body sheeted with sweat, saliva frothing from its mouth.

A length of rope dangled from around its neck, the reins connected to a broken block of wood, part of the hitching post to which it must have been tethered before it broke free. Startled to see the humans, the mule reared with a heehawing cry and boxed its forelegs. Then it darted past them, dragging the block of wood in its wake, and vanished into the forest.

Rhonda lowered the shotgun with a heavy sigh of relief.

"The hell did that thing come from?" Lonnie said, still crouched behind Rhonda as if expecting a stampede of mules to run them down.

Rhonda peered along the path the beast had plowed through the brush.

"Let's find out."

36

Mike's eyes flickered open, a crust of dried tears crumbling from his lashes. Darkness cloaked him. He smelled dirt. Gasoline. Blood. At first he feared he was blind. Had the man he thought of as Crossbow fractured his skull when he clubbed him unconscious, robbing Mike of his sight? He'd never been hit so hard. It was a miracle the blow hadn't killed him on impact.

Unable to see – *blind, oh shit, I'm blind* – the sounds he heard were terrifyingly loud: Gravel crunching under tires… the *squeak-creak-squeak* of ancient shocks as whatever vehicle he was riding in jounced along an uneven dirt road… nocturnal insects chirring… a distant rumble of thunder… a man and woman singing "Peace in the Valley" on a tinny car stereo. Loudest of all was his own panicked breathing… his hammering heart… the blood roaring in his ears… and the ghastly whistling sound his broken nose made as he hyperventilated.

At last his eyes adjusted to the darkness, and he saw that he lay beneath a sheet of tarp tied over the flatbed of a fast-moving truck. He tried to piece together what had happened, struggling to think clearly through his pain. The bastards must have tossed him on the back of the truck after Crossbow knocked him unconscious. And now they were taking him…

Where?

He couldn't remember.

Think, damn it…think through the pain!

The tarp flapped and popped in the wind above him. It reminded him of the tarp covering the hole in the floor of Jezebel, which reminded him of—

"Lonnie," Mike croaked, tasting coppery gunk at the back of his throat.

He'd always wondered if Lonnie Deveroux would be the death of him – from the day they first met back in high school, through the wild and crazy nights they had spent together in Wrathbone – but he never would have dreamed his old friend would leave him to die.

Worry about Lonnie later. Right now you've gotta think this through. Work out how you're gonna—

The truck hit a chuckhole and shuddered violently. Mike was hurled up against the tarp and crashed back down on the flatbed like a missile fired from a slingshot. He thumped his wounded ankle, shrieking at the white-hot stab of agony. He bit his bottom lip till it bled, fighting not to pass out again.

And suddenly he remembered.

Bring him to the church, the voice on the walkie-talkie had said.

What horrors awaited him there? He remembered what Becca had told them about her visit to the church…and he let out a whimper of terror.

*

Mike could have counted on both hands all the times he had been to church since he was a kid, and finished with fingers to spare. While he had always considered himself the kind of guy who didn't hold grudges, experience had taught him that the pews were mostly filled with self-righteous assholes.

His parents had attended the same church to which their parents before them had been so loyal – Trinity Baptist, at the corner of Blythe and Merrimon Avenue. They tithed regularly, volunteered their time when asked, and young Mike was an active member of the youth group. When the church doors opened, the Rawsons were dressed in their Sunday best, sitting third row from the back next to their lifelong friends, the Whitfields. It was only when Mike's cousin Amanda started attending Trinity Baptist that his views on the church and the people in it were changed forever.

She was four years his senior. They had been the best of

friends. Mike remembered when they were in grammar school he had innocently sworn that they would be married one day. Even as they grew older, he'd continued to carry a small crush for her, despite the fact that they both perched on the same branch of the Rawson family tree. She was just so COOL. He fondly recalled Mandy's "tomboy" ways, how she could always talk him into the craziest stuff (like climbing the tallest tree in the woods, or jumping into Juniper Lake on the coldest day of winter). They remained close throughout their teens, even after she graduated and began dating a fellow named Trae at the local community college. The two sweethearts started attending Trinity Baptist not long after things turned serious between them, and Mike couldn't have been happier.

Then he started to notice the side-eye glances the young couple received from the church elders, the expressions of distaste on the faces of other churchgoers as the two held hands while singing hymns. He heard the whispers, even from the Whitfields; to the chagrin of Mike's parents, their oldest friends in the church eventually moved to another pew. Mike tried to ignore what was happening. He never said anything to Mandy, because the thought of breaking his cousin's heart was just too much to bear.

A few months later, Trae and Amanda announced that they planned to marry, but first they wished to become members of the Trinity Baptist family. Their request was denied. The preacher met with the couple privately, and informed them that it "might be a good thing" if they found another place to worship altogether. If the Lord had meant for races to intermingle, he explained, He would have made us all one color. Their relationship was "upsetting" to the other churchgoers, and the time had come for the church leaders to "do the right thing." The preacher left the young lovers with a list of Bible verses he hoped would help them understand.

Mike's cousin and her fiancé never returned to Trinity Baptist. Neither did Mike or his family. Trae and Amanda moved away not long after that, and the last Mike heard they were still together. Mike hadn't set foot in a church ever since, save for the occasional funeral or wedding, and the baby's baptism three months ago.

Rachel had attended a local United Church of Christ since she was a little girl. She had insisted that they baptize the baby as soon as he was born. Mike didn't see much use for it – his discontent with the holier-than-thou "Christians" he used to know notwithstanding – but he didn't argue. There were fights worth picking and this wasn't one of them. Truth be told, he had no problem with the peace Rachel found in her religion. Sometimes he envied it.

He remembered the pretty woman preacher touching her fingertips to the infant's forehead…the baby gasping at the cold touch of water…the way the sunlight shining through the stained-glass windows behind the church pulpit haloed Rachel's smiling face. Mike had felt like the world's biggest fake, standing in church before 'man and God,' but that smile had made it all worthwhile.

He wondered if he would ever see it again.

*

The truck skidded to a stop. The engine died. Doors squealed open on rusted hinges, then slammed closed again like gunshots. Footsteps crunched across gravel to the back of the truck. The sheet of tarp was ripped away. Rough hands gripped his legs and dragged him from the truck.

Mike hit the dirt with a *woof* of pain. His assailant was a muscular man with a port wine birthmark patching his left eye, which made him look like Spuds Mackenzie, the dog in those Budweiser commercials. Mike yelped as Spuds snatched his injured ankle and began dragging him like a caveman taking a wife. He scrambled for purchase on the hard earth and gravel, but his efforts were futile. He saw where Spuds was taking him, and was helpless to stop it.

The church squatted on a plot of dead brown grass. It was a barn-sized rural gothic, its clapboard exterior painted crimson with black trim. The paint had faded with age to a scabby deep purple color. The church steeple stabbed at the stormy sky like a skeletal finger poking at an infected wound. The man-sized cross at its apex was in need of repair. Missing half of its horizontal beam, it listed like a lower case 't' scrawled by a palsied hand. Three stone steps led up to the church's main entrance. Its double doors were propped open like a hungry mouth waiting to be fed. Candlelight guttered within. Two burly figures stood statue-still on either side of the doors, waiting to receive Mike with clenched fists and glaring eyes.

Ignoring Mike's cries – *"What is this? Please! What do you want?"* – Spuds dragged him up the steps. The back of Mike's skull struck against each of the stone slabs, but he was no longer aware of the pain. Somehow he knew there would be worse to come. Spuds dragged him inside the church, and the two burly sentries followed. The doors slammed shut behind them with a resounding boom, muffling Mike's screams to the outside world.

37

Rhonda followed the path the mule had plowed through the brush. The others tramped through the undergrowth behind her.

The mule-trail led to the edge of a clearing. A strange humming sound filled the air. Rhonda froze at the tree line.

"What's that noise?" Lonnie said. "Electricity?" The hope in his voice was almost pitiful, that somehow they had stumbled upon a thriving metropolis in the ass-end of nowhere.

Rhonda glanced back at Pork Chop and the girl on his shoulders. The big guy's front and back were smeared with blood. Becca's wounds were bleeding again, and no doubt she had collected some new scratches as they clawed through the wilds. Her flesh was so pale she seemed almost to glow in the darkness, like some strange deep-sea fish.

"Is she still out?" Rhonda asked.

"I think so," Pork Chop panted.

Rhonda nodded. *Just as well.* "Whatever happens," she said, "she mustn't see this."

Lonnie frowned. "See what?" He brushed past Rhonda to see into the clearing. "Jesus fucking Christ!"

The humming wasn't electricity; in fact, it wasn't humming at all.

It was buzzing insects.

In the middle of the clearing was a ceremonial circle of stones. Within the circle loomed two wooden poles connected by a crossbeam. The stilted structure stooped slightly to one side, straining with the weight of the butchered animal carcass hanging from the crossbeam. Except this was no field-dressed deer. Rhonda knew from the story Becca had told them; it was the girl's mother. A storm of flies swarmed about the carcass in an orgiastic black swirl, their feast uninterrupted even by the rain.

"What is this, Shaughnessy? What the fuck *is* this?"

She could only shake her head.

On the other side of the clearing stood a tumbledown wooden shack.

"Wait here," Rhonda said.

"You see us running ahead?" Lonnie muttered.

Rhonda stalked from the cover of the woods, shotgun raised, sweeping flies from her line of sight with the barrel. The butchered carcass creaked in the breeze beneath the crossbeam. She glanced at the stones that surrounded the hanging body. Most of them were chalk-white, except for seven, which were blood red, almost black. *Crazy fuckers.* She kicked angrily at the stones, breaking the border of the ceremonial circle, before she continued on toward the shack.

Outside was a hitching post. Beside it lay a pile of plump animal turds. The wooden beam of the hitching post was sheared in half where the storm-spooked mule must have busted loose.

Rhonda struck the shack's flimsy door with the butt of her shotgun. It clattered inward. She stormed inside, clearing the room with a practiced sweep of the barrel. She lowered the weapon and looked about the single room for anything that might help them.

A lantern hung from a hook on the ceiling. A threadbare mattress lay in one corner of the room. Piled atop the mattress was a ratty gray blanket that made Rhonda's skin itch just looking at it. On the floor beside the makeshift bed sat a well-thumbed Bible and a silver pocket-watch on a chain. Tacked to the wall was a metal crucifix that had long since lost its shine.

No phone. But then, Rhonda hadn't expected to find one.

On a crooked table below the shack's single window sat a hardened loaf of bread, some cheese and smoked meat bundled in a scrap of cloth, and a drinking bladder filled with what she hoped was water – she hadn't realized how thirsty she was. Next to the food was a wrinkled piece of paper…*a map!*

Rhonda grabbed the map, and hurried back outside.

"All clear!" she called to Lonnie and Pork Chop.

The men emerged hesitantly from the woods.

"Is there a phone?" Lonnie asked.

"Phone, color television, VCR, even a hot tub. The hell do you think, Deveroux?"

Pork Chop looked about ready to collapse under the weight of the girl. The guy was clearly out of shape, a heart attack on legs, but how a big lug like Miller could struggle to carry the weight of a waif like Becca, Rhonda didn't know.

"Bring the girl inside," she told him. "There's a bed."

The men followed Rhonda inside the shack.

Pork Chop sank to his knees beside the bed, peeled Becca from his shoulders with a Velcro-crackle of caked blood, and lay her down on the mattress. Impossible as it seemed, the girl appeared to have lost another ten pounds since they'd abandoned the RV. She was wasting away before their eyes, her skull showing through her skin. Reminded Rhonda of a starving kid in a famine commercial.

"We don't find help soon," she said, "she's not gonna make it."

Lonnie made a beeline for the drinking bladder on the table. "Is that what I think it is?"

"If you mean Budweiser, no."

Lonnie gulped from the bladder.

"How 'bout you save some for the rest of us?"

Lonnie came up for air, smacking his lips heartily. "*Ahhh!*" He nodded at the scrap of paper Rhonda was holding. "What's that?"

"A map."

He snatched it from her.

It was a crude, hand-drawn affair. A series of backroads crisscrossed one another like worms brought to ground by a summer storm. Here were the railroad tracks they had come across earlier…there was the stream that ran parallel to the tracks. Only two major landmarks were marked on the map. A place called Little Enoch…and something called The Circle of Purgation.

Lonnie jabbed his finger at the latter. "Looks like we're here."

"Thank you, Captain No-Shit," Rhonda said. "We're so lucky to have you along."

If Lonnie heard the dig, he ignored it. "What kinda map is this, you reckon?"

"Not entirely sure," she said. "I'm guessing it's the route between wherever the hell we are now…and wherever these bastards came from."

"So how does this help us?" Lonnie said. "We wanna get as far as we can from those fuckin' Jesus freaks, not go knocking on their goddamn door!"

"Deveroux," she said, sounding beyond exhausted now. "If you've got any ideas then I'm all ears."

Lonnie opted for a softer tone, "So what are we gonna do?"

Rhonda backed against the wall, slid down it as she sank to the floor.

She glanced at the crucifix on the wall and thought but didn't say: *We pray.*

38

The men dragged Mike through the church, the toes of his shoes raking the floorboards, kicking up dust in their wake. He clutched at the corner of a pew but one of the men slapped his hand away. As well as Spuds, there was a no-necked bruiser with bad teeth and worse halitosis, and a lanky goon whose elongated forehead and bristling black uni-brow reminded Mike of Bert from *Sesame Street.* His eyes darted between the stained-glass windows lining the walls, and he let out a moan at the horrors they depicted.

The men delivered him within a few feet of the pulpit. No-Neck restrained him with a chokehold. Spuds and Bert reached for the chains dangling from the rafters and wasted no time shackling Mike's wrists with the steel bracelets. Mike remembered Becca's story; he assumed these were the same chains they had used on the girl when they carved her up.

Jesus, God… please, no—

The door behind the pulpit creaked open. A large man wearing a black shirt with a white clerical collar emerged. Blood spattered the hardwood floor in the preacher's wake. His back was bleeding but he seemed not to notice. The preacher paused in mid-stride, apparently surprised to discover his people manhandling Mike.

"Oh," he said, "I think we can do without the chains…"

The men obeyed, releasing Mike from the shackles.

Mike gave a pitiful sob of gratitude. "Th-thank you."

The preacher turned his attention to the shrouded figure on the communion table. He gently combed a strand of hair from the boy's brow. The boy's head lolled to the side, the hollow of his ruined eye glaring at Mike. The ball of cotton stuffed inside the socket had turned pink with blood and optic fluid.

Mike stifled a cry as he recognized the corpse. All that was missing was the coonskin cap…and the stick in his eye. This was the boy Becca had killed.

"No," the preacher said. "No chains for this one. I want this one *on his knees.*"

"Wait!" Mike cried. "No! It wasn't me—"

Spuds stamped on his wounded ankle.

Mike shrieked, crumpled to his knees.

"*'For it is written,'*" the preacher said, "*'every knee shall bow, and every tongue shall confess to God.'*"

"Please," Mike sobbed. "I just want to go home."

"And I aim to send you there," the preacher told him.

He asked his men, "Where's my brother?"

"Still looking for the 'goat," Spuds said.

The preacher nodded.

Returned his attention to Mike.

"And who do we have here?"

Mike didn't answer...*couldn't* answer.

Spuds ripped Mike's wallet from his jeans and tossed it to the preacher.

The holy man snatched it from the air. He flipped the wallet open, nosing through it until he found Mike's driver's license, and read his name aloud.

"Michael Rawson..." With a wistful smile, he studied the photo of Mike and Rachel at the beach. "A family man."

Mike felt a hot flash of rage, sickened by the thought of this demented stranger laying eyes on his wife. "Fuck you!"

No-Neck clubbed him in the kidneys with a wrecking ball fist. "You'll watch your mouth in this House, sinner!"

Mike grunted in pain.

The preacher's lips pursed in a tight smile.

"Son," he said to Mike, "your fornicating days are over."

He snapped the wallet shut with an air of finality. Nodded to his goons.

Spuds and No-Neck shoved Mike forward, pressing his palms onto the hardwood floor. Bert scuttled away to retrieve something from under the preacher's podium, and returned seconds later with a tool chest. He slammed it down in front of Mike, kicking up a layer of dust that swirled into Mike's face and made him cough and splutter.

Bert rooted inside the tool chest, pulling out a hammer and two shiny silver nails that looked as large as railroad spikes to Mike.

"What... what are you gonna do?" Mike stammered.

Bert nodded at Spuds and No-Neck.

The grip on Mike's wrists tightened.

His palms were pinned fast to the floor.

Mike glanced in terror from the hammer and nails…to the looming figure of the crucified Christ behind the pulpit. "No! Please, *no*!"

Bert clenched one of the long silver nails between his crooked yellow teeth. He pricked the sharpened tip of the other nail into the back of Mike's left hand. The flesh dimpled around the tip of the nail as Bert rolled its head back and forth between his finger and thumb, sadistically slow. He arced the hammer high above his shoulder…

Mike flinched, struggling frantically against Spuds and No-Neck.

Bert swung the hammer down.

The BOOM was gunshot-loud. It echoed through the church.

Mike gaped in horror at his pulped pinkie, haloed by a spray of blood, the fingernail jutting sickeningly from the ruined digit. The dumb bastard had missed. Well, not *missed*, exactly. Hot waves of agony charged through Mike's body as if he'd stuck a wet finger in an electrical socket. He screamed.

"Dang it!" Bert cried, with an accusing glance at Spuds and No-Neck, to excuse his own sorry aim.

"Can't aim for spit," Spuds said.

"Let me take a turn," No-Neck said.

"Not a chance," Bert said. "Just hold him still."

The preacher gave a heavy sigh. "We haven't got all night, boys."

Bert repositioned the nail on the back of Mike's hand, then raised the hammer once more. His eyes narrowed. His tongue poked from the corner of his mouth. He looked like a child concentrating on a crayon drawing.

Bert swung the hammer down.

BOOM!

The force of the blow splintered the glass face of Mike's wristwatch.

Mike threw his head back and screamed again. Tears poured from his eyes. Blood burbled from the back of his hand, welling up around the embedded nail like a pump jack striking oil.

"There!" Bert cackled in triumph.

Bert positioned the second nail on the back of Mike's right

hand, took aim with the hammer. He seemed to be enjoying himself. "Hold him now."

If Mike had hoped that the pain of the first wound would somehow nullify the second, he was mistaken.

BOOM!

As his agonized screams resounded through the church, the preacher produced a walkie-talkie. He thumbed the TALK button.

*

When the screaming started, Rhonda's first thought, crazy as it seemed, was that the cries were coming from Becca's mother. That the butchered woman was somehow still alive. Everyone in the shack startled at the sudden sound. Even Becca gave a shuddery intake of breath in her sleep. Then Rhonda realized the screams were coming from the walkie-talkie…and she recognized the voice.

"Oh, God…someone help me, please!"

"Hey…" Pork Chop said, looking at Lonnie in confusion. "That's Mikey."

Lonnie had turned deathly pale.

"I thought you said Rawson was dead?" Rhonda said.

Pork Chop looked at him sharply. "Yeah, man. What gives?"

Lonnie's eyes welled with tears of shame.

"There…there was nothing I could do," he insisted, in a cracked voice.

Rhonda shook her head in disgust. "Unbelievable."

Mike screamed once more.

"…they're killing me…"

*

PAIN was all Mike knew.

Sinking down to his stomach, his arms outstretched before him, he could only watch as the blood pooled around his ruined hands. Nothing – not his pulped pinkie, his broken nose, his twisted ankle – *nothing* had ever hurt like this. He tried to calm his breathing, tried to stop his hands from shaking. The slightest movement caused his wounds to tear and sent fresh waves of agony flooding through him.

The preacher loomed above him, the walkie-talkie reporting

Mike's every agonized cry to his friends.

And just when Mike feared his situation could not get any worse…

The preacher began to sing.

Have you been to Jesus for the cleansing pow'r?
Are you washed in the blood of the Lamb?
Are you fully trusting in His grace this hour?
Are you washed in the blood of the Lamb?

The preacher's hymn was loud and proud. His voice wasn't bad, a rich baritone. In fact, Mike was forced to admit, he was quite good. Not that his knack for carrying a tune made him any less crazy.

Spuds tapped a mud-caked boot in time to the song. Mike hissed in pain as the vibrations traveled through the floorboards and tormented his hands anew.

No-Neck and Bert joined the preacher for the chorus.

Are you washed in the blood,
The soul-cleansing blood of the Lamb?
Are you garments spotless? Are they white as snow?
Are you washed in the blood of the Lamb?

I'm in Hell, Mike thought. That's what this is. I've died and gone to Hell.

The preacher smiled down at Mike as he sang. He might have been leading the choir at Sunday service.

Lay aside the garments that are stained with sin,
And be washed in the blood of the Lamb;
There's a fountain flowing for the soul unclean,
Oh, be washed in the blood of the Lamb!

The preacher thrust his arms suddenly to the heavens.

"Lord!" he cried. "We pray for Your patience as we strive to complete our ritual. The first 'goat you received. But the second…she has been stolen from us. Transference is not enough. Without Purgation there can be no Salvation. The sins of Man must perish in flame. The fools who absconded with the 'goat have no idea the hell they have wrought. I beseech You, Lord. Lead them to the light! Have them return the 'goat to us within the hour – else I humbly offer You blood atonement, in this agent of Satan who kneels before You."

The preacher nodded to the men behind Mike.

No-Neck stomped on Mike's ankle.

Mike screamed, instinctively attempting to curl into a shell, wrenching the nails in his hands, which only made him scream louder.

The preacher laughed. "Hark, Lord! Hear his cries!"

"Please," Mike wept. "*Please…*"

The holy man raised the walkie-talkie to his lips.

"You have one hour," he said. "Bring me the girl or your friend dies."

39

The walkie-talkie went silent. Static hissed over Rhonda's radio. Apart from the storm outside, the only sounds were Becca's ragged breathing…the creak of floorboards beneath Pork Chop's feet as he anxiously paced the cramped room…and Lonnie's stifled sobs of shame.

"You bugged out on your friend to save your own sorry ass," Rhonda scolded him.

"How could you, man?" Pork Chop sounded heartbroken.

"I… I still can't wrap my head around it," Lonnie said. "One minute I'm going back for Mike…the next I'm running away like a pussy."

Rhonda shook her head at him. "Piece. Of. Shit."

"I know! I know… But you wanna know the worst part? Even as I'm bailing on him, there's a voice in my head says Mike deserves it. That I wouldn't be in this mess if he hadn't quit the band like he did. Right now I'd be sunning myself next to my guitar-shaped pool in Laurel Canyon…a Playmate either side of me…drinking Pina Coladas from coconut shells…"

He looked up sharply. His eyes were watery but his expression was one of intense anger.

"Why would Mikey take that from me? For a piece of tail and a rugrat. Things I'll never have. So *fuck him*, is what I think. And I keep running."

Rhonda let out her breath. "Jesus…"

"My best fucking friend," Lonnie choked, "and I just left him to die."

"It's because of her…" Pork Chop said.

He pointed at the girl on the bed.

Becca's breath wheezed like a broken accordion. By now she resembled little more than scabby skin and bones wrapped in a filthy cloth.

"There's something *wrong* with her," Pork Chop said.

"You said that already," Rhonda said. "And it didn't help us the first fifty times."

"Why won't anyone believe me?" Pork Chop whined.

"'Cause you're drunk as a skunk, high as a kite, and you're not the brightest bulb on the Christmas tree even when you're sober."

Pork Chop winced at her honesty.

"You asked, big guy."

"What are we gonna do, Shaughnessy?" Lonnie asked her.

Rhonda stared down at the girl. "There's only one choice I can see."

Lonnie nodded. "We give her to them."

"What? No, dumbass. They'll kill Rawson anyway. Us, too."

"So what *are* you saying?"

"We get him back ourselves."

"You really think we can do that?"

"I really think we can try."

"Yeah," Pork Chop said. "Fuckin'-A, Cyndi!"

Lonnie staggered to his feet. "Do I get a gun this time?"

Rhonda reluctantly handed him the revolver. "Just try not to—"

"Shoot my dick off. Yeah, yeah." He shoved the gun in the waistband of his jeans.

"Try not to shoot *me*, is what I was gonna say," Rhonda said. "By all means, shoot your dick off. *Please.* You'll be doing the gene pool a favor."

Lonnie cracked a smile in spite of himself. "You're a real piece of work, Shaughnessy."

"And you're a real asshole, Deveroux."

"What about me?" Pork Chop said.

"You're an asshole too," Rhonda assured him.

"Do I get a gun?"

"We don't *have* another gun. And you're staying here with the girl."

"No!" Pork Chop said, in sudden terror. "I don't wanna—"

"We didn't go through all of this just to let her die."

"She's right, P.C." Lonnie patted Pork Chop's gut affectionately. "You'll only slow us down, bro."

P.C. cut a frightened glance at Becca. "Dude, *please.* Don't leave me with her."

"It's gonna be okay, man. Have I ever let you down?"

"More times than I count!"

Lonnie glanced over his shoulder at Rhonda, making sure she was out of earshot. Then he whispered to Pork Chop: "If we're not back by dawn, ditch the bitch and split. Follow those railroad tracks to anywhere but here. Get help. And...tell Rachel I'm sorry. I did everything I could. Okay?"

Pork Chop nodded reluctantly.

40

Pork Chop watched from the door of the shack as Lonnie and Cyndi vanished into the darkness. He might have waited there all night, like a faithful dog pining for his master's return, had the storm not driven him back inside. The storm was getting worse, gathering above the shack, like it was following them...or the girl.

Rain drummed on the roof in a white noise roar. The shack creaked and groaned in the wind, teetering from side to side as if it might collapse at any second. An icy breeze breathed through the gaps in the wooden slats, swaying the lantern on its hook.

The lantern light cast creepy shadows across the sleeping girl. Her rasping breath made him think of some multi-legged insect skittering through dry leaves. He remembered the centipede from his dream, nightmare, *vision*, whatever it had been...slithering from his daddy's mouth like an obscene tongue—

Nope! P.C. pushed the thought away.

He checked the time on the silver pocket watch he had found beside the bed. Lonnie had said he could leave at dawn, but that was hours away. The wait might've been tolerable if the shack was stocked with beer and Cheetos. *Stop thinking about your own fat ass,* he scolded himself. *Mikey's in trouble!* But his stomach growled at the thought of snacks, so loudly that at first he mistook the sound for another roll of thunder. He investigated the provisions on the table. Sniffed the block of cheese. Gnawed one corner. He didn't drop dead, so he decided after a minute or two that it must have been okay, and devoured the rest of the cheese in two giant bites. Without a beer to wash it down with, he made do with the dregs of spitty water Lonnie had left in the drinking bladder. He belched. It crossed his mind that maybe he should have rationed what little food and water he had. *Too late now*. He checked the time again. It was gonna be a long night.

Something rustled behind him. He flinched, dropped the watch. The glass face splintered on the hard earthen floor. He turned his head slowly toward the noise.

The girl had moved in her sleep. A corner of the blanket had peeled from her shoulder to reveal the word carved crookedly down her throat:

SLOTH

The scab seemed to shimmer in the lantern light.

Pork Chop wondered what it meant. Wasn't Sloth the name of a character in that movie *The Goonies* from a couple of years ago? The hulking retard with the head like a deflated basketball… who Pork Chop looked *nothing* like, he didn't care *what* Lonnie said. That dude was funny. *Hey, you guys!*

Also, wasn't a sloth some kind of weird-ass animal? He remembered writing a paper about them when he was in tenth grade, a last-ditch effort to pass Remedial Science.

That was the day he met Lonnie.

One moment, he'd been perched at the top of the high school stairwell, proudly proofing his science report: "'*—the three-toed sloth climbs down from his tree just once a week to use the bathroom. He digs a hole and then buries his poop after pooping. I enjoyed reading about the three-toed sloth very very very very very much.*'" He added one more '*very*' to meet the assignment's five-hundred-word requirement. "'*THE END.*'" A solid D if he said so himself—

The next moment, he was crashing down the stairs like a husky human Slinky.

Sprawled at the bottom with a bloody nose and a chipped front tooth, he'd flopped onto his back with a pained groan, and saw the bullies looming over him. Larry Treadway and his snickering yes-men, Brian Ferrell and Chad Winslow. They'd made his life a living hell ever since the sixth grade. Because he was poor, because he was big-boned, but mostly because he was weak.

Before he could scramble away, Brian and Chad pinned his arms and legs to the ground. Larry straddled his chest and gripped one of his tits, wrenching it like he was wringing a wet towel. Pork Chop screeched in pain. The bullies cackled and jeered. And then a voice said, "Let the fat kid go."

Pork Chop gazed past the bullies, gaping in awe at the heroic figure silhouetted at the top of the stairwell.

"What's the matter?" said Pork Chop's shining knight. "You homos get tired of jacking each other off, had to find some other way to entertain yourselves?"

"Deveroux?" Larry sputtered in disbelief.

Lonnie Deveroux had recently transferred from another school. He and Pork Chop were in Shop class together. They had never spoken, but P.C. knew the new kid was cool because of the band logo patches (*AC/DC, Sabbath, Led Zep*) sewn on his denim jacket. He'd hoped they might make friends under better circumstances.

Lonnie swaggered down the stairs to confront the bullies. He peeled off his *Enter the Dragon* T-shirt, flung it aside, and assumed a karate stance.

"Whoa…" Pork Chop breathed.

He'd seen enough kung-fu movies to tell Lonnie was the real deal.

"Last chance, fuckheads," Lonnie said, slashing his hands in the air.

The bullies exchanged dumbfounded glances.

Started laughing.

Blitzed Pork Chop's would-be savior.

As the bullies beat the Bruce Lee out of Lonnie, P.C. scuttled away from the dog-pile on his hands and knees, and activated the fire alarm on the wall. The bullies cut and ran before a teacher arrived, leaving Lonnie sprawled on the floor. P.C. returned his *Enter the Dragon* T-shirt to him. "Dude, that was bitchin'! Where'd you learn that stuff? Would you teach me some moves?" Lonnie just murmured something unintelligible as he sank down into unconsciousness.

Ever since that day in the stairwell, when Lonnie saved his ass by sacrificing his own, Pork Chop had worshipped the guy – in a strictly platonic, one-hundred percent hetero way. All Lonnie had to do was ask, and P.C. would have followed him to the ends of the earth.

Now, alone in the shack with the girl, P.C. feared that's exactly where Lonnie had brought him.

42

Jacob gunned the four-wheeler through the storm, slitting his eyes against the stinging rain as he followed the path of the railroad tracks. He had expected to catch up with the other sinners by now. Where were they? Had they abandoned their friend and jumped the train without him? Jacob would not have put it past them – selfishness was the very least of their transgressions – though he thought it more likely they had fled back into the forest, making the hunt even harder.

He prayed for the Lord to guide him, fighting the fear in the pit of his stomach that the Almighty had abandoned him and all his good people.

Please, Lord. Won't you send me a sign?

Instead the Lord sent Old Moses.

The mule loomed suddenly in his headlights. Jacob tried to swerve, the mule tried to dodge, but the four-wheeler T-boned the beast, the sudden impact and the jolting stop hurling Jacob from the saddle. He flailed through the air like a tossed cat, before crashing to the cold wet ground.

It was hard not to feel forsaken.

Moaning in pain, he teetered to his feet, the world seesawing sickly around him. He wiped mud and rain from his eyes, along with the blood trickling down from the gash in his forehead, to find Old Moses crumpled beneath the four-wheeler's tires. The mule shrieked in pain, thrashing his head pitifully. Jacob drew his sidearm and ended the animal's suffering with a shot to the head.

He rolled the bike back off the dead mule, and tried the engine, but it refused to start. He kicked the bike in frustration. *Damn it, goddamn it!*

He glared at Old Moses, blaming the dead mule for his predicament, when he knew it was Noah to blame. The runaway mule was yet another example of how Brother Noah had failed in his duties. The beast should have been tethered securely at the—

At the Circle.

Jacob smiled.

"Oh, Lord. Forgive me for ever doubting you."

The Almighty had sent him a sign, after all.

43

The girl awoke with a gasping cry.

"They're here! Oh, G-God…they're here!"

Pork Chop staggered to his feet, thumping his head on the lantern. It swung back and forth from its ceiling hook, casting nightmare shadows through the shack. "What? Who? Where?"

He scrambled to the window. Couldn't see anyone outside, but he wasn't about to take any chances. P.C. overturned the table in the corner of the room. He wrenched off one of its legs and whapped the makeshift club against his palm.

Behind him, the girl gave a tortured-cat yowl.

P.C. wheeled around. "What is it? What's wrong?"

"They're…coming!"

The club shook wildly in his hand as he took a slow step toward the bed.

"Who's coming?"

Becca's face was an agonized rictus. She began bucking violently, driving her heels into the mattress, thrusting her hips up and down, her spine arching almost to breaking point. Her fingernails clawed at the floor until they snapped from her fingers like flipped switches. The mildewed blanket peeled away from her body. Blood bloomed through her bandages, through her HULKAMANIA shirt, and soaked the mattress beneath her. Something darker than blood, viscous and bubbling and stinking of rot, oozed from the symbols and words carved into her flesh. The words seemed to glow like molten lava in the lantern light.

Pork Chop crouched beside the girl, wincing as he took her hand. Felt like he'd grabbed hold of an ice sculpture. He was almost afraid to pull away in case he left a patch of his own flesh behind. "It's gonna be okay," he said. "Take it easy. The others are gonna be back soon. They'll know what to do. We'll get you to a hospitaaaaa— *Awww, shit!*"

Her fingers crunched his hand with knuckle-cracking force.

The girl's head cranked towards him.

And suddenly he was face-to-face with his Daddy. Pork Chop could see his own reflection in the milky blue cataracts of the dead man's eyes. Pop's lips had withered away to reveal crooked brown teeth, fuzzed green with lichen. *You deserve everything you're gonna git!* Daddy said, rocking with laughter. One of his eyes spilled from the socket and slid down his cheek, revealing a festering mass of maggots—

Pork Chop shrieked and tore his hand free, losing his balance and landing on his ass. He shoved himself back against the far wall, away from the rotting thing.

He blinked. Daddy was gone. It was just the girl again.

"What the fuuuuu—"

Becca's belly began to swell.

Where only moments before it was famine-flat, almost concave, now it ballooned before Pork Chop's eyes. Her blood-sodden HULKAMANIA shirt split down the middle, as if the Hulkster himself was shredding his shirt in the wrestling ring. Livid purple veins cobwebbed the girl's bulging belly. The jagged letters the crazies had carved there widened into dripping-red smiles. And still her stomach continued to grow…and grow…like a slowly inflating blimp. For a moment P.C. thought he saw something moving inside her…like oddly shaped fish swimming inside an opaque bowl.

"Stop…" he whimpered. "Please stop…"

And she did. For several seconds she lay deathly still. Silent.

Thunder rumbled outside. P.C. felt the vibrations under his feet.

The girl sucked a sharp breath. Her eyes rolled over white in her skull. Her mouth yawned open, so wide that the corners of her mouth ripped jaggedly to her cheekbones, and fresh blood streamed from her lips. Then her jaw snapped shut with trap-like force, her teeth exploding in a blizzard of enamel that sprayed Pork Chop's face.

He covered his mouth, and could only sob, watching helplessly as the girl clutched her stomach and gave a lowing moan. Her still-swelling belly had assumed the stretched-white color of a balloon about to—

Burst.

Bloody viscera painted the walls, drenching P.C. in a red rain.

Gore splashed the glass case of the lantern, tinting the shack's interior an unholy devil-red.

The girl's head slumped back on the mattress with a sickening squelch. Her mouth hung open in a silent scream, her torn lips lending her the leer of an insane Harlequin. Her arms and legs flopped lifelessly by her sides.

A blast of putrid air and gray-green smoke billowed up from her gaping abdomen. A fierce gale tore through the shack. The door crashed open, slammed shut, again and again.

Pork Chop crawled on his hands and knees toward the girl. Unable to stop himself. Even as his rational mind screamed at him to *GET UP AND RUN!*

Reaching the edge of the bed, he leaned forward, peering down into the gory cavity in Becca's torso. He gibbered in mindless terror as he found himself gazing into an impossible abyss. He clutched at the sides of the bed for fear he might tumble into the hole and never stop falling. An icy wind ruffled his hair. His breath frosted before him.

Smoky gray clouds scudded past him, miles below.

Lightning flashed down there, revealing an endless vista of jagged black mountains, like the mountains of corpses he had climbed in his dream. Something moved in the darkness below. Something monstrous and vast. A lumbering leviathan crushing everything in its path. It was not alone. There were at least half a dozen of them, surging up through the inky black nothing toward the light shining down through the chasm…and towards Pork Chop's gaping face, framed there in the light.

Pork Chop lurched back from the pit, staggered to his feet, and bolted for the door. He fled the shack and stumbled into the night, pelted by rain. He wheeled in a panicked circle.

Railroad tracks, which way are the railroad tracks?

Fuck it. Just RUN!

Something punched the air from his lungs. He grunted in pain and sank to his knees, staring down in confusion at the glistening steel rod spearing his belly.

He only looked up from the gushing wound when he sensed someone looming over him.

"Where is she?" the bearded man said, as he loaded a fresh bolt into his crossbow.

Pork Chop tried to warn the man, but when he opened his mouth only bloody froth burbled out. He jerked his head toward the shack…then toppled backward and crashed to the cold wet ground. Rain spattered his face, filling his eyes and nostrils.

The man kneeled beside Pork Chop and took his hand. Pork Chop had never been so afraid…of what he had seen in the abyss, and of where he was going now. He squeezed his killer's hand, just grateful not to die alone. His grip was no stronger than an infant's. His vision was fuzzy-gray at the edges.

"Son…" the man said.

The man's voice sounded distant, echoing far above him.

"Do you accept Jesus Christ as your Lord and Savior?"

"Okay…" Pork Chop said, as he faded away.

44

Jacob closed the fat man's vacant eyes. The sinner's plaid skirt had flapped over his hips when he fell, exposing his private parts. Jacob hesitantly pulled down the skirt, covering the fat man's nakedness. Why was he wearing a skirt? Was the situation worse than they'd thought…were they dealing with sodomites here? According to Heaton, such hellbound deviants were rife these days – men wearing women's clothes, and vice versa. With a shudder of disgust, Jacob wiped his hands on his pants.

He turned his sights on the shack.

Praise God, they had found the 'goat at last.

He smiled.

I found her.

Not Heaton.

Me.

His chest swelled with—

A shiver stole through him.

"Dear God…" Jacob gasped.

The shack exploded in a storm of slats.

The blast hurled him off his feet.

Sprawled on his back, hacking for breath, Jacob raised an arm to shield his face from the fiery debris raining down from the sky. He teetered to his feet, his ears ringing from the blast. His eyes widened in horror as he saw the columns of smoke billowing from the ruins of the shack.

Within the smoke, seven nightmare shadows swarmed.

Jacob clamped his hands to his ears, wincing as the demons rejoiced in their freedom, the sound of their malevolent laughter turning his blood to ice.

He fumbled for the walkie-talkie on his hip.

"Heaton… Heaton, we…we're too late."

The earth thrummed beneath him.

"Do you hear me, brother? It's over. They walk among us now."

Jacob dropped the walkie-talkie and sank to his knees.

He thought of his wife, Ethel. They were only thirteen when Jacob's father brought them before God's people and announced that the Lord had paired them. With her horsey teeth and freckled face, her brick-red hair and lazy eye, her beanpole frame and boyishly flat chest, Ethel was not the buxom bride Jacob might have chosen for himself. But he had known better than to question the Lord. And love had come in time.

He thought of their children. The four-year-old twins, Henry and Hannah, who were already learning to read, making Jacob so proud as they slowly made progress through the book of Exodus every night before bed. And poor, simple-minded Virgil. He adored trains more than anything in the world, so much that the rest of the family had to mind him whenever he heard the 'choo-choo' in the distance. He had wandered off before, and it had scared them all half to death.

Jacob tried not to grieve as he thought of his loved ones. He would see them all in Heaven soon. And when they were together again, there would be no more suffering. No more pain. Even sweet Virgil would be normal like everyone else. And they would all have a special place by God's side.

Jacob removed his sidearm from the leather holster on his hip. He chambered a round, cocked the hammer with his thumb, and genuflected with the 9mm Browning. "God have mercy on us all," he said.

And then he brought the barrel to his temple and squeezed the trigger.

PART / THREE

EVIL WALKS

45

Ledbetter repeated his brother's last words to him, "They walk among us..."

The color drained from the preacher's face, leaving him as white as his clerical collar. The walkie-talkie slid through his fingers, shattered on the church floor.

Mike flinched, turning his face from the spray of radio parts. The preacher's fear was contagious; Mike felt his own heart hammering against the floorboards.

"What...what does that mean? What's going on?"

The preacher silenced him with a slashing hand motion.

He turned toward the Christ behind the pulpit.

"We failed You," he said, in a cracked voice.

He stumbled against the communion table where Daniel's body lay. The young man's hands came unclasped from his chest. One arm slid from beneath his shroud and dangled from the table.

The preacher stood with his back to the others for some time, staring up at the Christ, and whispering something no one else could hear. Blood had soaked through the shredded back of his clerical shirt in flame-shaped crimson blotches.

At last the preacher said, "Ethan."

Spuds stepped forward. "Yes, Reverend."

"Sound the horn."

No-Neck and Bert shared an anxious glance.

Spuds paled, swallowed hard. "Sir—?"

"Do what I say!" the preacher barked at him.

Then, softer: "The hour is upon us."

Spuds scuttled toward the door behind the pulpit.

The other two men dropped to their knees and began to pray.

"Lord, hear my confession—"

"Father, forgive me—"

"And Ethan?" the preacher said.

Spuds paused at the door.

"Play the recording."

Spuds nodded dumbly.

Ledbetter turned his attention to Mike.

He slowly approached him, the toes of his boots threatening to crush Mike's splayed fingers.

Mike recoiled from the advancing madman, yelping as the nails ripped his hands.

"Please!" Mike cried. "What's going on?"

The preacher squatted on his haunches before him.

"Are you right with God?" he asked Mike. "I know I am."

46

Rhonda led the way through the woods. Shotgun in one hand, map in the other. As much as she would have welcomed Lonnie to take point, if only to act as a human shield, she didn't trust the dumb bastard to guide them. She paused to consult the map. Rain spattered the parchment as she plotted their next move.

"This way," she said, hoping she was right.

The map brought them to a rutted dirt trail. The trail snaked through the woods before circling an apple orchard. The air smelled tangy with ripening fruit as they cut through.

A two-story farmhouse loomed into view. The house was dark save for a single dim porch light. Kamikaze moths dive-bombed the bulb. A dirty kewpie doll lay neglected in the yard, next to a pink bicycle with rainbow ribbons tied to the handlebars. Behind the house was a crooked brown barn, its doors lolling open. A stake truck was parked inside the barn, a rusted orange International Harvester with its flatbed converted to carry fruit.

"I guess it's too much to hope the keys are inside," Lonnie said.

"But you know how to hotwire, right?" Rhonda asked him.

"I should be offended by that… but yeah."

Stalking across the yard towards the barn, they'd barely taken ten steps when an alarm began to wail. They froze in their tracks in the middle of the yard. After the initial shock had passed, they realized the siren was coming from the town common. They were hearing its echo, bouncing off the hills that bordered town.

It was an ominous, hackle-raising sound.

"What the hell is that?" Lonnie said.

"Whatever it is, it can't be good."

An upper-story light blinked on in the house behind them.

"Shit, move!" Rhonda whispered, giving Lonnie a shove.

They ran for the house, as it was closer. Pressed themselves tight against the wall, and held their breath. The light cast an orange rectangle down into the yard. A woman's silhouette appeared in the window. There was a sound like fingernails on a chalkboard as she raised the window on rusted hinges. Rhonda and Lonnie pressed themselves tighter against the wall, Lonnie sucking in his gut as if *that* would be the giveaway. The woman leaned from the window, cocked her head to listen…then gasped. Lonnie raised the revolver. Rhonda grabbed his wrist and shook her head. The woman was reacting to the siren, not them.

She ducked back inside the window.

Still not daring to move or make a sound, they listened as the woman crashed and banged through the house. She woke her children. *"Teri, honey. Go get your brother and sister. And remember to mind the baby's lil' fontanel. Hurry now. Everyone downstairs. Quickly!"* Groggy complaints from the little ones. Urgent footfalls and creaking floorboards.

A downstairs light blinked on. A radio crackled to life; a preacher began speaking. It was not the same man they had heard before, the one who had vowed to pluck out Lonnie's tongue. This time the speaker was a very old man with a shrill, rasping voice.

"I tried, brothers and sisters!" The ancient tape recording warped the old man's voice even further. "How I tried to lead this community in a way that was pleasing to the Lord. Yet, in spite of my efforts…if you are hearing this, then I have failed you. I have failed each and every one of you. Because…I am just a man."

He paused for breath; it sounded like he was sucking on an oxygen mask.

"I always knew there would come a day when God's people could no longer hold back the denizens of Hell. We tried. How we tried. We said the words. We performed the ritual. Blood was shed, and our sins consumed by cleansing fire. And still, it was inevitable that the Day of Judgment would one day come.

"It is foretold in the Book of Revelation: *'Blessed are those who hear the words of prophecy, and take to heart what is written, because the time is near.'* That time is NOW. Are you listening? Man and woman, young and old, the Almighty is calling. Calling you home. Will you answer? *'Do not be afraid,'* He tells us, *'of what you are about to suffer. Be faithful, even unto death, and the Lord shall give you eternal life.'*"

Rhonda peeked above the window ledge into the house.

Four young girls wearing nightclothes lined a mustard-colored sofa. The eldest girl appeared to be about Becca's age. She cradled in her arms a fussy baby boy wearing a sky-blue onesie. Their mother stood with her back to the window. She wore a floral-patterned housecoat and slippers. As the preacher's voice rambled on, the woman sank to her knees in prayer.

"Brothers and sisters, just as the Lord has never lied to you, I will never lie to you. That is why you must trust in me. Be strong, and know that what waits on the other side is glorious beyond comprehension. The time has come for us to step off this plane of existence. We've waited our whole lives for this moment. A lifetime of pain, of growing old and feeble…from the moment we are born, we wither and die. So let us be done with it. Let us depart for a place where there is no death or disease, no sorrow, a place where there is only light and love and peace for all eternity."

Lonnie nudged Rhonda, mouthed: *What's going on?*

Rhonda shook her head: *I don't know.*

The woman rose to her feet, moving purposefully to the mantle where a bolt-action Marlin was propped on a gun rack. She pulled the rifle from its mount and loaded a round in the chamber. Her daughters watched her every move, waiting patiently, expectantly, as if they had rehearsed this moment many times.

"The bottomless pit has opened," said the man on the radio. "Soon those who inhabit the chasm will rise, and they will walk among us. But we need not worry. For we are the chosen. We are God's people. *'And it was commanded that they should not harm those who have the seal of God upon their foreheads.'*

"That is *you*…that is *we*…the good and righteous people of Little Enoch.

"So come now, brothers and sisters. Enter the Kingdom of Heaven. Do not hesitate. Help those who cannot help themselves. The old, the infirm, the innocent. It is an act of mercy. We are in this together and we shall leave no soul behind. We shall die with dignity and live for all eternity."

"Oh my God," Rhonda said, with dawning horror. "I think she's going to—"

The woman turned, pointing the rifle at the girls on the sofa, and pulled the trigger…drew back the bolt, reloaded, and did it again…pulled the trigger and reloaded…killing her daughters one by one. The final shot pulped the baby's head, passing through his tiny skull and piercing the eldest daughter's chest.

The smell of gunsmoke and blood drifted from the living room window as the woman chambered one last round.

Then she swung the gun towards herself, jammed the barrel under her chin and groped for the trigger. Her head exploded from her shoulders like a champagne cork.

Lonnie lurched back in shock, tripping on the pink bicycle in the yard and thudding to the ground. Rhonda turned her eyes from the window. The world around them was silent, save for the storm and the distant wail of the siren. The preacher's sermon had ceased, as if the holy man had paused to revel in the slaughter.

"What the fuck is this, Shaughnessy?" Lonnie said. "What are we dealing with here?"

"We have to move," Rhonda told him. "I don't think Rawson has much time."

They made for the truck in the barn.

In the farmhouse, on the radio, the old preacher's sermon began again from the top, playing on a loop that would continue forever… or at least until the End.

47

As the siren wailed, and the preacher beckoned, in every home throughout Little Enoch, God's faithful answered His call…

*

Not far from the church, an elderly couple, woken by the siren, sat side-by-side in the bed they had shared for some sixty years. His and Hers dentures grinned at each other from within cups of water on their respective nightstands. On the wall above the headboard was framed an embroidery which the missus had cross-stitched before rheumatism stole the pastime from her:

"For here we have no lasting city, but we seek the city that is to come."
Hebrews 13:14

He asked if she was ready. She replied that her only regret was that they couldn't meet the Almighty with their hands entwined. He promised his beloved she would beat him there by a minute, no more. They kissed as if they were eighteen again. Then she lay back. He placed the pillow over her face before pressing down and holding it there until she stopped moving beneath him. When that was done, slightly breathless from his efforts, the old man reached for the antique Luger he kept in the drawer of his nightstand. He placed the end of the barrel against the roof of his mouth, staring at the embroidery as he pulled the trigger, and making good on his promise to his wife with twenty seconds to spare.

In another house, a rake-thin man in his forties, wearing only horn-rimmed glasses and pajama bottoms, injected himself with nine vials of insulin. He had tended to his wife's diabetes for thirty years, and knew exactly what to do. When the deed was done, he settled down in his recliner with the framed photograph from their wedding day. Noreen had weighed three-hundred-pounds when they married, twice that when she died; he himself had never weighed more than a hundred and ten pounds, making them the proverbial Mr. and Mrs. Jack Sprat. By the time she went to live with Jesus two winters ago, the sugar had taken both of her legs below the knee, she was unable to roll over in bed without assistance, and required him to help her bathe and go potty. Yet he had loved her with all his heart. "I'm coming, sweetheart," he said. His eyelids grew heavy. The photo frame slipped from his slackening grip. "And when I get there I'm gonna make you a chocolate cake as big as the moon."

A few miles outside Little Enoch, two fifteen-year-old lovers embraced on a rocky ledge overlooking the town. The girl had recently discovered she was pregnant. The boy had sworn he would never leave her. Secretly he feared that once their secret was out, they would be exiled from the church – *only* exiled, if they were lucky – and they might never see their families again. As the young lovers kissed, they remembered the first time their lips had touched, right here, at this very spot. Their relationship had been innocent then, holding hands as they watched the setting sun bleed across the forest before it ducked behind the mountains; it was only a matter of time before they caved to temptation, and their fleshly desires led them into sin. But now they could enter the Kingdom of Heaven along with their unborn child. He cupped her face in his hands, telling her there could be no regrets for those who would soon bask in the everlasting light of the Lord. The young lovers shared one last kiss…and then they stepped off the ledge, certain they would ascend, even as they plunged to their death on the craggy rocks below.

In the dim light of the cloud-choked moon, Malachi Brunswick, wearing a parka over long johns and galoshes, moved purposefully through the pigpen, killing each of his "girls" with a single shot to the head from his rifle. Tears coursed down his face as he carried out his duty. He could barely hear the wail of the siren over his own sobbing. But he would not allow his girls to suffer. When every snuffle had been silenced, every snort had ceased, and the final oink had faded into the night, Brunswick turned the gun on himself. Sadly his aim was not as true as his faith. He blew off only half his skull, dying the slow and painful death from which he had spared his girls, before at last he passed into merciful oblivion.

On Main Street, where the siren was loudest, the owner of OSBORNE'S ALL-YOU-NEED emerged from the general store / gas station that had been in his family for three generations. He paused on the porch to cinch his robe around his waist, shot an anxious glance toward the stormy sky. Stepping down onto the forecourt, he removed one of the gasoline pumps from its stand and began spraying the forecourt, porch and storefront with gas, as if he were watering his yard with a garden hose. Once that was done, Osborne raised the nozzle above him, and drenched himself from head to toe. His gasoline-sodden slippers squelched beneath him as he returned inside. It had been several years since he quit the habit, but now he took a pack of Newports from the cigarette stand, and prodded a coffin nail between his lips. Then he struck a match across the counter…experiencing the pains of Hell on his way to Heaven.

In the cluttered bathroom of a doublewide mobile home, a young mother kneeled beside the claw-foot tub, watching as her month-old triplets sank like stones in the water. Bubbles blurred their munchkin faces. She did not attempt to save them; she *was* saving them. The bubbles slowed…then stopped completely. Her babies were in Heaven now. Rising to her feet, she turned toward the sink, staring down at the hairs her husband had left in the basin after he shaved that morning. He'd been out all day helping Jacob and the others search for the 'goat. The siren told her that he would not be coming home. She opened the medicine cabinet, took out her husband's razor and raked the blade across her wrists, the wounds describing a crude cruciform. She returned to the bathtub, smiling as she climbed inside it to be with her little ones. The water turned red as she held them, and her life slowly ebbed away.

Two hundred yards east as the crow flies, Jacob's wife Ethel used a pestle and mortar to pulp a vial of pills to powder atop the kitchen counter. She sprinkled a heaping into each of the four bowls on the supper table, then mixed the powder into the porridge, as if stirring the ingredients of her husband's favorite dish (chicken pot pie). She took a taste, smacked her lips, wrinkled her nose at the bitterness, but decided it would have to do – she doubted poor Virgil would even notice. Ethel called the children to the table, and then sat down to join them for one last meal. For once they did not say grace, since they would soon thank the Lord face-to-face for the blessings he had bestowed on them.

*

Throughout Little Enoch, gunshots echoed like fireworks on the Fourth of July. Shotguns boomed. Pistols popped. Muzzle flash lit up windows. Blood flowed.

On and on it continued, through every home in town.

The tri-tone beckoned.

The faithful answered.

One by one…

48

It was a keening melody comprised of three distinct chords, repeated in an endless loop. The closest comparison Mike could make were the three dissonant chords of the song "Black Sabbath" by the classic band of the same name. Mike remembered the first time he'd blasted that tune through his stereo headphones. Ominous and foreboding, he'd thought it sounded like the end of the world. But he'd been wrong…

This was the soundtrack for the Apocalypse.

The rumbling bass quaked the church to its foundations. Mike screamed as the floorboards juddered beneath him, and the nails tore his hands. Pews moshed across the hardwood, coughing up great swirls of dust that blinded and choked him. The stained-glass windows rattled in their frames.

Through tears-blurred eyes, Mike glimpsed the apocalyptic horrors depicted in each of the windows. The hellish creatures shared vague anatomic similarities with beasts of the earth. Was *that* something akin to a lion… and *that* some kind of snail? *Maybe.* In more than one scene, humanoid limbs sprouted from reptilian or insectoid torsos, as if the subject were the offspring of some unholy coupling of man and monster. These were demons from the bowels of hell, Mike knew, and no mortal mind could comprehend their true forms while remaining sane on the other side of it.

Below each of the abominations scrolled a wrinkled yellow banner:

GREED ~ ENVY ~ LUST
WRATH ~ PRIDE ~ GLUTTONY ~ SLOTH

The preacher loomed over Mike, clutching his Bible before him.

"We are fallen, Rawson. The people have turned their backs on the Lord. They scoff at His commandments. They mock His faithful. They wallow in sin like swine in soil. And the agents of Satan grow e'er stronger."

His eyes bugged wildly in his skull. A sweaty forelock hung down across his fevered brow. With violent thrusts of his Bible, he gestured between each of the stained-glass monstrosities. "The demon *Lust* spreads disease among the fornicators and the sodomites… *Greed* and *Envy* compel men to covet material possessions over spiritual grace… *Gluttony* has transformed our once-great nation into a heathen hellhole… *Wrath* has turned brother against brother… *Prideful* women paint their faces like modern-day Jezebels… And *Sloth* has forced the faithless to accept it, to idly sit and watch as every precious thing God created withers and blackens like rotten fruit."

Mike could only shrink in horror as the lunatic raged. "Jesus Christ—"

"*Oh, no!* You don't get to call on Him now. You had your chance. You had your whole *lifetime* to repent. The Lord's patience is at an end. The Day of Judgment is upon us…"

He pointed at Mike.

"Upon *thee.*"

49

Lonnie gunned the fruit truck through town. Rhonda huddled in the flatbed behind the cab, checking the load in her shotgun. The tri-tone siren wailed from speakers, erected on flagpoles or attached to storefronts on every other block. The endless droning was driving Rhonda crazy. She might have started shooting the speakers if she didn't need to conserve what little ammo they had.

Main Street was choked with billowing black smoke from the burning general store. Before the porch collapsed, Rhonda glimpsed the charred sign out front of the place: "OSBORNE'S ALL-YOU-NEED." Flames licked at the properties on either side of the store; it was only a matter of time before HANK'S HABERDASHERY and an unnamed BARBERSHOP were consumed. Before long all of Main Street would be ablaze. Not even the rain would douse the inferno. Gunshots echoed here and there as if some macabre festival was underway.

Under different circumstances, Little Enoch might have been a nice place to visit. The town had a quaint, old-timey feel. Of course, Rhonda knew why. The people who called this place home were living in the fucking Dark Ages.

Lonnie suddenly hit the brakes. The truck shuddered to a stop.

"Shaughnessy!" he called from the cab, directing her attention ahead of them.

Upon a small rise, at the end of a snaking path, stood the church.

50

Lonnie fished the Wrathbone cassette (*Rode Hard/Put Up Wet*) from the butt pocket of his jeans, kissed it for luck, and then slammed it in the tape deck.

For a moment he almost regretted it. This was the only copy in existence. He half-expected the stereo in the rattletrap truck to eat the tape and start puking out loops and coils like the entrails of his gutted rock n' roll dreams.

But instead: Feedback whined, guitars squalled, drums pounded, bass *chugga-chug-chugged*...and then the ear-piercing screech of nineteen-year-old Lonnie 'Love Gun' Deveroux proclaimed his undying love for raisin' Cain and chasin' tail.

"Jesus, *really*?" he heard Rhonda mutter from the flatbed behind him. "*This* is gonna be the last thing I ever hear?"

Lonnie looked at himself in the rearview mirror and smiled.

His dreams of rock n' roll stardom might not have come true as he'd hoped, but there was no reason why he couldn't *go out* like his heroes: Jimi, Bon, Randy Rhoads, Ronnie Van Zant… Lonnie was a blaze-of-glory kinda guy.

He adjusted the rearview for one last look at Rhonda's perfect, sweat-shiny—

"Stop looking at my tits!" she shouted at him.

Lonnie revved the engine. "Ready, sweet thang?"

Rhonda spared one last thought for Billy, knowing she might not live to see justice for her brother, but hoping he would understand… Hell, if this went wrong, then maybe she'd get a chance to apologize to him in person.

"Hit it!"

Lonnie stamped the gas pedal, and the fruit truck surged forward.

51

Mike sucked a deep breath. It took almost every last shred of energy he had left, but he refused to die without saying what he wanted…because: *fuck this guy.*

"I was raised in the church," he said, "but these days I guess I'm an agnostic."

The preacher sneered. "The Lord has no love for fence-sitters."

"I don't believe much in anything," Mike went on, "but I've seen how my wife's faith gets her through each day. I see the hope it gives her when things are at their worst."

"Your point?"

"This is wrong…*so wrong.* And you're so far gone you can't even see it. God is love. At least, that's what I was always taught as a kid. He sent His son – that guy up there on the cross behind you? – to save man from his sins. Isn't that right? Way I remember it. Which means… the world doesn't *need* saving. Our sins are already forgiven. Everything you've taught these people – it's all bullshit. You've cherrypicked from that precious Bible of yours and warped it all to hell. But you can't see it 'cause you're crazier than a shithouse rat!"

Mike gave a bark of unhinged laughter that opened the floodgates; soon he wouldn't be able to *stop* laughing. He was quite sure he'd lost his mind, but he no longer cared. "All this…" Tears streamed down his face. "It's for nothing!"

Mike's laughter joined the cacophony of noise echoing through the church: the tri-tone siren… the raging storm outside… the desperate prayers of No-Neck and Bert…

Then another noise joined the chaos. Louder than the thunder and lightning outside, even louder than the siren within. The preacher cocked his head, turning slowly toward the church doors, as the noise grew louder… LOUDER.

A squeal of tires.

The roar of an engine.

A chugging guitar riff and pounding drums.

And above it all: A high-pitched rebel yell, as if the Devil himself had a red-hot grip on the singer's nuts, and was squeezing them like a stress ball.

Mike would have recognized that voice anywhere.

And even after all these years, he knew the lyrics by heart:

Spread 'em wiiide, honey
If you got the love, then I got the money!
Spread 'em wiiide, baby
You got what I need, and I don't mean maybe!

"What in God's name?" the preacher said, as the music grew louder… LOUDER.

Mike bared his teeth in a defiant grin. "Guess again, asshole."

52

"Silas," the preacher barked at Bert, "go see what that is."

Bert's prayers ceased for now. He hefted himself to his feet, snatched his Browning automatic from the waistband of his pants, and checked the load as he strode past Mike—

The truck exploded through the church doors like a last-second objector to a marriage doomed to fail.

Bert gave a helpless shriek that was cut short when the truck thundered over him, leaving him smeared on the hardwood as the vehicle roared down the aisle toward the head of the church.

No-Neck scrambled to his feet, snatching up the shotgun he'd left propped against a pew. He racked a round and fired at the truck. Buckshot peppered the windshield. Lonnie jerked his head to the side, ducking low in his seat, driving blind. Rhonda jacked up from the flatbed, firing back at No-Neck, her shotgun punching a hole through his chest, slamming him against the organ, which echoed a few melodramatic low-notes as he crumpled lifelessly to his knees.

The preacher's face betrayed no fear as Lonnie gunned the truck toward him. He extended his arms in cruciform pose, mimicking the crucified Christ behind him. "'And He laid His right hand upon me,'" the preacher bellowed, "'saying unto me, *Fear not, for I am the first and the last! I am He that liveth and was dead...and I have the keys to Hell and Death—*'"

Lonnie crunched the stick into higher gear. "Ah, blow it outta your ass!"

He floored the truck at the crazy fuck.

Wait—

Why wasn't Mikey moving out of the way?

"Mikey!" he yelled. "Make a hole, man!"

But Mike only glanced back over his shoulder.

His wide-eyed face glowed in the onrushing headlights.

Lonnie suddenly saw why Mike couldn't move: *He was nailed to the floor!*

He stomped the brake pedal, wrenched the wheel and tried to swerve, but the heavy wooden pews were blocking both sides of the aisle, like kiddy bumpers on a bowling lane. The truck shuddered onward, pinballing off the pews.

The jarring impact hurled Rhonda from the truck. She crashed down into the pews, thudded against a bench. The shotgun spilled from her hands and skated away across the hardwood floor.

Mike shut his eyes, pressing himself flat to the floor as the truck jerked to a halt above him. The blistering-hot undercarriage scorched his back, making him scream.

The truck hit the preacher head-on, hurling him back through the air. He struck the crucified Christ with skeleton-shattering force, thudding to the floor in a heap of twisted limbs beneath it. The heavy wooden sculpture swung wildly from its ceiling mounts, its shadow swishing like a pendulum across the preacher's motionless figure.

The truck engine died, along with Wrathbone's racket. Tire-smoke and cordite choked the church in a swirling gray mist. Lonnie shook his head, amazed at the hell he had wrought, not to mention that he'd survived. Then he grinned.

"That's what happens, motherfuckers, when you screw with Lonnie Dev—"

Spuds charged from somewhere at the back of the room. An M-16 blazed in his arms. He advanced on the truck, raking it with fire.

Lonnie ducked below the dash as bullets tore through the cab. "Shiiiiit!" The windshield shattered. Broken glass rained down over him.

Mike cowered beneath the truck, sparks flashing off the chassis all around him. All he could see of Spuds was a pair of legs, scissoring forward as the gunman advanced, a hailstorm of smoldering shell casings clattering on the hardwood at his heels.

On the floor to Mike's left, through the choking clouds of gunsmoke, he saw Bert's Browning automatic. The sonofabitch must've have dropped it when the truck ran him down. It lay just a few feet away. Within easy reach… or it would have been, if Mike's hands weren't nailed to the floor. Mike sank against the hardwood in despair.

Then he spotted something else, to his right. His wallet. It had flopped open, revealing the photo inside: Mike and Rachel vacationing in Myrtle Beach, and the baby in her belly.

He choked down a cry.

He refused to die here.

"Fuck this—"

Ducking his face toward the nail in his left hand, Mike gripped the head between his teeth, and started prying it loose with savage jerks of his neck, adrenalized by the pain, even as he tasted blood, and his guts churned, and stars burst across his vision, roaring like a trapped beast as he wrenched the steel spike from his flesh and spat it from his lips. The nail plinked on the hardwood floor and rolled away from him.

Ignoring the blood burbling from the hole in his hand, Mike reached across the floor to snatch up the pistol. He prayed it was loaded as he raised it toward the advancing gunman, and squeezed the trigger.

Spuds screamed as the bullets sheared his legs to bloody pulp beneath him. He crashed to the floor, took two more shots to the chest and another to the throat. He seemed surprised to see Mike beneath the truck, clutching the pistol in a hand pissing blood, and he died with that dumbfounded look on his face.

The pistol clicked empty. Mike dropped the gun and drew his wounded hand back toward him, pressing it against his shirt in a futile attempt to staunch the flow of blood. He looked helplessly at his right hand, still pinned to the floor.

At the ceasefire, Lonnie peeked above the dash. Seeing Spuds lying dead, not knowing how it happened, nor caring, he clambered from the cab and dropped to his knees beside the truck. Peering under the vehicle, he feared he would find his friend mangled in the tires. But instead he found Mike gaping back at him with wide wet eyes that said: *I can't believe I'm still alive…or that you drove a truck over me.*

Lonnie choked down a sob of relief. "You okay, man?"

"I'm nailed to the fucking floor!"

"Apart from—?"

"Just get me out of here!"

Lonnie noted the nail pinning Mike's hand to the floor. The color drained from his face as he realized his gruesome task. He looked away and dry-retched.

"You know," he said, "they're doing some amazing things with prosthetics these days."

"You're not cutting my fucking hand off, Lonnie!"

"Right. 'Course not." But apparently amputation was Lonnie's one and only idea. "What do you suggest?"

"There's a hammer in the tool chest." Mike nodded behind him. "*There.*"

Lonnie fetched the hammer from Bert's tool chest. He glanced between the claw-end and the nail in Mike's hand and swallowed hard, trying not to hurl.

"I… I don't know if I can do this, man."

"Lonnie, look at me. You have to. I don't dress these wounds soon, I'm gonna bleed out. Please. Don't let me die here. Not here."

Lonnie sucked a steely breath. "All right, okay… I can do this."

The hammer shook in Lonnie's grip as he lowered the claw-end toward Mike's right hand. He trapped the head of the nail between the steel claws. Mike flinched in pain, hissing through clenched teeth, his face pale and dotted with sweat. Lonnie looked at him apologetically. Mike nodded for him to continue. Lonnie hesitated, not sure if he should act fast or slow. *Was this like removing a Band-*

Aid? Mike said, "Just do—"

Lonnie pumped the handle like a tire-jack, uprooting the nail from Mike's hand with a screech of wood, a squelch of flesh, and a scream from his friend. Lonnie winced, tossed the hammer away. He grabbed the scruff of Mike's sweater and dragged him out from under the truck. Mike moaned in pain as Lonnie propped him up against the side of the vehicle. He was barely conscious, his eyes heavy-lidded and rolling in his skull. Lonnie tore off his HULKAMANIA shirt and used the strips to bandage Mike's bloody hands. The yellow fabric was dyed red in seconds. When that was done, Lonnie slung an arm around Mike's waist and hauled him to his feet.

"Shaughnessy?" he called over his shoulder.

"Here…" came the groggy reply from the logjam of pews.

Rhonda teetered to her feet a few seconds later, clutching one of the benches for balance.

"You okay?"

A stream of blood trickled down the side of her face from a nasty cut on her scalp. "The stupid questions aren't helping any," she said, fetching her shotgun from the floor.

Lonnie gave a *thatta girl* grin.

"Start the truck," he told her. "We've gotta—"

"*Woe to the wicked!*" cried a voice at the head of the church.

The preacher sat slumped against the fallen pulpit, wreathed in swirling gunsmoke. His legs were tangled beneath him like spaghetti, quills of fractured bone spiking through his pants. Blood streamed down his face from a ghastly gash in his forehead. The dome of his skull glistened white within the wound. He raised a pistol in his shaking fist. "*For what his hands have dealt shall be done twofold unto him!*" The pistol *pop-pop-popped.*

Bullets pounded the truck, shearing off the side mirror as Lonnie wrenched the door open and shoved Mike inside. He clambered in after him, shielding his friend from the shots like a Secret Service agent protecting the President.

Rhonda ducked for cover behind the truck. She racked the shotgun, down to her last round. *Gotta make it count.* Pinned down behind the truck, she couldn't get a clear shot at the preacher. She glanced in desperation at the Christ hanging precariously from the ceiling above him…and experienced an epiphany.

She fired at the ceiling mounts from which He depended.

Sparks flew from the chains. Plaster rained. The mounts tore free from the ceiling.

The preacher glanced above him, and gave a helpless cry – as the heavy wooden cross slammed down upon him like a judge delivering a death sentence with a thud of his gavel.

Rhonda dropped the empty shotgun. It clattered to the floor at her feet. She limped to the front of the truck, hauled herself in the cab, and slid behind the wheel.

"Everyone okay?"

"No," Lonnie and Mike said at the same time.

"That makes three of us."

Praying for one last miracle, Rhonda wrenched the screwdriver in the ignition, which Lonnie had used to hotwire the vehicle back at the orchard. The shot-to-shit truck spluttered to life. She crunched the shift into reverse and hit the gas. The truck rumbled back down the aisle, juddering over Bert's lifeless body as it exited the church.

53

The siren screamed on. The truck tore through town. Sporadic gunshots still sounded in the distance, as if a drummer with no rhythm was attempting to keep time with the tri-tone melody. Every building along Main Street was aflame now, spewing fiery embers into the stormy night sky. Thick black smoke choked the road.

Mike stared in numb horror from the splintered passenger window.

An elderly couple sat snuggled on a porch swing outside their A-frame. The only sign of life came from the insects haloing the moth light. The wall above their heads was slimed with blood and brain matter. The shotgun with which they had taken their lives lay at the husband's feet… In a well-tended yard, a younger couple and their children, the boy and girl pint-sized likenesses of their parents, hung like Christmas ornaments from the outstretched limbs of a fir tree… At the end of another drive, beside a mailbox with reflective stickers that read 281 – PRESTON, a plump bulldog lapped greedily at his owner's slashed throat… And still the siren screamed on, even though Mike suspected there was no one left alive to hear it.

His eyes welled with tears, his vision blurring between the town and his own fractured reflection in the window.

"How do we tell people what happened here?" he said, in a choked voice.

Rhonda could only shake her head.

Lonnie suddenly coughed, hacking blood across the dashboard.

"What the hell, man!" Mike cried. "You've been shot!"

Lonnie was clutching a hand to the side of his gut. Tar-black blood burbled between his fingers. He forced a smile, his teeth smeared with blood.

"It's…just a scratch."

"Let me see. *Jesus, Lonnie!*"

Lonnie clamped his hand back over the wound, squeezing his eyes shut in pain.

Mike and Rhonda exchanged a grim glance.

Lonnie said, "Nothing a Band-Aid…and a little T.L.C. won't fix."

He winked at Rhonda. "Did I do good, sweet thang?"

"Yeah, Lonnie," she said. "You did good."

Lonnie gave a pained grimace, the closest he could manage to a smile.

Then he shut his eyes, sank down in his seat, and slumped against Mike.

"Drive faster," Mike said.

He put his arm around his friend.

54

The Reverend Ledbetter lay broken beneath the wooden likeness of his Savior.

The Christ had landed facedown across his chest, pinning him to the floor. Ledbetter stared into His agonized features, as if into a mirror. His breath came in weak, ragged gasps. His fluid-filled lungs gurgled like a blocked drain. His broken ribs stabbed his insides, burning like branding irons. He coughed up something stringy and wet and no doubt vital, but he lacked the strength to wipe the bloody tissue from his lips. His legs, twisted this way and that, prickled with a strange numbness, as if his bottom half was enveloped by an alien cocoon slowly sapping the life from him. He knew escape was impossible, as he had personally supervised the hanging of the cross – during a remodeling project shortly after his father's death – and it had taken three strong men to do the job. He also knew that he was dying. Yet he felt no sadness, no fear. Only joy.

He would soon leave this world of suffering and take his rightful place by God's side in the Kingdom of Heaven. He could hardly wait to watch the Lord judge the faithless. How they would plead for mercy. And yet He would not grant it. They would be cast into the Lake of Fire and burn for all eternity. How Ledbetter would laugh!

He had been loyal all his life. *Blessed are the dead who die in the Lord, that they may rest from their labors, for their deeds follow them.*

His bloody lips twisted into a smile. He was ready to accept his reward for all the good work he had done here.

"Show me, Lord..." His voice was a sandpapery rasp. "Show me that my deeds...have pleased...You."

The storm raged above the church. A flash of lightning seemed to animate the stained-glass beasts that surrounded the dying preacher. Thunder boomed like mighty footsteps, the lumbering advance of some vast behemoth.

Ledbetter frowned.

The wooden Christ gazed down at him dispassionately.

A foul gust of wind breathed through the hall, snuffing out the votive candles as one, and cloaking the church in shadow. The room grew cold. The floor beneath the preacher's back became chill as a mortuary slab. His breath frosted before him. A fear he had never known – *uncertainty* – gripped his heart in an icy fist.

"Oh, Lord..." he gasped. "Oh, Jesus Christ!"

The stained-glass windows exploded inwards, showering Ledbetter in jagged rainbow shards...

...and into the church came the sins of mankind, beasts from hell that now stalked the earth because the Reverend and his people had failed to complete the ritual that had held them at bay.

The first was a bloated, bilious, wart-mottled thing. It considered Ledbetter with toad-like eyes. Its cavernous mouth yawned wide and vomited forth a ropy gray tongue. Ledbetter cried out as the tongue unfurled across the floor toward him, before it abruptly changed course and coiled around the shrouded body of his son. He screamed the boy's name as the tongue, clutching its prize by one ankle, whipped back into the creature's mouth and

Daniel disappeared down its gullet. GREED belched its satisfaction.

The second beast was coated in coarse black fur. The pupils of its seven bulging eyes were slitted horizontally. Walking on two legs, its cloven hooves clip-clopped on the floor as it advanced on the helpless holy man. Gigantic bone-white horns crowned the creature's skull, their points scraping the church ceiling with a nails-on-chalkboard screech. A tree-trunk-size phallus swung from between the demon's legs, drizzling ejaculate that sizzled through the floorboards like acid. LUST's hot snuffling breath reeked of deviant sex.

A serpentine creature slithered through the next broken window. Its hind legs were multi-jointed, bristled and barbed like those of an insect. The thing's tail was tipped with a silently screaming human skull, which it switched back and forth with a furious staccato chattering. The demon's forked tongue flickered inches from the preacher's face. ENVY smiled, relishing the taste of his fear.

An obese, snorting fiend crashed inside next. Its elongated trunk suggested the hellish offspring of swine and pachyderm. The pungent stink of rotting food and excrement baked from the hairless pink body. The porcine beast appeared to be blind; mucus had crusted shut the single eye in the center of its forehead. Rows of rigid brown nipples stippled its swollen, swaying belly. Each of them ended in a puckering mouth that salivated as GLUTTONY waddled toward the preacher.

The gaping maw of the fifth demon was a pit of fanged teeth that receded in rows down the plunging blackness of the creature's throat. Its lion-like mane was formed of skeletal quills that quivered and twitched. It walked on four muscular feline legs, each ending in the wrinkled hand of an old man, palms slapping on the hardwood as the beast padded forward. WRATH's voice belied its monstrous appearance; instead of a bellowing roar, its shrill, keening cries recalled the screams of tortured women and children.

Through the next window struggled a cumbersome monstrosity weighed down by the great spiraling shell on its back. The shell was etched with arcane symbols the like of which Ledbetter had never seen before, not even in the most obscure and esoteric religious text; his eyes burned and his brain ached just to look at them. The creature's body was a pulsating mass of snot-like ooze, save for the two spindly arms that dragged SLOTH forward, inch by resolute inch.

The demons surrounded Ledbetter.

"Almighty Father!" he cried. "Have mercy! Spare your servant!"

His eyes darted from one abomination to the next:

GREED, LUST, ENVY, GLUTTONY, WRATH, SLOTH—

Ledbetter gave a sharp intake of breath.

There was still one demon yet to reveal itself.

In fact, it was already upon him.

PRIDE birthed itself from the holy icon pinning the preacher to the floor. The cross began to shudder and twitch in violent throes. From the horizontal beams sprouted two limbs, slender and gaunt, each at least six-feet long. The gangly arms were veined with wood-grain, and ended in hooked claws. Enormous hands slapped to the floor. The beast braced itself for what remained of its metamorphosis. The preacher gave a wheezing cry as the crushing weight eased from his chest. Crab-like legs burst from the base of the cross, scrabbling for purchase on the hardwood. Then the abomination stood, rising slowly toward the shadowy rafters of the church. The vertical beam of the cross was still part of the creature's body; it scraped across the hardwood floor like a tail.

The demon loomed before Ledbetter.

His bowels released.

Gone were the features of God's Only Son, carved into the cross years ago by Little Enoch's finest woodworker… now the demon wore the face of his father.

"We were wrong," said the thing with his Daddy's face.

Its grating voice sounded like a shovel scraping cement. The head lolled, the scrawny neck barely able to support it. Scraggly wisps of bone-white hair clung to the emaciated skull. Only its eyes – piercing blue, like Ledbetter's own – possessed anything like life, though they seemed to plead for death, a mercy they knew would never come.

"All our lives thinking we were doing God's work. The faggots, the niggers, all of it… we only bought our place in Hell."

A mirthless laugh croaked from his father's lips.

Ledbetter shook his head. "Daddy, no… it's what He wanted."

"All He ever wanted was for His people to do good!" Daddy roared at him, his dead man's breath blasting Ledbetter's hair back from his forehead. "We did everything but… now we're damned.

Goddamned. For all eternity—"

Daddy gave a gasping cry. His wooden face petrified, his features frozen in an agonized rictus. With a slash of its claws, the demon sheared Daddy's face from his skull. Ledbetter wept as he saw himself reflected in the bloody open wound.

The demons mocked him, the sound of their laughter alien to mortal ears. They closed in around him. The faceless thing that had looked like his father plunged its claws into his chest. The preacher gasped as the last earthly breath was snatched from his lungs. Then the demons dragged him down through the church floor…down, down…the hellbound holy man screaming all the way.

And that's where the *real* screaming started.

For all eternity. Just like Daddy said.

55

The truck passed a billboard on the outskirts of town, where blood-red letters proclaimed:

BY THIS ALL MEN SHALL KNOW YE ARE MY DISCIPLES, IF YE HAVE LOVE TO ONE ANOTHER JOHN 13:35

Mike snickered, covered his mouth with his bandaged hands, fearing he might laugh himself all the way to the nuthouse. Once he started he knew he would never stop.

Rhonda glanced at him in concern. "Get it together, Rawson. We're almost home free."

They continued on. Rain spit inside the truck through the broken windshield. The wind whipped their faces raw. A flash of lightning revealed a weathered wooden sign that read: HOG FARM, 2 MILES.

"Pork Chop," Mike said. "Where's Pork Chop? And the girl?"

Something clawed Mike's leg. He flinched in surprise, glancing down to see Lonnie's bone-white hand squeezing his knee. Mike assumed the movements were involuntary spasms of pain.

Then Lonnie croaked, "I…tuh-told P.C. to bug out." He grimaced an apology to Rhonda. "They'll be long gone by now. Assuming…they muh-made it."

Mike tried to picture Pork Chop and Becca boarding a

Greyhound bound for Louisville – P.C. in his stupid kilt, and the girl carved up like a grisly game of tic-tac-toe. Tried to picture it, and couldn't quite manage it.

"Maybe we should go back and check?" he halfheartedly suggested.

But Rhonda's foot never eased off the gas pedal.

"We go back," she warned, "I don't think Deveroux makes it."

Mike stifled a sigh of relief that she had called his bluff. He hated himself for it, but the last thing he wanted was to go back. Pork Chop would be okay. Just like Lonnie said.

Rhonda nodded at the blood seeping through Mike's bandaged hands. "You could use a doctor yourself."

No shit, Mike thought. *I went to Little Enoch and all I got was this lousy stigmata.*

"I'll call it in," Rhonda assured him, "first chance I get."

Mike nodded, grateful to relinquish responsibility – and his guilt – to her.

Lonnie's hand slid from Mike's thigh, squelching on the blood-sodden seat.

Jesus, Mike thought. *How much blood does he have left* inside *him?*

Slumped against him, Lonnie's face was ice-cold on Mike's shoulder.

"Mikey?" he said, gazing up at him like an adoring kid brother.

Mike leaned forward to hear his pained voice. "Right here, man."

"Listen…"

"I'm listening."

"You remember that song…we were working on…before you left? Killer riff. Best thing…we ever wrote. Too bad…we never got to…show it to the world."

A tear trickle down Mike's cheek, dripping onto Lonnie's upturned face.

He didn't have the heart to remind Lonnie that his killer riff had sounded exactly like "Hot Blooded," even though Lonnie had always insisted that a real rock warrior wouldn't be caught dead listening to fluff like Foreigner.

Better to let his friend have his moment.

"Man, that song…was sweet," Lonnie said. "Remember…what we called it?"

Mike shook his head. Hell, it had been years—

Then it came to him, and he grinned.

"'Don't Go Out Like a Bitch—'"

"'—Go Out With a Bang.'"

The double entendre was, of course, intentional; and their proudest moment as lyricists.

They smiled at each other.

"Hey, Mike."

"Yeah, Lonnie?"

"I'm sorry I ran out on you, man."

"You came back for me," Mike said. "That's all that matters."

Lonnie started to hum the melody of their blockbuster hit that never was. Mike chimed in for a few seconds (mostly just humming "Hot Blooded"), before Lonnie stopped and said, "Shit, I'm dying…aren't I?"

Mike choked down a sob. "I love you, man."

Lonnie smiled. "*Fag.*"

He died in Mike's arms.

56

Rhonda floored the truck through the maze of backroads… the same roads on which they had first gotten lost. Hard to believe barely twelve hours had passed since then. It felt like forty days and nights since Deveroux took his ill-fated "shortcut," and landed them all in this living nightmare. Little Enoch was nearly three miles behind them now, but she refused to ease her foot off the gas. Maybe when they reached the East Coast she might feel safe again, like they had put enough distance between themselves and that fucked-up church. But it wasn't happening any time soon. She adjusted the rearview and checked the mirror for any sign they were being followed.

"Holy shit," she said at last. "I… I think we made it, Rawson."

Mike said nothing. His bandaged hands clutched the cracked plastic cassette case with WRATHBONE scrawled in Wite-Out on the cover. He choked back tears at the band photo of his younger self posturing with Lonnie 'Love Gun' Deveroux and Arthur 'Pork Chop' Miller. All glam-metal hair and try-hard macho pouts. Dumbass kids with a dream that never came true. *And never would…*

Mike tucked the cassette in his pocket, before bending with a grunt to retrieve an old gray blanket that lay on the floorboards at his feet. It smelled like apples.

He draped it over Lonnie's lifeless body. A patch of green-black mildew covered his friend's face like some white-trash Turin Shroud.

They rode in silence for some time. Rain spattered the dash through the broken windshield, the wind whistling through the bullet holes in the truck body.

"How is it possible?" Mike said, breaking the silence. "All those people… how could they fall for it? How could *one man* have such a hold over an entire town?"

Rhonda shook her head. The gesture appeared to take every last shred of energy she had left. She said, "Men like the preacher… they've got something. Call it charisma, I don't know. His people were born into servitude. Blind faith. It's all they've ever known."

Mike looked unconvinced.

"You can't underestimate people like that, Rawson. It's easy to write them off as loonies. But they believe what they're preaching. That's what makes them dangerous. Guy I used to date worked in the Bureau's Occult Crimes Division. He told me most of the Satanic stuff is bullshit – parents flipping out, thinking Little Johnny's into drinking blood and killing kittens 'cause he listens to Iron Maiden and drew a pentagram once on his Trapper-Keeper… But *these* holy rollers? They're the ones you've gotta watch out for. Look at Jonestown. And that Mormon thing a few years ago. Assholes like the preacher are a ticking time bomb. And it's only a matter of time before—"

The truck shuddered, died, its engine suddenly cutting out, its headlights fading to black, like an old man nodding off in the middle of a conversation.

"No!" Rhonda shouted, pumping the gas to no effect. "No, no!"

She hit the brake.

The truck skidded to a stop in the middle of the road.

"What is it?" Mike cried. "What happened, what's wrong?"

"Engine crapped out?" she guessed. "I'm surprised it got us this far. And that's before those bastards shot it all to hell."

She jimmied the screwdriver in the ignition, as she'd seen Lonnie do when they requisitioned the vehicle back at the orchard.

Nothing.

She smacked the wheel with the heel of her hand. "Damn it!"

"What now?" Mike said.

"Let me think," she snapped. "Just… *relax*."

"Yeah, sure, right."

Rhonda climbed from the cab, stiff-jointed and sore, her whole body aching.

What I wouldn't give for a hot bath right now. Calgon, take me away…

A sick, humorless laugh escaped her. Mike asked her what was so funny. His voice seemed to come from a million miles away. She ignored him.

Limping to the front of the truck, she popped the hood and frowned at the engine. Didn't have a clue what she was looking at, but she thought it was important that she went through the motions. Rawson was in bad shape. Looked like he was about to lose it. Understandably so. She was the professional here, needed to act like it. Easier said than done. She wasn't trained for this shit.

Mike joined her at the front of the truck. "Well? What's it look like?"

She stepped back, gestured to the engine. "Be my guest."

"Lonnie would have known what to do," Mike said with a heavy sigh.

She didn't have the heart to remind him that Deveroux had been unable to restart his beloved camper – *motorhome*, she corrected herself, stifling another sick chuckle – so what the hell could he have done with *this* clunker?

Mike flinched as she slammed down the hood.

"Looks like we're walking," she told him.

"What about Lonnie?"

"We can't bring him with us, Mike," she said, gently.

He knew it was true – he could barely walk on his wounded ankle, let alone carry Lonnie's deadweight – but he needed her to be the one to say it.

He shot a guilty glance at the shrouded shape in the truck. "I'll come back for you, man. I promise."

Hot tears splashed his cheek. Mike brushed them away with the back of his arm… and then blinked in confusion at the Nike swoosh of blood smeared on his skin. *Where… am I cut again?* He glanced at Rhonda for reassurance.

She wasn't looking his way. She was staring slack-jawed at the sky. A shower of oily raindrops spattered her upturned face, running red down her cheeks and throat.

Slowly, she turned to face him.

"Mike...?" she said, in a tiny voice.

He followed her gaze, staring up at the sky.

The roiling clouds above them burned fiery red, like a thin veil stretched across the mouth of a vast furnace. Veins of lightning shot through the clouds… thunder cracked like a bone wrenched from a carcass… and then the clouds burst, and Hell rained down from the heavens, as if God had finally given up on His creation and slit His wrists in despair.

Within seconds, they were soaked to the skin, gore slopping down their faces and arms like scarlet slime, their eyes shining wide through crimson masks.

The wind banshee-howled.

The blood-rain hissed on the road, churning to pink froth.

"Mike!" Rhonda shouted above the deluge. Blood streamed down her face like red tears. "Mike… what the hell is this?"

Mike didn't answer – *couldn't answer.* He had a horrible feeling she'd just called it. He struggled to remember what he had learned about the End Times so many years ago, when he had attended church with his family. He thought of Rachel and the baby, and despite the horror unfolding before him, he felt a strange sense of peace. If this was truly the End as foretold in the Book of Revelation, Rachel and the baby should have vanished in the blink of an eye the instant it began. Rachel was a believer. The baby's soul was not yet tarnished by sin. The two of them should have been zapped up to Heaven already, leaving nothing but their clothes behind… Wasn't that how it worked?

At least his family was safe. His wife and child were out of harm's way. They *had* to be. *Please, God…*

But then that feeling of relief at the thought of his loved ones' welfare was replaced by a smothering black despair like nothing Mike Rawson had ever experienced, a mortal dread he felt in the marrow of his bones. Because this was unlike anything he had ever been taught about in Sunday School. The Good Book never said anything about *this.*

Mike sank to his knees. The road was already flooded. Blood soaked through the legs of his pants. It was warm.

"They were right… the crazy bastards were right." He looked up at Rhonda. "What have we done, Shaughnessy? What the fuck have we done?"

Rhonda shook her head, flinging blood from her hair. "No," she said. "No! I… I don't believe in this."

"I don't think that matters anymore."

Rhonda dragged Mike to his feet.

"Come on!" she cried. "We have to…" The words died on her lips. "Have to…"

He yanked his arm from the pincer-grip of her hands.

"Have to what, Shaughnessy? HAVE TO WHAT? Look around you!"

He remembered what the preacher had said, back in the church.

"*They walk among us now,*" Mike said.

The ground began to rumble beneath them as something mighty and terrible roared in the distance, back toward town.

It was not alone.

Mike's guts turned to ice.

Six years ago – *a lifetime ago* – he had caught AC/DC on the band's *For Those About to Rock* tour. When Angus and the boys played the title track from that album, twin cannons on either side of the stage BOOMED out an epic "twenty-one-gun salute" during the song's finale, an eardrum-rupturing climax to the greatest rock n' roll show Mike had ever seen. He had attended the concert with a co-worker. Hadn't thought about inviting his old Wrathbone buddies until it was too late. But he remembered thinking guiltily at the time that P.C. would have loved it when those cannons went off; he pictured the big lug grinning ear to ear, clapping out of time with the music like a hyperactive kid watching a fireworks display. He also recalled, quite vividly, how those cannons produced *the loudest sound he had ever heard.* With every thunderous BOOM it was as if someone had punched him square in the chest.

The chorus of earth-shattering roars that resounded now through the crimson skies over Little Enoch… *this was ten times louder, at least.*

On either side of the road, the forest turned black, as if the trees were in the radius of a nuclear blast. They withered to dust and were cast to the wind in a storm of scorched leaves and ash.

Agonized screams filled the air… wails of soul-wrenching anguish… legions of doomed souls dying in unison. Mike and Rhonda's screams joined them.

Before long, as the ash swirled around them, mixing with the blood-rain, they could no longer tell which way was forward…

backward… up… or down.

The sky was an open wound, drowning the world in blood.

Again, something roared in the distance. Another answered. Then another. A call-and-response between infernal beasts let loose upon the Earth.

By us… Mike thought. *We did this…*

Back toward Little Enoch, he saw monstrous shapes lumbering over the town. Leviathan things straight from Hell, colossal demons as tall as the neighboring Blue Ridge Mountains. Their forms blacked out the sky as they came. Closer. Closer. And with every step they took the ground cracked and ruptured like diseased flesh leaking fluids of infection and rot.

He glanced back toward Rhonda, but could no longer see her through the thick scarlet sheets that gushed from the sky. He called her name, his voice barely audible over the howling wind, the hissing rain, the screams of the damned, and the roar of the things from the Pit.

"Shaughnessy!" he cried. "Where are—?"

He barely felt the pain as she took his wounded hand. In fact, he welcomed her touch. To know he was not alone… nothing else mattered. He could not see her… but he could feel her. He squeezed her hand, and she gently squeezed back.

The feel of her hand in his, even through the bandages, made him think of Rachel, and he could almost imagine he was holding his wife's hand one last time, as they began to walk down the Highway to Hell.

THE END

ABOUT THE AUTHORS

Adam Howe writes the twisted fiction your mother warned you about. He lives in Greater London with his partner, their daughter, and a hellhound named Gino. Writing as Garrett Addams, his short story JUMPER was chosen by Stephen King as the winner of the international ON WRITING contest. He is the author of TIJUANA DONKEY SHOWDOWN, DIE DOG OR EAT THE HATCHET, BLACK CAT MOJO, and the editor of WRESTLE MANIACS. Stalk him on Twitter @Adam_G_Howe

James Newman lives in North Carolina with his wife and their two sons. His published work includes the novels MIDNIGHT RAIN, THE WICKED, ANIMOSITY, and UGLY AS SIN, the collection PEOPLE ARE STRANGE, and the fan favorite novella ODD MAN OUT. SCAPEGOAT is the most recent of several successful collaborations for Newman, following the titles DOG DAYS O' SUMMER (w/Mark Allen Gunnells), THE SPECIAL (w/Mark Steensland), and DEATH SONGS FROM THE NAKED MAN (w/Donn Gash).

STORY NOTES:
HERE BE SPOILERS

ADAM HOWE

The genesis for "Scapegoat" came from a BBC travelogue of the American South by comedian Rich Hall. During the documentary he made passing reference to the etymology of the word 'scapegoat,' and the biblical ritual attached to it, in which ancient communities would cast their transgressions onto a literal goat before banishing the unfortunate beast into the wilderness to die, and their sins along with it. This struck me as a good premise for a horror story. All I need do was switch the goat for a human, and the story would "write itself."

They never write themselves, dammit.

As I often do, I used movie templates to help me structure the story.

This time it was 1975's RACE WITH THE DEVIL, directed by Jack Starrett, in which RV-trippers Warren Oates and Peter Fonda, and their gals, battle devil worshippers after witnessing a human sacrifice in the Texan backwoods. Not a great movie, by any means, but a lot of fun if you're a fan of killer B's. Much of the film is made up of Oates and Fonda riding dirt bikes through the badlands. In fact, you get the sense that the movie was loosely structured around Oates and Fonda taking an actual motorcycle vacation. For all its flaws, RACE WITH THE DEVIL has an absolutely killer climax. I won't spoil it for you, just in case you haven't seen the movie, and want to track it down. For me, it's an ending up right up there with that of THE WICKER MAN… the 1973 original, I hasten to add, not the Nicolas Cage abomination. (Much as I admire Mr. Cage's commitment to the "not the bees!" scene.)

The other movie I riffed on was 1993's JUDGMENT NIGHT, directed by Stephen Hopkins, in which Emilio Estevez (playing an unlikely badass), Cuba Gooding Jr. (at his bug-eyed best, he hams his ass off here), Jeremy Piven (pre-hair transplant, pre-Ari Gold, pre-MeToo allegation), and Stephen Dorff (I got nothing), are luxury-RV-trippin' to a boxing match… when they blunder into the middle of a gangland execution, and subsequently find themselves hunted through the ghetto by Denis Leary (an unlikely villain to parallel Emilio's unlikely hero) and his House of Pain-looking goons. Remembered mostly for its soundtrack, in which rock n' rap groups were tag-teamed, JUDGMENT NIGHT remains a solid street-level action/thriller, and is worthy of your attention.

Mixing these elements together, I had what I felt was a pretty good opening for a story… Then I hit a brick wall; I found I was intimidated by the religious angle.

I'm an agnostic, as opposed to atheist. I believe in… *something*. I just feel it's beyond any human comprehension and probably isn't worth killing each other over. I was raised Protestant, within my grandparents' church, but my religious education ended at Sunday school. We never covered the particulars of ritual human sacrifice, the eternal torments of hell, and the Apocalypse; maybe we were building up to all that good stuff before I stopped going to church?

I felt the story would benefit from the assistance of another writer with some actual knowledge of this stuff…

Someone like James Newman, a card-carrying Christian whom I know for a FACT has ritually sacrificed BUSLOADS of non-believers in tribute to God.

James and I have never met in person. I'm English, for those of you who don't know; James is American (with an accent best described as Kenny Powers meets Karl Childers, *mmm-hmm*… and though I have seen photographic evidence to the contrary, I prefer to picture him as the banjo boy from DELIVERANCE.) As admirers of each other's work, we'd struck up an online friendship… a friendship I may have just destroyed thanks to that DELIVERANCE reference, but whatever.

James had been kind enough to write the foreword to my TIJUANA DONKEY SHOWDOWN – I say "kind," he spent most of it threatening me, his mouth writing checks his body can't cash. Around that time, James casually suggested we might collaborate on something some day. I'm sure he was just being polite, but I called his bluff, and pitched him the idea for SCAPEGOAT.

He responded with yee-haws, thigh-slaps, a burst of fiddle

music, and other signs of enthusiasm I assumed were native to North Carolinians. It turned out JUDGMENT NIGHT was a "date movie" back when he was courting his wife, so right away he dug the set-up. (What a fuckin' romantic; my "date movie" was HENRY: PORTRAIT OF A SERIAL KILLER.)

Aside from sharing a fondness for B-movies, James, like me, is fanatical about doomsday cults, especially the Reverend Jim Jones, his Peoples Temple, and the Jonestown massacre. Using Jim Jones as our primary influence, we started shaping the sinister church led by the Reverend Heaton Ledbetter Jr.

From there, the story began, if not "writing itself," coming to life.

To the influences of RACE WITH THE DEVIL and JUDGMENT NIGHT we added Kevin Smith's RED STATE. James and I agreed that Smith missed a trick with his ending. Those of you who have seen RED STATE will remember the climactic moment in the standoff between Michael Parks's church cult, and John Goodman's feds, when an unearthly horn begins to sound. Goodman freaks out. Parks rejoices at the sound of Gabriel blowing his horn on Creation. The Apocalypse has arrived… or has it? Turns out the sound is part of an elaborate prank. Man, what a letdown. James and I agreed; how ballsy Smith would have been had he ended the movie with the actual Apocalypse.

Fortunately he didn't, which meant we got to do it.

We wondered, what if our cultists are right; what if the scapegoat ritual truly is preventing (or at least, postponing) the Apocalypse? Of course, there remains in our story some ambiguity; the reader is free to interpret it as they choose. Our cultists, to their surprise, find themselves damned along with all the other sinners. The cultists may be right about the scapegoat ritual, but they are wrong in their overall interpretation of the bible: a case of right message, wrong messengers… which reminds me of the Bill Burr skit about heaven being just Fred Phelps, of Westboro Baptist Church "fame," and God, saying "I hate fags."

For more influences, check out the Suggested Viewing / Listening appendix.

*

Our writing process worked like this: From the opening section I'd already written (in which our RV-trippers encounter the intended human sacrifice of a religious cult), and with our apocalyptic ending in mind, we bounced an outline back and forth until the rest of the story took shape. Following the outline, we wrote lengthy sections in turn, rewriting each other along the way. Once we had a good working draft, having rewritten and revised until we lost all objectivity – until we hated the damn thing, and each other – we brought in James David Osborne, of Broken River Books, to edit and help the hone the structure. This is the end result. We hope you dig it.

*

I'll leave James to relate more details of our collaboration, if he's recovered from the trauma; I know I can be an exacting writing partner… so expect him to say lots of nasty things about me. For my part, I enjoyed the experience immensely, and hope to repeat it; I think James and I make a good team.

What say you, genital reader? Let us know.

*

Lastly, this book was written between some incredible highs and lows in my life. My daughter Georgia Mae was born around the time I first started planning the story. And during the writing itself, my partner Suzie lost both of her parents within the space of a year. My in-laws, Norma and Mike, were huge supporters of my work… even if they didn't always care for the subject matter! They are greatly missed. This book is for them.

Adam Howe / Aug.18

JAMES NEWMAN

First off, I want to respond to Adam's comment about how he "knows for a fact" that I'm a "card-carrying" Christian who's sacrificed a bunch of people who don't believe the same way I do.

Dude's so full of shit he's swimmin' in it. I've never carried anything other than my driver's license – if there's some sort of nifty membership card that's handed out to those of us who aren't godless heathens, the upper echelon failed to let me know. I have no idea where to get one of those (is there a number I should call?).

It's been said that writers of fiction are professional liars. Adam Howe is walking, talking proof of that.

But on to SCAPEGOAT! I'm supposed to talk about my part in the book you just read, instead of defending myself from my co-writer's baseless claims…

I would like to get a bit more personal in my story notes, for better or worse. SCAPEGOAT wears its influences on its ragged denim sleeve, so I won't take up too much of my allotted word-count here by rehashing the stuff that inspired the story because Adam already covered that well (once you get past the filthy lies). JUDGMENT NIGHT was indeed a date movie for my wife and me way back when. It's been a not-so-guilty-pleasure of mine ever since, because I can relate to those characters. I can relate to being the sap who drifted away from his rowdy group of friends to settle down and start a family, the guy who gave up his dreams of rock n' roll stardom to pursue a career that entailed sitting in front of a computer all day (how many office drones do you know who sport "ROCK" and "ROLL" tattoos on their knuckles? Yeah, that's what I thought). The best tales of suspense and horror are those populated with characters we know, real people with real problems who suddenly end up in a terrifying situation. Those characters don't always have to be likeable, as long as they're anything but boring. JUDGMENT NIGHT is a perfect example of what I'm looking for when I kick back to watch a movie or read a book – it's entertainment that might not win any awards or ever hope to be hailed as a "classic," but it's fun with a capital F. That's what matters to me. I'd like to think SCAPEGOAT follows suit. It's certainly what Adam and I set out to write.

Moving into the personal insight here, you might be surprised to learn that there are elements of SCAPEGOAT that are borderline autobiographical, as bizarre as that might sound. We'll get to that shortly…

I have to talk for a moment about Christianity. Most of my readers know that I'm a believer, as I have mentioned it before in interviews and such. While I won't get into the specifics of what I do/don't prescribe to when it comes to my religion -- that's a bit too personal and this ain't the place for it anyway -- I was raised Southern Baptist but have since moved on to a much more progressive outlook on such matters. You wanna know the truth, I can't stand 99% of those bigoted, sanctimonious assholes you see on TV or read about in the news who claim to follow the same God I do. They embarrass me. That said, I never wanted SCAPEGOAT to be an attack on religion, and contrary to what you might think neither did my agnostic co-conspirator. In some ways, it could be argued that SCAPEGOAT is pro-Christianity, in fact. Think about it (you were warned about spoilers!) . . . Reverend Ledbetter was kinda right all along, wasn't he? The wrath of God is a terrifying thing, especially when those who are supposed to be spreading His message of Love fuck it up so royally. Speaking of ole' Heaton, I've been infatuated with cults for as long as I can remember, and that was another thing that made SCAPEGOAT so enticing when Adam first pitched his idea to me. It's incredibly fascinating to me how seemingly normal, rational people fall for the lies of a megalomaniac, trusting anything their leader tells them even it goes against their best interests (kinda like yours truly when I came onboard this project). Then again, I guess there are a lot of folks out there who would argue that what I believe is pretty crazy. Fair enough. Don't worry, I'm not gonna cut ya.

Now for that autobiographical stuff I mentioned. Although I didn't realize it until we were approaching the finish line on this project, there's a lot of me in SCAPEGOAT. No, I'm not referring to the psychotic Bible-thumpers, ya smartass. I'm talking about in the character of Mike Lawson, specifically. I think my own kinship with Mike brought something special to this collaboration. It gave the story more heart, if you will, alongside all the blood n' guts n' rampant sacrilege.

Adam and I have a joke that goes something like this:

"Yeah, this Mike guy's based on James."

"Oh, really?"

"Yeah, he's a love-struck pussy."

You can guess who came up with that one.

All joking aside, though, I'll be the first to admit that it's true.

Like I said, there's a lot of Mike in me. Particularly in that moment when Mike and Lonnie are reminiscing under the railroad tracks…

In 1991 I was working at a local fast-food restaurant (that cushy office job I mentioned earlier was still about 25 years in the future). I had recently been promoted to Customer Service Representative, which meant I was a glorified cashier in a grease-stained tie. One afternoon, a young lady walked in looking for a job. Sexiest hair I'd ever seen, and a smile that instantly made that burger joint grow brighter. Fast forward to a few months later: This smiling, sexy-haired girl who now works directly under me (heh, heh), I've been spending a lot of time with her. Being the big-spendin' ladies' man that I am (read: a grade-A geek who wouldn't know how to be cool if I fell into a tub full of ice water), my idea of showing this young lady a good time is late-night walks together on the nearby railroad tracks. Sometimes we stay out there till dawn, and once or twice we even build a fire beneath the trestle bridge outside of town, and we do nothing but talk and talk until we grow hoarse, holding each other as a midnight train thunders overhead like something out of . . . well, like something out of a story about the End of the World. She's a girl who enjoys the simple things, and although it seems too good to be true she seems to be digging this no less than me: the early-morning breeze running its fingers through our hair . . . the smell of pine trees and honeysuckle . . . and the sound of highway traffic so distant the rest of civilization might exist on another planet entirely. On one of these walks, my girl says she has to tell me something. She seems nervous. Whatever it is, I can take it, I assure her. But she insists she's not quite ready. This conversation happens several times as we stroll along beneath the immense ebony dome of night sky, the stars blinking down upon us like the eyes of an audience waiting to see how our story will end. Finally she says she'll tell me now if I promise not to laugh at her. She takes a deep breath, squeezes my hand, and says, "I think I'm falling in love with you." Without hesitation, I reply, "I feel the same way." She looks relieved. Tears glisten in her eyes as we kiss. I think we kissed for hours that night. Just held hands and kissed.

Yes, you have my permission to vomit now.

But now you know what I mean when I say that there's a lot of Mike Lawson in me. His story is mine. My story is his.

Except . . . my story doesn't end with blood raining from the sky, zealots committing mass suicide, or demons crawling up from the bowels of Hell to rip mankind asunder.

At least it hasn't yet.

Let's be patient, shall we? Wait and see what happens.

James Newman / Aug.18

*Recommended Viewing

Race with the Devil, 1975 Jack Starrett
Judgment Night, 1993 Stephen Hopkins
Red State, 2011 Kevin Smith
Prince of Darkness, 1987 John Carpenter
Martyrs, 2008 Pascal Laugier
Safe Haven (VHS2), 2013 Gareth Evans
The Wicker Man, 1973 Robin Hardy
The Beyond, 1981 Lucio Fulci
Pumpkinhead, 1988 Stan Winston
Brimstone, 2016 Martin Koolhoven
The Hills Have Eyes, 1977 Wes Craven
Guyana: Cult of the Damned, 1979 Rene Cardono Jr.
The Decline of Western Civilization Part II: The Metal Years, 1988 Penelope Spheeris
Wrestlemania III, 1987

*Required

"SCAPEGOAT" PLAYLIST

Real American, Rick Derringer
Highway To Hell, AC/DC
Heading Out To The Highway, Judas Priest
Piece Of Your Action, Mötley Crüe
Party All Night, Quiet Riot
Orion, Metallica
Stonehenge, Black Sabbath
Disturbing The Priest, Black Sabbath
Overkill, Motorhead
Believer, Ozzy Osbourne
To Hell With The Devil, Stryper
Watch the Children Pray, Metal Church
Jump In The Fire, Metallica
Welcome To My Nightmare, Alice Cooper
Run Through The Jungle, Creedence Clearwater Revival
Locomotive, Motorhead
Good Mourning / Black Friday, Megadeth
If You Want Blood (You've Got It), AC/DC
Burn In Hell, Twisted Sister
Raining Blood, Slayer
Evil Walks, AC/DC
In The Mouth Of Madness, John Carpenter
In The Face Of Evil, Magic Sword
The Torture Never Stops, W.A.S.P.
The One You Love To Hate, Halford
Judgment Night, Biohazard & Onyx

ACKNOWLEDGEMENTS

Devil horns to the following reprobates, without whom this book could not have been written: Our editor, James David Osborne, of Broken River Books… Joseph Hirsch, David Dubrow, Fred Fischer, Pete Kahle, Tod Clark, Andi Rawson, Kent Gowran, Marc Tams, Dan Studer, Justin Woodward, Judy Haigh, and Andy DeVore; for reading early drafts and offering sage advice… Thanks also to Michael Patrick Hicks, Sean Costello, Eryk Pruitt, Niki Mackay, and Keshini Naidoo… Bang your heads: Mike @ Tenebrae Studios for our cover art, Alex McVey for our author art, and Duncan Bradshaw of EyeCue Productions for formatting and all-around cool-dudeness… And eXXXtra special thanks to our gals, Suzie (Adam) and Glenda (James).

ALSO BY HONEY BADGER PRESS

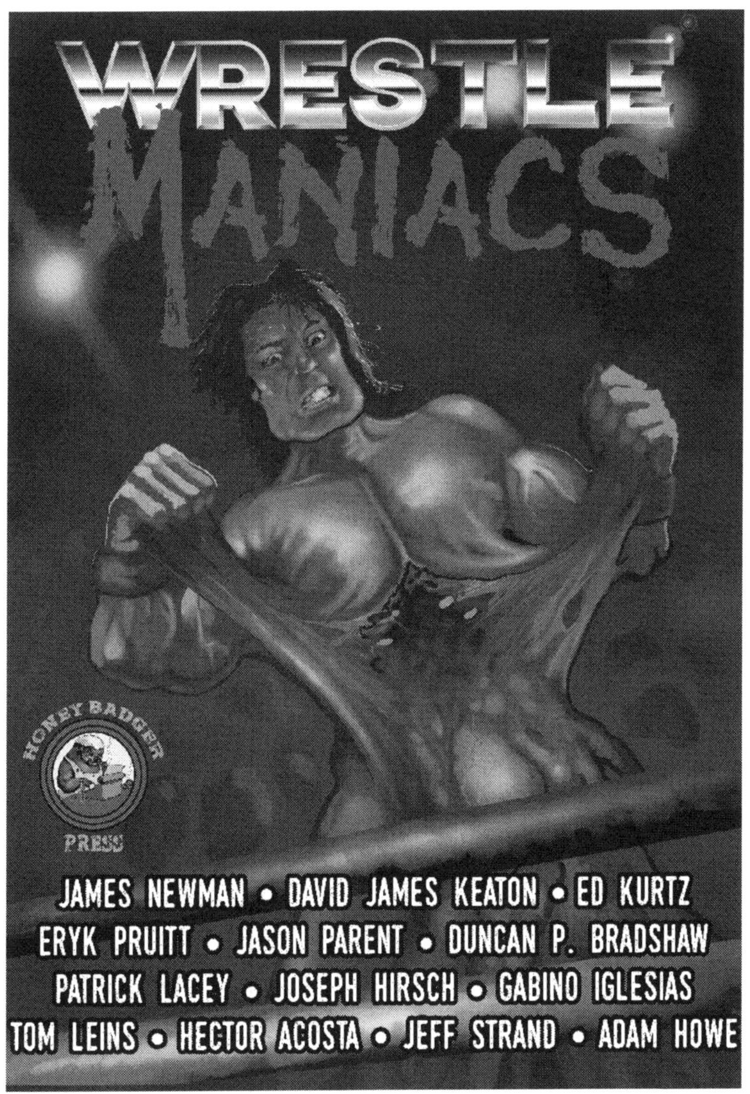

A dozen dark fiction masters bring their twisted vision to the world of professional wrestling. Twelve original stories of crime, horror, humor, and taboo. Ohhh, yeahhh! This ain't no kayfabe, baby. This is hard-hitting wrestling fiction that grips like a Camel Clutch, and pins the reader to the page for the count of one, two…THREE!

Includes a confrontational foreword by ring legend 'Pulverizing' Pat McCrunch (as told to Jeff Strand)… An all-new story starring Nick 'The Widowmaker' Bullman from James Newman's wrestling noir, "Ugly as Sin"… And ex-boxer turned strip club bouncer Reggie Levine ("Tijuana Donkey Showdown," "Damn Dirty Apes") returns for another action-packed misadventure.

Available on Amazon

Coming November 2018 from EyeCue Productions

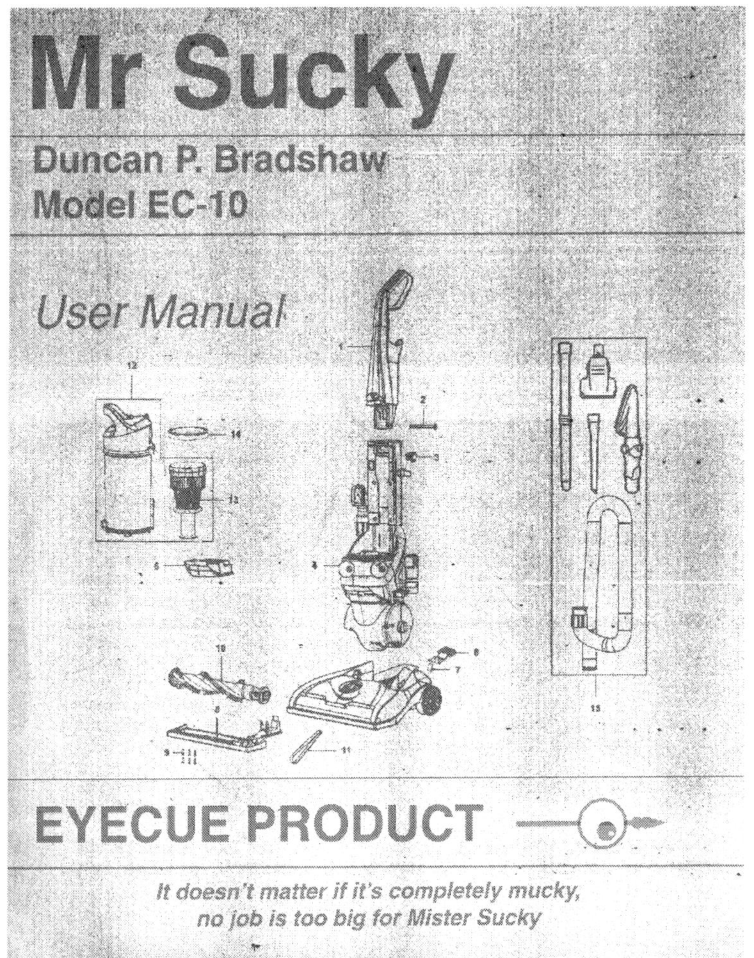

Serial killer Clive Beauchamp has checked into his hotel room and is all set to increase his death toll by one. However, intended target Angela Foxe has other ideas and murderer becomes murderee. Determined to save Clive's soul from eternal damnation, an ancient evil instructs one of his acolytes to intervene. Unfortunately for Clive, the hired help is not the brightest bulb in the box, and instead of Clive being born anew within an avatar of unparalleled strength and brutality, his spirit is interred inside a vacuum cleaner.

Irked but undeterred, Clive decides that the only course of action is to finish what he started, taking care not just of Angela, but everyone else involved in the plot to kill him and stuff his corpse in a dingy cleaning cupboard. The only thing that can stop him comes not from the other hotel guests or staff, but from within, as a growing, nagging voice threatens to escalate a simple case of revenge, into something far, far worse.

Mike Tenebrae
The man behind the cover and the Honey Badger Press Logo

MEET THE ARTIST

Mike Tenebrae is a freelance illustrator working from his studio in Cape Town, South Africa. He enjoys a wide list of clients from around the world, and has worked on everything from book covers to fantasy games such as THE LORD OF THE RINGS and TALISMAN. He enjoys working both in digital and traditional mediums.

http://tenebraestudios.net